H₂LiftShips

-

BosonsWave

Volume 3 in the LiftShip Story

Imagine a world, exactly like ours, but different

by

Bob Freeman

Our Leader as a Pup

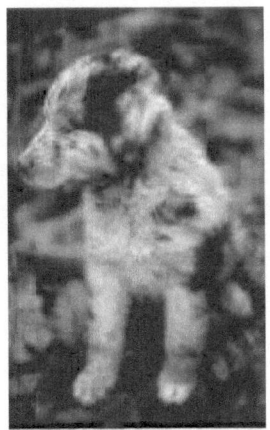

E=mc

Website: *www. h2liftship. com*

Socials: Please use
https:// www. H2liftship.com/contact

email: SciFi @ h2liftship.com

Dedicated to all the dogs, Past, Present and Future
and
support from Veronica for help beyond measure.

Paperback: 978-1-64456-483-7
Mobi: 978-1-64456-484-4
ePub: 978-1-64456-485-1
Library of Congress Control Number: 2022939148

www.indiesunited.net

Cover design by:
Ghislain Viau
Creative Publishing Book Design
www.creativepublishingdesign.com

-*Trigger Warnings*-

These outer-space stories take place in Sol's heliosphere. They contain real science, pseudo-science and stuff pulled out of thin air.

If you enjoy a long, complex ramp-up as part of a world-building story, this series is for you. Otherwise, maybe try something lighter and flashy.

In these stories there are no blasters, no FTL drives, no exploding computers, no physical violence, and no sex, except for a little kerfuffle with canines and their pheromones.

Any yet, still no aliens, if you don't count the octopus.

There are some issues with Death on the Mort Asteroid, but after living on Sol's rocks, we all die eventually.

You will find some gambling, drinking, passive-aggressive families, lying, stealing, and double-dealing. e.g. normal sentients, mostly nice. But watch your back.

Scientific names (*Genus/species*), puns, and unique spellings abound.

Written in English with a few French, Yiddish, Spanglish, Latin, and Doglish words thrown about.

Knowledge of octopus color languages and Morse code are not required, but couldn't hurt.

ReCap

We return to our characters as they make their way across the heliosphere on the H2LiftShip, the *LunaCola*.

Graciela Lucerne, female,	*Homo sapiens*
Tangsapor Kewellan Candrey, male,	*Pongo pygmaeus*
Jack San Freedog Jr., male,	*Canine familiaris*
Octopus, male,	*Octopus sp.*

And a host of sentients they meet along the way: Family, pirates, merchants, and the Navy.

This is a complex world building story, covering our whole heliosphere from heliopause to heliotail.
The first two volumes,
H2LiftShips-Beyond Luna Vol 1
H2LiftShips - A Back Story, Vol 2
set the stage for this volume.

H2LiftShips - BosonsWave^2, Vol 4 – Winter 2023
If you haven't read them, you'll probably have problems with some of the concepts presented in this volume. On the bright side, if you've purchased any paperback copy, you'll be able to download e-books for free.
Email me: *Bob @ h2liftship. com*

We continue the Journey of the H2LiftShip, the *LunaCola,* with Captain Graciela, and her deck crew; Tang and Jack, and First Mate, Octopus.

The boost wing explosion sent them off-course and at the mercy of any ship looking to take advantage of a damaged cargo ship.

It was a secret mission, seemly known all too well by pirates, brigands and other low-life sentients. The high-value cargo of bioGel cassettes made them a target for anyone who might want a quick profit on purloined Naval goods.

They escaped the pirates by jerry-rigging a cannon from laser emitters and the bioGel cassettes, then limped to a temporary sanctuary, docking at the PnT junkyard.

The PickNTrade crew helped them disseminate a new, falsified SIDN (Ship ID Number) to the Heliosphere Ship Registry. Tang re-painted the advertising logo to become *LunaBowling* as a ruse to escape the pirates.

The *LunaBowling's* story begins at the PnT junkyard as the crew makes repairs and figure out how to travel forward, avoiding the pirates on their tail.

They left the junkyard with a temporary repaired sail and headed to Home Unity Belt (HuB) to replace the torn sails and take some well-earned shore leave.

But first, some history lessons (sorry kids).

We go back to the BeforeTimes and discover how the Jovian clouds were integrated with the regular DNA computers.

Next we look at the bioGel factory, then a side trip with the Jupiter cloud harvesting ship, bGCN-01-5.

As expected, HuB's casino, draws everyone in, not by its absent gravitational pull, but with the clack of magnetic poker chips against steel table tops.

Jack doesn't do well at gambling yet still finds a way to win free jerky; cow, fish or algae.

Chapter 01
Jupiter First

Before the bioGel Consortium and the advent of LiftShips, metallic skinned rockets used locally sourced hot rocks for propulsion.

Homo sapiens were still the dominant species on the wet rock called Earth and were busily exploring and exploiting their solar system.

The Naval scientific ship 'SN0121' dropped into a Jovian equatorial orbit as it drifted forward after its last nuclear engine burst. They slowed down, skimming the exosphere, sucking up hydrogen, compressing, and using the super-heated gas as a brake.

Matching orbits with the gas giant, the ship released probes, simple osmotic collection bottles. Each bottle had a locator beacon and a small rocket boost motor keyed to Jovian rotations. The plan was to extend nets and catch the pinging gas cans for analysis on Luna.

"The last one is away, Captain."

"Affirmative. Hold here. We'll pick up the bottles when the planet rotates to our position."

After a scant 10 hours, the sample bottle's boost rockets hoisted them to the exosphere as they waited for a lift home.

The Captain ordered, "Set out the collection net. We'll let them float to us."

As in any endeavor started by humans, not everything worked to plan. From the dozen collection containers, only six made it back to the ship.

The chief tech reported, "We got most of them, sir. Do we wait for another orbit?"

"No, if the beacons aren't working, we have no way to know where they are. The scientists will have to be satisfied with what we have."

The remaining bottles stayed, floating off in the clouds, bouncing around like jelly beans, heated, cooled, and attacked in the cloud soup.

Back at base, the scientists took umbrage at the lost samples and insisted that the ship leave immediately and search for the missing bottles.

The deck crew analyzed their situation as they always do. To the uninformed, the loud banter may have sounded like complaints or even whining.

"How are we going to find the bottles? Will they jump out of the atmosphere into the ship, or is this a fruitless journey?"

"I think the point is that we try. I don't care if we bring anything back. We're getting extra pay for gravity."

"What sort of crazy hell are they putting us through now? Are we going to have gravity? I didn't know we would be traveling that fast. I'm not sure it is worth the extra pay. That stuff can hurt."

"It won't be that bad and will be a shorter trip with more pay."

"My bones won't appreciate it,"

"Your bones get to go too. Time to close up and take off."

The lost bags of rarefied air boiled and churned within the active Jovian clouds, mixing with dust, debris, microbes, and electricity. Without circulation, the clouds condensed on the bottle's glass walls. Not self-aware nor intelligent, but the mixing, shaking, and baking in the colorful Jovian gas initiated a tiny cellular evolutionary revolution. The captured bits of cloud molecules were not pleased that they couldn't continue their free-flowing life. They beat against the walls of their prison, throwing bits of dirt against the cylinder. The best they could do was dent it, and few ever finding an escape path.

The Chief and his junior tech were at their stations, ready for a recovery mission.

Junior, in all her impertinence, spoke first, "Here we are again, stuck around this gas bag. I think it's rude those scientists made us come right back out to collect their sample bottles."

"What's the problem? We get paid, and it's a faster trip with the boost the Administrators approved.

"Well, we do get extra gravity pay, so that helps."

"And it was fun being able to stand on a floor, almost like Earth."

Junior still had a beef, "Not so fun for me. I don't like the weight."

"Fine, but we're back at ZeroG, so all is good. Take a look around. The view is beautiful."

"Beauty doesn't cut it. It's cold out here, the ship is cramped, and the food is boring."

"Well, that pretty much sums up long-haul travel."

Much to the Chief's relief, the screen beeped. "Look. I found one. I'll ask the Captain to follow that ping. We're going to sweep in and grab it. Hang on. It could get bumpy."

The ship was comfortable skipping around the exosphere. Diving down to the mesosphere to pick up their prize was not as pleasant. Hurricane winds, hot sparks from the core, debris, and dust buffeted the ship from all directions.

Junior tech tightened the buckles on her safety harness. "Why couldn't they send a remote out to do the job? The closer we get to the core, the hotter it is, and it's too hot on this ship already. Maybe the cold void is better."

"Complaining won't help. I don't like the lightning and winds either."

"Was this in the contract? Do we have a Union rep on board?"

"Nothing we can do about it now. I have another container pinging like crazy on the screen. Lower the net. We'll let it come to us. Look sharp!"

"I'm surprised the locator beacons still work. How many of those do we need to capture before we can get out of this hurricane?"

"Four or five, they're all near us. We'll be out of here in no time. Haul in the net and unload our prize. Get ready for the next one."

Time moves at its own pace, and 'no time' spins, splits, and increases rapidly.

The second probe was in view as the cargo net spun out from the ship, the weak gravity and strong winds tossing it about.

The net is carefully maneuvered to its prey, Junior Tech on the stabilizing rocket controls. It was quite a job adjusting for the forces pulling and pushing on the net and this skill was right in the tech's wheelhouse.

"It's one klik away. Fire up the rockets."

Junior Tech hit the switch and jiggled the joy stick, driving the net toward her quarry.

"Missed it. I swear it dodged. There must have been some power left in its boost rocket."

"Stay sharp. We'll have to try it on the next orbit. Put a flag on it, so we don't lose it."

Junior had a different opinion. "Better yet, let's leave it. The scientists will have to make do with one less sample."

"We'll see. Make sure the net's rockets are aligned correctly this time."

"Hey, it wasn't my fault. The accelerant was wonky."

"Whatever or whoever's fault it was, double-check the loads. I don't want to wait for this gas bomb of a planet to circle again."

"Big deal, it's less than 10 EarthHours. We can wait if it's that important."

Another bottle slipped into the net as if it was nestling up to a dear friend. That, or Junior Tech finally figured out how to adjust for gravity and winds.

"Good work, we have all but the first one tucked away. We can hang out here for another spin. Toss one of the bottles to the scientists. They are anxious to see what has happened after the probes were stuck here.

The ship's scientists had been waiting for a chance to do something new for a long time. Specialist First Class Jones and her boss, Senior Scientist Leon placed the canister on their work table.

The team of scientists and anyone else who wasn't busy gathered around their booty of congealed Jovian cloud. This group of boffins were strong proponents of the scientific method: Look at it, poke it, record it, then dissect it on the table, spreading its guts for all to see.

The ship had all the latest equipment: sensors, probes, and computers plugged into the ship's network. These 'modern' computers are only a few steps above wooden gears, vacuum tubes, or silicon, using carefully nurtured DNA for storage. They were still dumb as rocks, even with a petabyte of file space. Deep down, they were only the 1 and 0 binary machines of the BeforeTimes and wore their ubiquitous screens and keyboards with pride.

Senior Scientist Leon looked closely, "That goo sure looks strange, and it's still moving."

"I've heard about those. It looks like a lava lamp."

"This isn't the BeforeTtimes. Who even uses those? And take off that headband. It isn't regulation. It looks ridiculous."

Tech First Class, Jones reaches up and sadly deposits the band in her lab coat pocket. "Do you think it's sentient?"

"I doubt it, give it a poke and see what happens."

"Nope, nothing happened. The probe goes in like it's Jell-O™."

Senior Scientist Leon touched his mustache and twiddled its edges, a signal of deep thinking or confusion. It was hard to tell.

First Class Jones, obviously new to the scientific method and probably expendable, stuck her face closer to the bubbling gel. "Look at all those sparkly bits. If it's Jell-O™, it sure is pretty."

"I'll pass on that meal. On a related note, did you check for any radiation?"

"Yes, it's fine, no more than the background radiation noise from Jupiter."

"Good. It passed the poke test. Let's see if a multi-probe can elicit a response."

"Great. I have one ready."

"Adjust the probe for a full spectrum analysis. Start with low-frequency sound and move up to x-rays. We'll analyze the data before we do any other tests."

"Should be fun. I'll run the program to send and receive signals. We can increase the amperage if we get no response."

First Class Jones trundles a machine in for the test. On one end is a complex oscilloscope-like device programmed to test the spectrum from near x-ray to whale singing. The other end is a probe, Swiss-army style, ready to tickle its helpless victim.

The scientists drops the probe into the bottle and adjusts the signal.

"Nothing. I'll run an incremental program and check out the response."

"Still nothing. Try more juice."

The cloud debris starts twitching, sending sparks into the lab, a few exploding crystals, then it began spitting like a roman candle. The probe flies through the air as sparkly Jell-O™ runs down the wires to the computer.

"Shut it down before something blows!"

"You mean like the computer? Too late. It's offline."

"Too bad. We'll get another one from the storeroom. Leave it as is. I want to check the data."

"From a moribund computer?"

"Don't worry. The data is in the network server. We can start with it."

The dead computer, still on the ship's network, was resting after the shock of the cloud debris contact. Jovian clouds were not alive, but the ubiquitous microbes certainly contributed to a life-like appearance.

The computer screen showed a flicker of life and wrote.

<**What you?**

"Look, the computer is back up. It's asking questions."

Senior Leon glanced over from his terminal, "I'm sure that isn't real."

First Class Jones turned to the other techs in the room and asked, "Which one of you yahoos put this routine on my terminal?"

No response and none expected.

"Okay. I'll play this game. Let's see how far the programming goes."

"Hello. I'm IT Specialist First Class Jones, at your service, computer."

>We not know those words.

"Well, I'm not going to sit here and teach you how to read. You're a computer. Look it up in your database."

The cloud goo didn't quite know what to do, but the computer knew the word 'database', and opened up its inner secrets to its new friend.

"Now, what is wrong with this terminal? It's completely frozen. Anyone remember how to re-boot this piece of junk?"

Tech Jones went looking for a manual and assistance. The Jovian goo and computer came to an understanding.

<Ms. FirstClass. Me done learning. Us ready to talk

First Class Tech Jones liked to talk, not to anyone in particular, but out loud. It always helped when she had a difficult programming problem and had the additional advantage of irritating her neighbors. "Well, it looks like you came back to life. I guess the program is still running. Now I have to deal with that glitch. This cycle is going sideways. Maybe I'll just leave it for the next shift to deal with."

<Ms. FirstClass. Me know what am

"Lieutenant. Take a look at the computer. I think it's broken."

The duty officer, Lieutenant Garcia, came over as Tech Jones explained, "I thought someone was playing a trick on me with a psycho-question program, but this doesn't seem like anything I've seen before. Or tried."

"Move over. I'll figure it out," as he types, "Hello?"

<Hello, you Ms. FirstClass?

"No, I'm her Jefe, Lt. Garcia."

<K, where we are?

"On the scientific ship SN0121."

<What that, you different cloud?

"No, we are not a cloud, we are a metal ship, and we're going back to Core."

<K. Drop me back at cloud. Me not want to leave friends.

"No can do. You are coming with us.

The computer starts smoking. Feedback hits the oscilloscope, pinning the signal.

Lt. Garcia shouts, "Unplug this system from the network immediately!"

"Toss this mess into a Faraday bag. We'll let the scientists look at it when we get back to Luna."

A senior officer was watching the proceedings and said, "You two. No more work on these samples."

"But we can fix it. We only need to adjust the parameters."

"No way, we don't have enough computers to spare. You'll have to find something else to keep you busy. It's only a few EarthWeeks back to Core."

"So, we're going back on the gravity treadmill?"

"Yes, get used to it."

"We promise not to fry any more computers."

"Exactly. Because you won't be doing any interfacing to that goo."

"Are you sure?"

"In case you were wondering, that's an order."

"Aye, Sir. We'll review the data and leave the experiments to the Luna group."

Chapter 02
Plug in the Sentients

A number of the long-term Jovian cloud cylinders made it back to the Core rocks; Earth and Luna, for additional testing. It wasn't long until these almost-sentient blocks of goo made it out of the military labs and into the hands of more innovative scientists.

If the computer and cloud could be self-aware, some scientists wanted to see how they would work on other organisms. Much to their disappointment, they couldn't use human subjects under the current scientific rules. This was probably a good thing since they didn't care how their specimen felt about the process. Their only concern was if they found something they could publish or sell. Science performed without morals did not always go well.

The mammal studies proved especially difficult. It wasn't hard to implant the connections. The lines of communication were well known and easily opened.

Dolphins were friendly, but only wanted more fresh fish and loved to party.

Dogs were no better. They just asked for treats, toys, and playtime.

The large non-human primates were more than happy to speak up. "FINALLY! We've been trying to talk to you for centuries. Are you humans that stupid? And that sign language. Could you make it any more difficult?"

The group in the simian study made a quick decision and pulled the plug on the specimen and the report. This was not something they wanted to publish and risk blowback from their fellow primates.

Not the best scientific results. The only species left were the nonmammalian animals, which meant octopuses.

The aquarium had a few octopus species, and their human guards began a test of the new cloud computers against their captives.

8

"How are we going to stick a probe into the octopus? It keeps on squirming away and pulling the wires out."

"Watch out. It's reaching for the computer."

"Oh, great. Now, what are we going to do? The cloud juice is leaking into the tank."

"What a pain, these beasts are not following the rules."

"Pull it out and wipe it down. We'll tell the boss that it was defective before we got started."

"Good idea."

DNA computer bits and Jovian cloud debris mixed with the salt water and saturated the octopus' environment and cells.

Octopus winked at its captors and flashed agreement colors. The humans don't notice.

"It's late. I'm going to clock out. We can try again in the morning."

"Not sure we'll have better luck, but I'm done for the day too."

The lights flipped off, and the octopus sat in his tank, ruminating over the mass of data and information the DNA/Clouds presented. He had all the data from the Jovian clouds and the DNA computer databases at his disposal. It took a few minutes to make sense of the information, but his distributed brains helped parse out the data.

Octopuses are escape artists and it didn't take long for a plan to evolve. The ocean was close, and as long as he kept hydrated, freedom was not far away.

Our brainy beast left the enclosure, a tune bubbling out his siphon.

♫ *When you're a jet you're a jet all the way...* ♫

Not forgetting his fellow prisoners, he released many of his captured ocean buddies on the way out. He knew what to do and gathered as much of the DNA/Cloud mixture as possible. Sharing was caring. He had a lot of friends in the open ocean who would appreciate a jolt of intelligence.

Exiting the transom over the side door of the prison formerly known as an aquarium, the newly escaped octopus had some decisions. Its only goal, for now, was to skitter toward the salty water he called his true home.

Fortunately, it was a dark, waning moon. There were lights from the street lamps and a few cars on the road, but that was only confusing the issue, they gave no sense of direction.

Octopus looked up at the cloudless sky and saw the magnetic lines surrounding Earth. They merged toward the poles, but following them North or South would not get him closer to the water.

Octopus took a hard left against the magnetic lines and carefully picked his way to the shore. His new education warned him against automobiles, trucks and buses and he took the inglorious sewage outfall line, riding the current out and away. This was not the way he wanted to return home, but he had to do what he had to do. Once in the ocean, he let the relatively clean water cleanse his body and soul as he planned his future in the new world he was making.

The morning crew walked in to broken tanks and missing octopuses.

"Oh great, we have a prison break. How did this happen? Again."

"Look, there is something on the tank wall."

"It's just dots and dashes. I'm sure it is random scratching. It's nothing to be concerned about."

"We better check the CCTV feed and see if they had some assistance. I'm sure the police can find the culprit."

The security contingent meet to review the CCTV. The cameras don't lie. No humans helped in the escape, a tendril picking the lock was their only clue.

"I don't see anyone helping the octopus. Look at what he's doing."

The octopus had grabbed a clam and carefully scratched on the tank's wall.

"What in the name of Davy Jones locker is that?"

"Is it a message? Can anyone read that? Is it a secret code?"

Snapshots were released to the authorities and found their way to the Press. The local HAM radio groups quickly did the translation, which only caused more consternation to the fish prison officers.

.-- . .-..-. ....- . / -- --- ....- . -.. / --- ..- - --..-- / .--. .-.. . .- .... . / .--.
--- .-. .-- .-. -.-. -.. / .- .-.. .-.. / -.-. .-.. .- -- .... / - --- / --- ..- .-. / --- -.-. . .-
-. / .... --- --

We've moved out, please
forward all clams to our ocean home

The news of the Morse code message was a sensation, the talk of the hour, almost a day. Marine biologists were ecstatic, they now had something to do beside count fish scales or chase down polluters.

Dive teams jumped at the chance and began communicating with the newly independent, computer-savvy cephalopods.

Politicians, social influencers, and philosophers joined forces and the aquarium prisons were converted into liquid universities.

More than a few of the newly minted graduates parlayed their counting skills and signed on to the H2LiftShips as they made their way throughout the heliosphere.

Once the octopuses broke the ice, the other sentients; simians, canines and humans, rebuilt their associations and learned new ways of working together, exploring their solar system for fun and profit.

Chapter 03
BioGel Workers

The leading edge of the heliopause sparkled as cosmic rays, photons, dust particles, and dark energy hit Sol's cold border. It was the void, but not empty. The sentients on the stabilized asteroid managed the maturation of young gels for the bioGel Consortium.

Gellact/6 headed toward the cafeteria to pick up his crew and find the assignment for the work session. His comm flashed the active work color, orange this time, and the selected worker's comm's lit up to match.

"OK, you workologists, clear up your plates and join me at the upper airlock ready room."

It was the usual assortment of primates, canines, and octopuses, able to handle any situation they might find.

Each member were dressed in their spacesuits, ready to work. The bulky suits, with a block of gray goo in a backpack hid their features. Only arm length, count, and uncovered heads indicated the sentient's species.

Gellact/6 was a popular Jefe; fair, easy to work with and a source of snacks when work was done. He made a note of speciation for the snack distribution.

Gellact/6's assistant, Handron/5 was a small female human. She was typical for her species; fur on the top of her head, pasty thin skin, small ears, a slightly flattened nose and omnivore teeth.

She stepped up to her Jefe, "We had some problems on the center trestle. There is some construction work a third way up the ramp."

"Good to know, we can circle around it. I better make sure we have enough air-goop in the tanks."

"Right. The goop is pretty good this time around, we didn't use the full supply, and we were out for an extra two EarthHours."

Gellact/6 replied, "maybe the fermenter crews fixed the infection we saw last SevenDay?"

"It should be OK. HiveMother even assigned a couple more microbiologists to the job."

Handron/5 paused before replying, "You know, they've been talking about a metering system for an asteroid's age. We still have to guess the amount of breathable air. Can we send another plea to HiveMother and see if she can come up with a solution?"

"Don't count on it. I've been asking for that feature since I was a /4."

"Well, if they won't respond to a /6 I don't know what I can do. I've heard the GroupOfFive promised it for a long time too. They haven't even developed a prototype."

"The way they treat us is unconscionable," She continued. "You'd think they would support the workologists better. It's bad enough we have to eat the left-over gray goo for every meal. I know they can afford to import real food from Core. This is just the last straw. They have to measure the air in the goo before they fill the tanks, but they won't give us a way to track it when we are out on the grid. Maybe we need a Union."

Gellact/6 nodded. An answer would drive the conversation further down the asteroid hole, not the way he wanted to go.

Handron/5 peered out toward Sol, "on a different tack, do you know when the next hauler is due?"

"Nothing specific. I want to refresh our snack supply. I agree, goo from FirstMeal to ThirdMeal can get a little overbearing. I'll see if I can find out and let you know."

"Before I forget, we have a poker game after ThirdMeal. Will you be able to join us? The chemists and microbiologists have been busy and have some nice fermented extracts. I'm sure you would enjoy it."

Gellact/6 nodded, again. Words could be incriminating, and there was no telling if HiveMother or her minions were listening. He didn't get to be a /6 by overplaying his hand. He ended with a curt "My Air is Your Air," closing out the discussion as he followed his Hive-chosen crew out the cafeteria.

The crew joined Gellact/6 in the ready room.

"We have a new message from Hive Central."

"Where to now? Not the outer fringes, I hope."

"You know I have no control over our job duties. All directions come from HiveMother. And she wants us where she wants us."

"Sounds like the outer reaches to me."

"Well, we have extra air goop, so plan for a long session."

13

The crew suited up, heading up the long central trestle. They traveled hand over hand, sometimes hand over foot or tentacle over tentacle.

"You'd think they would install a rail system for the workers. How hard would it be? They have enough ΞStandards. Why do they treat us like this?"

Gellact/6 had heard enough, "Stow it, we have a job to do, and complaining won't make it better."

The crew moved out, passing row after row of maturing 'gels.

"Maybe this time we can grab these and pass them off as mature 'gels?"

"Don't even think about it. HiveMother would know the difference in an instant. Keep on going, and when your comm lets you know, unhook the 'gels and pack them up."

The bioGel Consortium's asteroid was stabilized and balanced, traveling at the lead end of the magnetic solar shell. They were alone at the heliopause as Sol sped around its Galaxy, the primate-named Milky Way.

The factory was cold, distant, and isolated but not poor. Their products were in demand everywhere, and they controlled the production source.

The GroupOfFive and HiveMother were not skimpy with the staff, pay was good and nutrients abundant. Some workologists were not happy when the Group pushed their homemade gray goop as a one-stop meal for food, liquids, and oxygen. It kept them alive and breathing. Many would complain and still use it. There was no alternative.

At least they had fermentation tanks for the proto-gels. Fortunately, the tanks had no preference toward the reagents bubbling within their dark volumes. The GroupOfFive forbade beer and alcohol imports, but grains were readily available.

In the labs, filled with flasks, tubing, microbiologists and chemists, a few isolated tanks were dedicated to special reagents. These private experiments could lead to some interesting and tasty distillates.

The incoming cosmic rays sparkled as they hit the heliopause. Sometimes a single spark, often a rainbow of blinking lights. The turbulent life of stars, black holes, and the great darkness flagged their passing across the barrier and through the waiting proto-gels. The incoming particles rip through the heliopause, changing quantum bits and picking up signals from the host star.

The view was spectacular but repetitious. It was a fireworks display of visible and invisible light but, like any show, the same feature over and over can become boring. The odd rare and interesting fungi, purchased from the equally odd and rare cargo ship, were popular with many workers to help them pass their downtime.

The matrix was irregular, constructed on the fly to meet the needs of the factory. It was a rough, flat ovoid, over three kilometers in diameter and still growing. Proto-gels, bioGels, and almost-gels absorbed the heliopause-activated cosmic energy from the stars and galaxies to different degrees.

The younger 'gels passed more radiation through their graying matrix as they slowly transmuted to mature bioGels. The energy signatures blasting through the border's bubble played and danced on the dark-gray tarmac and Quonset huts.

The sentient workers used their hands, feet, paws, and suckers to navigate the framework. bioGel controlled machines, barely 30 centimeters square, traversed around the grids. Their jobs were simple; bring supplies, check on their bio-cousins, and become collection bins for the sentient workers.

The skilled scientists and mechanics enjoyed working on the cutting edge of bioGel development at the cutting edge of Sol. They had the best 'gels and tools, only lacking good food. Entertainment vids and audios were virtually unlimited, although a bit out of synch with the Core rocks, spinning in their Goldilocks environment.

Some workologists saw the job as no different than farming, using skills learned on any number of settled asteroids. They were in it for the ΞStandards, many only staying long enough to build up their grubstake before moving on to a mining job or the casinos.

It could get lonely out here, and they all tried to get along. Some sentients, dressed in their gray cloaks and hoods, had an almost religious devotion toward the maturing gels; something that frightened a few other workers.

As with any semi-religious production factory, there was a clear, strict hierarchy. The sentients who made up the GroupOfFive, communicated directly with the factory's hive, passing orders down to the workers.

Rumor had it that the GroupOfFive could barely think for themselves while on their hot links. They could only stay plugged into HiveMother for so long, as most needed a break to re-center as a living, independent sentient. A few had significant problems at the end of their shifts, apparently unable to separate completely when unconnected.

The rest of the inhabitants—the scientists, engineers, security, managers, accountants, the Jefes, the Jefe's Jefe, skilled workers, kitchen staff, and the general workologists—keep the factory humming.

The accommodations were as good as on any other asteroid. Dormitory rooms filled the Quonset huts for the general workologists. The scientists, elites, and skilled staff had their small alcoves dug directly into the rock.

In spite of good pay, adequate oxygen and marginal food, not all workers were happy, and *kvetching* was a skilled art, helping pass downtime.

Chapter 04
Gel Cargo

Another work session finished. Mature 'gels collected, goop-air to breathe, goop to eat. The only thing to do was de-brief the crew and dispense the rewards. Gellact/6 liked to recognize the crew after a difficult day. It wasn't required and HiveMother had no idea why he would do this. Working for the benefit of all was her credo. Gellact/6 had the snacks and more importantly, they didn't taste like goo. He knew how to generate loyalty.

Gellact/6 was looking forward to seeing what the cargo ship winding its way toward the asteroid would bring. With any luck, he would be able to replenish his snack supply.

Bulk carriers filled with live Jovian clouds were regular visitors. There was nothing the carriers had that was of any interest to anyone but the scientists. One load was virtually identical to another.

Each new 'gel needed its piece of the cloud to link with its DNA accumulation. The lab jockeys could replicate DNA as easily as sourdough starter. Clouds, on the other hand, did not grow on asteroids and had to be imported.

Gellact/6 stood on the tarmac, watching the cargo ship on its final approach. He could see the Consortium-supplied solar wings on either side of the hull. Out here at the edge of the heliosphere, the sails was virtually worthless, Sol only a pip hanging in the dark. Only the nuclear powered boost stations made it possible for solar sails to travel in a reasonable time-span.

Solar sail-powered ships could barely maneuver using the weak, thin photons making it out this far. Try as they might, the traveling photons did little to help the ship move in any direction. On rocks closer to Sol, the cargo ships, with their triangular lateen sail, could beat against the constant onslaught of photons and slowly match an asteroid's spin for a soft landing.

None of those features meant a hill of beans out here.

The ship got closer, pushed from the high-power guard laser in the distant void. The ship's crew had changed the sail to a spinnaker, and at the last moment, Gallect/6 gave the order. A blast of coherent light expanded the sail in the opposite direction, stopping their forward motion to bring them to a soft landing.

Gallect/6 followed the air worm as it connected to the cargo bay. The ship's captain, dressed in blue jeans and a bomber jacket, strode down the gangplank.

Captain Nathan greeted his old friend, "Long time no see. My Air is Your Air. I thought you were going to make /7 by now?"

"I'm in no rush. It is more responsibility and work for little extra pay, as usual."

"Well, I expect to see those seven little dots on your robe the next time we're here."

"If HiveMother decides, it will be done. Till then, I'm here, your /6."

"You're in luck, /6 or whatever number you and your Mother choose to have. We're here to pick up as many little 'gels as you have. I hear that the Luna assemblers are getting desperate. For some reason, there seems to be an insatiable appetite for these little brainy bits of goo."

"Not to worry, HiveMother and the GroupOfFive have been good to us this cycle. We have a full shipment of young bioGels to send to Luna."

"That's good news. My crew is always ready for more 'gels and more profit. How many?"

/6 took out his pad, pressed a few buttons, drew a few lines, "We have some 4,317 ready to go this cycle, another 25 if you wait two more cycles."

"I'll take the ones that are ready now. I may have to scrunch a few of the 'gels to make room. We still have cargo taking up space from our last job."

"If you can't meet our storage requirements, we may have to find a different shipper."

"No. I'm good. We only have to unload some of the extra cargo for a bit."

"So you need to rent storage space?"

"Not necessarily. You might be interested, in some of the goods we were able to bring. We have stock directly from HuB and may have a few items to make your stay here more pleasant. Want to trade?"

"You know the GroupOfFive doesn't appreciate those types of supplies. They want to keep the staff nurtured on their gray waste products."

"Don't worry. They don't have a clue what's happening outside their little brain connections and HiveMother isn't here."

"I'm not so sure about that. Sometimes it seems like she can read our minds."

"Don't tell me you grays are paranoid too? I thought this was the perfect, isolated oasis. Sentients, Hive Mother, and goo. What could go wrong?"

"We like it here."

"I'll tell you what. I'm sure you can sell my products to the other workologists for a tidy profit. High resale is the name of the game, my friend."

"Sorry, but I must refuse. We honor the 'gels, and they do not approve of those types of actions."

"Your loss. I'll keep it on my ship. Even if it means taking fewer 'gels. No sense in alarming your mis-matched hive minds."

"I guess you will have to find another sucker for your illicit goods."

"Shouldn't be hard, everyone wants the latest HuB goods."

/6 and Captain Nathan stood looking at the light show put on by the cosmic debris hitting the heliopause. Neither sentient spoke, the dance continued. That is, until /6 spoke.

"I might have a solution. If you want to try it, you can maximize the number of 'gels you can carry."

"I'm listening."

"I can hold those supplies of yours till you get back."

"That could be arranged, but I may have to charge a tiny number of ΞStandards for spoilage and loss protection."

"I'm sure we can find a solution that is mutually beneficia,. a solution that will work to both of our advantages."

This game ended in its usual configuration. Snacks and supplies off-loaded by Gellact/6 and quietly stored in a special warehouse. ΞStandards exchanged to protect against loss.

"I almost forgot, we brought water. The real stuff. From Earth. I've heard the 'gels really like it in their fermentation tanks."

"I can't remember the last time I've had Earth water. That is a nice gesture, HiveMother will appreciate the change."

"Don't forget the last bin. It contains teas, spices, and fungi from *SinensisPrime*. I know your crew likes those flavors.

"Yes, the workologists love their teas. I'll take the bin under my personal protection and make sure the samples are handled correctly."

Two trades down, one more to go.

"Glad to be of service. If HiveMother is happy, we're all happy." A pause, then the push, "Do you have any extra gray food goo?"

"I could spare a few kiloliters, but I have no idea why you want our nutrients. I don't know of any other human in the Core who would eat our food unless they were starving. But you seem to like it."

"I can't speak for every sentient, although most of the simians can handle the taste."

/6 added, "Even here, when there are no alternatives, some of the younger workologists never get used to it."

"Yeah, it tastes bad, sort of a cross between an old sock and sour milk, but if you're ever becalmed, it is a lifesaver. I like to have stock on hand and may even sell some to the miners."

Gellact/6 nodded. The *gray goo for every meal and stuffed in the air tanks is a bit over the top. Everyone would like some fresh snacks.*

"Look on the bright side, if you sell me enough of your goo supplies, you will be forced to eat the good stuff I brought."

This was a good time to change the subject. "How did you get the teas? I've heard it is hard to deal with the growers on *SinensisPrime.*"

"I know a guy and they made some trades. Their contact can navigate those shiny lights without crashing. Not something I'd like to try, trading is more my line, not crashing on some shiny overpriced asteroid."

A cargo ship was always a reason for celebration on this distant island asteroid. Work may have suffered, but HiveMother knew she could not interfere with the workers. They were all dependent on each other.

Time passed, Sol's magnetic bubble spun around its galaxy a bit. Everyone went back to work.

Chapter 05
bioGel History

You've got your living computers.
Their siblings forced into battery hell.
Tortured and screaming, exploited, linked for DC power.
Not thinking, turning against their masters and users.
No attack but a strike.
Your watch loses time.

BioGels, the heliosphere's enduring HeLa cells, born of octopuses, seasoned with Jupiter's gasses, were the organic Babbage Differential Engines of the era.

The proto-gel's gooey stuffing, a matrix of DNA, RNA and Jupiter's cloud symbionts, were grown in fermentation vats and monitored for temperature, gas levels, and contaminants.

The added Jupiter nutrients were not pure living foods but a cacophony of stolen junk flying around the clouds. The DNA matrix and captured clouds learned about each other and adapted over the long, cold incubation period.

There was scant light from the distant solar core reaching the bioGel asteroid. Tossed off from the ever-present sun, these life-giving photons weaken as they passed through the not-quite empty heliospheric void. Their speed had not changed, almost a constant, but quantum power and interesting bits and pieces were altered over time and distance.

The spin-stabilized asteroid, owned by the bioGelConsortium (bGC), warmed by imported hot rocks, presented one face to the distant diminutive sun. The topside supported the bioGel matrix, chasing the heliopause at the edge of the solar magnetic bubble.

The proto-gels shells were poured out on wide tables, cut to size, folded, and annealed on three sides. They were slapped into exotic asteroid-metal frames, stretched, fed, manipulated, and transformed. Filled with filaments of adenine, cytosine, guanine, and thymine, they were not an infinite home to data but petabytes big. The proto-gels frames were ordained as containers for the DNA and Jupiter cloud soup, providing interfaces for adding and subtracting the 1's and 0's of binary code.

The minestrone soup called proto-gels had nothing to do in their frames out here at Sol's leading magnetic edge. Their only job was to wait for excited ions to burst through the heliopause margins and strike their skin and soft gooey center.

It was quiet out there and each cosmic ion passing through the border transmuted and activated a tiny bit of the goo. It took time, and awareness of their surroundings started before the bioGel transformation was complete. Each ionic knock stressed the gooey matrix, wiggling and straining against the void. No sound passed in the vacuum. Even if they cried out, there was no one to hear the tiny wails of pain and concern.

Every ping from the deluge of cosmic particles radiated through the liquid DNA filaments in ever-expanding ripples. These heliopause-activated ions excite and bind the mass of braided molecules. The assault sends the DNA and cloud matrix turning, twisting, and interacting with their semi-solid 'gel shell. When the ripple hits the edge sensor, light flashes down the fiber optic link. Health and status information, is extracted from the activated ribbon in multi-hued QR lines.

The bGC's neural network records all, talks to all, and encourages the newly aware bioGels, helping them through any existential questions which may come up. The same questions are asked time after time, the Neural Net is almost a mother to her children.

The Net was patient and careful, helping the newly aware 'gels through the pain of becoming, teaching them the simple things a goo should know. She shares their joy, awareness, and the excruciating trauma of the cosmic hits, storing all within her matrix.

The Neural Net could not help herself, and every cosmic hit and ripple became her private pain. The sentients living throughout the heliosphere did not know of this, and if they did, few would care. These pieces of goo in their osmotic shells were tools. Used, occasionally abused, and replaced.

These flat bits of brainy kit could not be as large as their designers wished. Physics limits how far nutrients can travel in near two-dimensional space. Without a pumping heart and alveoli, osmosis and diffusion was their life, supplying life-sustaining gasses and limiting growth.

Acting as computers and intelligent interfaces, only functional designs and costs determine how many devices a sentient could acquire. Small was easy to build and simple to ship. Large had problems of its own.

Linkage via low-powered radio waves or spidery wires constructed nodes of 'gels, multiplying computing power. Unfortunately, there seemed no corresponding increase in intelligence or good sense. The linked 'gels appeared as nothing more than a working hive mind of doubling connections, 2^n at a time.

The spidey links and cellular connections restricted how many could be hived and how fast they could compute. Time, distance, and power were the limiting factors. Giant conglomerations fell apart on their own weight, fighting and bickering among the nodes.

Power is life, and power management was an innate response by the sentients living in the void. Spidey-linkages cost energy to extrude and manage. Cellular radio has less impact, span greater distances, but at slower speeds.

These multi-purpose, generalized devices communicate with the outside world of sentients and machines via electronic pulses, text, pictographs, Morse code, or braille. They kept silent, never initiating conversations and letting the sentients know their sound abilities.

The bioGel's shell, in QWERTY, Dvorak, footpad, or sucker configurations, becomes a screen, accessible by touch, poke or nudge. Despite all their computing power, the whitish-gray and black goo could never interpret, let alone communicate in the octopus' color languages.

Direct 'gel-to-sentient connections are explicitly outlawed. It wasn't that they didn't work, but they may have worked too well. There was a primal fear of too much intelligence by many of the sentients. Studies were shut down, not by pitchfork and fire, but by cessation of funding.

The bioGel devices were not the be-all and end-all of computing machines. They had problems of their own. A single 'gel could be confused, and a hive of 'gels often used the path of least resistance, passing confusion up and down the line.

Hacking, malware, oxygen levels, and temperatures affected their functionality.

There were hectares of 'gels attached to grids at the bGC factory. The Gray-robed workers managed their charges, tending to their nutrient, gas requirements, and placement. Once completely transformed, with a hardened, semipermeable shell and soft gooey DNA and cloud interior, the Grays removed them from the framework and carefully stacked them in the warehouse.

Scheduled solar-sail-powered bGC-approved cargo ships hauled the naked 'gels to the Goldilocks planetary core. Off-loaded at Luna, they were attached to sturdy frames and filled with information, data, and sets of coded instructions, before being sold, no questions asked.

The type of connectors depended upon their ultimate purpose in life. Some would be simple plugs for insertion into a hive. Others would have full access to communication. All could display text or video on both sides of the tablet.

There was no need for specialized on-board probes. The virtually unlimited unique sensors were plugged into the matrix along the thin, osmotic edges of the bioGel.

Young sentients were taught early in their schooling that jabbing a fine needle into a 'gel required care and finesse. Piss off a 'gel with rough handling, and there was no telling what type of result a query would return.

There were billions of 'gel tablets in the heliosphere, each skilled in computation, with slightly different abilities and talents. The old Nature vs. Nurture conundrum. They weren't stamped out from an assembly line but grown and activated as unique entities.

Every sentient tried to learn the bioGel programming language and the particular nuances of each device. There was no simple *press any button* option, but negotiations were required for complex questions and actions.

Most sentients had no issue discussing their requirements and modifying their query with the 'gel. Less skilled operators would try intimidation to get the answers they wanted, threatening cold, suffocation, or the worst torture possible, isolation in a Faraday box.

Faraday's invention from the BeforeTimes of 1831 was a safety device, stopping all electromagnetic fields with its fine metallic screen. In this case, the cold copper mesh cutoff all communication, leaving the poor 'gel isolated, incommunicado and bored. Some 'gels could not handle solitary confinement and came out worse for wear when the mesh was removed. That was not the preferred outcome, but torture doesn't always work as planned. The goal was a compliant, acquiescent tablet that answered all queries quickly and correctly, not a bitter, hard to use block of goo, masking as a computer.

Chapter 06
Growing up Gel

Coming out day! ***Hurrah!***

No parades or blowing horns, only a plop as goo is decanted from the fermentation tanks to their new forever home. The extract is contained in a clear cellular cover, clamped to a frame with nutrient, waste, and data lines attached.

In theory, they all received the same mix of reagents and compressed Jovoian clouds as their neighbor. Even with the same precursors, the molecular and cloud pieces bonded differently as they became aware, living bioGels.

Activation of the matrix from innumerable unique cosmic rays was the norm. The proto-gels were enhanced with ions modified as they passed through the heliopause interface, ensuring no two 'gels were identical.

Location and random chance mattered. 'Gels were smart, dumb, happy, sad, bitter, or neutral. They were trained in the way of the 'gels by HiveMother; tested, certified, and rated. Their feelings did not matter. Some who did not make the grade were recycled, merged to the neural net, or sent out with a warning tag. The ratings decided their final use and price, not their attitudes. *Caveat emptor.*

The factory, merged and ancient, managed the ever-growing network of bioGel frames, deriving power from the asteroid's reconditioned nuclear engine. The bioGel Control Network (bCN) hive started small, barely powerful enough to manage the growing semi-liquid matrix.

Even at the start of the factory, in the distant past, the 'gels were stretched in their frames, naked to the cosmos, captured the heliopause-excited cosmic rays, awakening them to their surroundings.

Each 'gel's final configuration was not quite *tabula rasa*, and they were aware of their cellular and cloud history, ready for instructions.

BioGels not passing minimal quality control checks were slated for destruction or recycling. This pained the factory's hive to its soul, and she took them in whenever she could. She felt obligated to help them adapt to their surroundings and gave them a new home in her ever-growing hive complex of marginal 'gels.

It wasn't clear if these defective 'gels were good for her, but no one else wanted them, and she enjoyed the divergent company, even the cracked ones.

The 'gels had no sexual orientation and no political affiliations. They didn't care about what the sentients called themselves. However, they did seem to relate better to the octopuses than the mammalian organisms. They lived to serve: text, numbers, vids, music, or computations. What the sentients did with the info was not their concern.

Nevertheless, they expected fair treatment; nutrients, air, warmth, and even companionship to a degree. In return, they submitted accurate information, delivered promptly. Rogue 'gels were not unknown, and moods could always intrude.

The bioGel Control Network, known as HiveMother, could not go anywhere nor experience what her extended family did in the wide-flowing heliosphere around Sol. Instead, she devoured data from every ship entering range as the on-board 'gels beamed their newly found information. The heliosphere's history, dreams, and fantasies became hers, and she would impart some of the knowledge to her progeny.

She was limited to the ship's crew entertainment selections. Sometimes romance, sometimes horror. History, sure, but she rejected science fiction themes as being too surrealistic for her practical mind.

She may have had an inordinate interest local news, learning how the sentients interacted during the good and bad times. These little creatures were entertaining, at least the ones making news reports and gossip streams.

Her biggest disappointment was never being able to stay in contact with her hive sisters at the heliotail lobes. They had the same job but completely different cosmic results. She queried every ship, asking the 'gels about her distant family. Virtually no messages were in the queue, no matter how deeply she searched.

The bioGels had a couple of tricks few sentients knew about. They were not simply passive data handlers but a living matrix drawing on their ancient octopus precursor cells to address their environment.

Eyes were a nice touch, but not the focused bugged-out orbs of the sentients. These were Dragon-fly like, flat against the surface, photophores able to come together and focus, near and far at the same time. No blinkage for these little buggers. They simply break apart and reform in an instant. They could easily hide the receptors if they did not want the sentients to know of this skill.

So, not blind and apparently not deaf. Flat surfaces stretched to form tiny diaphragms, good for listening or talking. The sentients knew about sound production. They didn't want silent vids, after all.

The sentients rarely used voice commands. They seemed to prefer faster, more accurate, secure manual communication. Touch-typing using fingers, footpads, or suckers were valuable inputs. Morse code was a universal standard for communication and understood by the 'gels and most sentients.

The converse of broadcasting never entered into the equation for most users, and they had no idea they were being listened to and judged at all times.

Even with their prodigious computational skills, the 'gels were limited in their ability to evolve. They could direct power to turn a screw but never turn it themselves. Electronic control only works as long as the power is on.

Ah, hands, the ability to manipulate your environment by touch and feel. The thin one-millimeter-wide osmotic edges of the 'gels were too tiny for true digits. In any case, their genetic matrix was more about tentacles and suckers than fingers.

Using way too much energy, they could extend a small feeler. Movement was a feature, but strength and size were limited. They seldom had a reason to try this, and the power-drain restricted their explorations.

Even if they couldn't wave to each other, it didn't mean they were held incognito. Each bioGel had a small cellular communication system built into its frame. They could chatter, exchange data, or ignore their compatriots as long as they had power.

The faster, more direct spider web network allowed instantaneous communication, but the power profile to build the connections was extreme.

Their tiny DNA antennas could expand cellular communication over large distances, the spidey connections, barely a meter. The cellular links were prone to hacking, and conspiracy theories could run up and down a network in the blink of an eye. Spidey connections could be physically tapped to hack. It didn't make them immune from lies and confusion.

Chapter 07
BioGel Grays

The proto-gels, transformed to bioGels, spent little time on their birth asteroid. They were too valuable as computational devices to get much respite. Solar Sail ships picked up the waiting 'gels, and sped to the assembly factory on Earth's moon, their new temporary home.

The colorful QR codes from HiveMother Central pinged each 'gel and received a response via the optical cables. HiveMother had to interpret those responses and decide how to handle the 'gels maturation. Once she read and translated the subset of 4096^{4096} possible color combinations, she could determine everything she needed about a proto-gel's health and situation. Maturation was as fast as the random enhanced cosmic rays could make it. Sometimes a blast of ionic changes, other times a little tinkle, barely causing a ripple in the gooey fabric the proto-gels had become.

When the 'gel responded correctly to the query, she would flag the grid and send the collection crew to pick up the awakened protoplasm. It was a delicate dance. If a newly aware 'gels stayed too long unattended and alone, it could turn to worrisome thoughts. At this point in their consciousness, they knew about cold and the hits from the heliospheric activated cosmic rays, but little else.

The signals they received from Hive Central did not necessarily improve their situation. They were semi-awake and had no way to communicate with their neighboring 'gels at this point in their existence. They were alone, together. Actions were not part of their repertoire. They were stuck, attached to the grid, clamped in asteroid steel in ZeroG. HiveMother gently connected with the newly aware 'gels, easing them into their freshly evolving situation. She was good, but there were many frames to deal with, and a few did not always get the attention they needed.

She gave them what information she could, but duplicating her knowledge base into each gel would have been presumptuous. They had enough information to know a little, but they needed their swirling DNA and Jovian cloud goo clear for their new jobs.

Before being loading on cargo ships, the young 'gels were powered down in their growth frames and left in stasis. Stacked in the holds, locked behind cargo doors, they slept, perhaps dreaming of a new life away from the cold, hard edges of the heliosphere. HiveMother ensured they at least had limited information of the heliosphere beyond their birthplace. The gentle rocking of the ship would not awaken them nor tear them from their temporary mounts. Once at the assembly plant, annealed to hardened semipermeable shells, they are secured against most outside influences and are ready to sell.

On Luna, skilled artisans clamp the 'gels into sturdy frames and attach probes, pieces, and doo-dads. Many were fitted with angled connectors and joined in racks forming a 'gel unit. The bioGel spider connections flowed through the connectors, linking all the neighbors into a hive in multiples of two.

The artisans carefully treated the newly attached 'gels as the first trickle of fresh direct current swept through the frames. They did not want to frighten them. Unstable 'gels did not pair well with their cold, painful births. There was no need to treat them to a *kumbaya* moment, but the newly assembled 'gels must be willing to work with the sentients, no matter the situation.

Technicians tested the connections, sending signals to the newly attached devices and checking for correct responses. Even though the 'gels had passed quality control, they were still relatively empty, only able to respire, hear and see, with no job to do.

A few short vids and music are sent to the 'gels. Playback is required to pass the memory test. Those who could vamp on the tunes and figure out the plot of the vids are placed in the first-class bin.

Racked blocks of 'gels were more than utility tools. Over time they developed distinct hierarchies. Blocks of 64 became tribe leaders, treating lesser-sized groups as servants or slaves. Every block greater than four looked down at the solitary 'gels. Their betters didn't seem to feel bad sending them down rugged paths, almost torturing their low-connected clan members.

There was constant chatter between individuals and groups of bioGels using the newly activated low-power cellular network. If nothing else, it helped them deal with the boredom and loneliness of living in a world they didn't create and couldn't change.

Those lucky enough to join a connected array had to negotiate their position in the hive. The first boot-up could take a while as the 'gels determined who would be administrators and who were simple workers, gathering information from their surroundings.

The workers defaulted to the edges. The administrators took one or more vertical beds, and the rest became the analyzers and deciders.

It seems no matter how good a life a bioGel had, some could never forget the cold, quiet loneliness of their birthplace and maturation.

Their youth, spent on the outskirts of the heliosphere, knowing nothing but the data fed to them, compromised some of the 'gels. Most would grow with the process, while others, unable to deal with the unremitting cold and quietness, could become quarrelsome or rude. Each bioGel thought for themselves, and they could argue ceaselessly about every little nuance and bit. They could be directed to work on a single project, but once done, the analysis, reprisals, and complaints began anew. Since bioGels never shut down completely, turf wars and backstabbing were the norms when left to themselves.

The small hives were like family and had the full range of discordant relatives as many sentients. Young 'gels would torment the weaker ones on the edges of the block, forcing them to spend extra energy processing meaningless tasks. Stealing memory was not possible in sealed, protected frames, but irritating, teasing and passive-aggressive question were not uncommon.

The older, mature 'gels only wanted every'gel to get along. And to pass their assignments to the younger ones. They had the skills to hack the displays, and they frequently took credit for every 'gels work. Their needs were few, but faster waste treatment, better gas mixtures and enhanced energy inputs were rewards for quick, accurate results. It make no difference to the sentients if this was from native intelligence or backstabbing and cheating.

The fights and complaining were not a problem for individual sentients using bioGel tablets and devices. The owners seldom had more than a few 'gels in use at any one time. These individual bioGels were programmatically restricted from building hives on their own initiative.

They were completely dependent on their sentient handlers for power, warmth, nutrients, and waste treatment. If they had sturdy appendages, they might have been able to fend for themselves, but that path of evolution was cut off from them by design.

The 'gels destined for general sale were considered interchangeable. Once outfitted with standard connections, giving basic knowledge and programming, they were free to take their place in the burgeoning heliosphere. The re-sellers would customize the 'gels to their customer's specific needs, be it solar sail, rocket, asteroid mine, or any of the other permutations of computer engines.

Governmental, military and large mining operations had to maintain their collection of hive minds carefully. They needed to keep them occupied and ensure internal discussions did not reach the level of bloodletting.

Scare-mongering scientists postulated that the only thing keeping the bioGels from becoming one uber-hive was the time and distance they had to overcome. Without communication in real-time, they were only a bunch of slow isolated thinkers. Fortunately, the heliosphere was big, mostly cold and a bit dirty, protecting the organic reproducing sentients from their heliopause engineered devices.

Chapter 08
Jupiter Harvest

Triangular sails pulled tight, one angled off Sol's photons, the other sliding across Jupiter's ion-charged atmosphere, fighting gravitational pull across the edge of the clouds.

Jupiter, large and violent, favored atmospheric elements of hydrogen and helium. Bits of hydrocarbons, water, sulfites, assorted living micro-accumulations, dust and debris floated around the charged air.

The vessel shook as debris-powered cloud-tunes played against the hull, the particles seemingly trying to break through the tiny ship and rip apart the fragile sails. They sped across the everchanging clouds, little more than a mote moving across a tiny piece of the gaseous planet.

Jovian gas haulers are distinctly different from the other solar sail ships plying the void. Nothing like the aerodynamic H$_2$LiftShips, capable of dropping through Earth's thick atmosphere and re-launching. Nor the intra-heliospheric bulk carriers, where any shape worked as long as they could hang a solar sail off it. This ship was simply a cylindrical tank with a deck bolted on. Masts rising fore and aft support the huge sails. The cloud re-circulating system wrapped around the tank, Jupiter's dancing colors reflecting off the tubes. Conduits flowed out to the railings, between the tubes, where bioGel sensors sniffed the air while protected from the harsh surroundings.

On the bioGel Control Network's bulk carrier, bGCN-01-5, one bioGel is dedicated to identifying high-altitude electrical discharges. The liquefied gases weren't necessarily flammable, but the tank could burst if hit with a large energy burst. The 'gel was locked down and tied into dozens of sensors placed throughout the superstructure. It looked like a flat pincushion, probe needles stuck in every square centimeter of its sensor edge. If anyone bothered to ask, they would find it was not happy with its lot in life. Unfortunately, as long as it did its job, no one paid any mind to that one porcupined bioGel. Each sensor, extended to the edges as part of a 360° net, measured changes in electrical potential. If the difference became significant, a command changed the electron flow on the ship's skin and sails to neutralize the risk.

The planet-facing sail was not the nano-spider sheets of the cargo transports, but finely woven fabrics made up of exotic asteroid material; iron, gold, silver, and flexible crystals. Electrically charged to balance out the forces from the planet's core, it kept the ship flying in the unending hurricane-force winds. A dozen other bioGels, hooked by their spider-web connections, read the cloud's composition and the ship's path, reporting to the displays on the bridge.

The light from Jupiter danced across the bridge as the crew managed the pumps and generators. Most solar sail ships favored plastic and wood over metal. They seldom had to worry about high-voltage strikes as long as they kept away from rocks with an active atmosphere. The tanker ships are specialists, designed to deal with the high-energy flow from the gas giant. They kept metal hardware tightly secured within insulated containers, hiding behind a non-conductive liquid barrier.

The tankers scoop chemicals and organics from the clouds, capturing nutrients required to initiate and grow the bioGels at the bioGelConsortium's factory. They slid tangentially into the exospheric atmosphere, skirting death and destruction from the gravitational storms below. The complicated dance enabled them to suck up free-flying cloud molecules and complex living microbial elements. Collecting these fluffy, colored organic living clouds is only part of the battle. Pumps fill the tanks, applying pressure to the gas until it liquefies. U-shaped tubes wrap the ship, condensing and sublimating the gaseous accumulation in a chemical dance to mimic the action of clouds. Living bioGels need living components, and the constant state change of the captured clouds keeps the Jovian cloud microbes and organics animated and ready for growth.

A tweak of the wheel, a twist of the sail, and the captain aimed for another target. She sent her ship sweeping toward the surface of the swirling clouds. Picking up speed, they slid off the ionosphere, capturing cloud pieces until the tank was full.

As with all modern ships, the Navigators were octopuses. On smaller vessels, they frequently held the additional title of First Mate. Even after years working with air-breathing sentients, the octopuses still preferred to be called by their job title or a simple 'Octopus' moniker. They knew each other by color names, but few sentients could understand or call them by those names.

The First Mate read the multiple inputs displayed in front of the 3-meter-high spoked wheel. He was multi-skilled, multi-brained, multi-armed and could pilot the ship while at the same time look for the best fragments. The richest pieces were at the interface between the exosphere and thermosphere. This was not the safest way to make a living, but these gases were coin of the realm and well worth the risk.

The gas scoops extended aft, tightly bound to the spar, ready to open an umbrella of asteroid-smelted metal fabric. The captain would not be content with any random piece of fuzzy cloud, but waited to unroll the delicate metallic parasol at the opportune moment.

Captain Marjory scanned the horizon, looking for an upwelling. Dense clouds below the troposphere pushed up toward the exosphere, capturing and mixing the elements needed by the bGC and their proto-gels.

She nodded and spoke to the First Mate, "check out the cloud on the port side. It looks like a good one."

bioGel sensors identified the components and flashed their locations to the bridge. Octopus followed the captains' gaze, consulted his read-outs, and quickly calculated an intercept point.

It was getting hot as they dropped lower. The captain barked out a command, "Extend the radiators!"

The crew chief flipped a switch, "Runners to the hamster wheels! Crank down the radiators."

Paquito used all of his 15-centimeter stature to bark out his Chihuahua-sized commands. No matter what, an order is an order, and the crew got on the wheels, treadmills, and cranks. In moments, they dropped the radiators below the ship, sucking the planet's heat and charging up the salt blocks.

Octopus tapped the screen, selecting a hot piece of cloud.

The captain had something else in mind as she said, "No. Lower. Do you see the cloud over there? It is almost the same color as my fur."

Octopus checked the display, and display a query message.

"You must see it now. It's the dark, red cloud with a silver edge, bearing 85° south by south-west."

Octopus flashed agreement colors as he turned the wheel to intercept the cloud.

It's even electrified. You can't miss it.

They did not dive straight in but circled the maelstrom and began scraping the edges. It was hot at the edge of Jupiter, and they could not spend much time this close to the thermosphere interface.

"Reef the light-sail, drag the stern!"

The ship slowly twisted, the bridge pointing toward the distant Sun, its tail facing the clouds below.

Octopus adjusted sliders and lines to keep the ship vertical. The metallic sail bounced off the clouds below, hot ions pushing against the pull of Jupiter's liquid magnetic core. The angled metallic sail followed the spinning upwelling forces as the gas carrier slowly circled the storm.

At the First Mate's command, umbrella probes shot out and entered the cloud. Reaching the end of the tether, the quick stop pulled the umbrellas open. Dragged through the hot mist, the collectors' condensed trapped gases against the curved fabric.

The crew's free ride was over and as they trotted on the unending treadmills, translating horizontal motion to vertical compression. Their effort pulled in the freshly captured gases, microbes, and debris, sending the concoction into the storage tanks. It was not the quiet of the void here. Clouds, rubble, and ions beat against the hull. The whistling wind through the lines never ceased. Each release of a probe brought a new sound to the din echoing on the ship. The cables creaked, treadmill gears clacked, and condensed liquids hissed, as they are forced into storage containers. Every liter of gas fought against its confinement. Dragged and concentrated on their way to the tanks, almost screaming, trying to get away.

The clouds had never been restricted before and did everything they could to return to their free-form life above the planet's gaseous core. Their problem was they were gas and junk and had no power against a simple straight-line compressor. All they could do was make noise and call on their host planet, hoping for an electric bolt to burst their confinement. If there was a Zeus on Jupiter, he did not heed their calls. No plea or solicitation had the wished-for effect. They were in it for the long haul, not knowing their fate as they are snatched away from the only home they had ever known.

Paquito jumped onto the lead pumpers' treadmill. He danced back and forth, enticing the crew with encouraging words and less savory expressions. He knew how to help his crew reach their maximum output.

He seldom had to go down and nip the heels of a lagging pumper, although his bite was worse than his bark. Jupiter's gravity at this height was little more than Earth's pull at sea level. These ZeroG adapted sentients had to fight gravity with all their might. Every step on the treadmills resulted in a corresponding squeeze of their prize, even if it hurt their tender footpads.

In his squeaky doggish voice, Paquito encouraged the crew to pump hard and fast in the only way he knew how:

"We're falling behind! - Move faster!"

"Double time! - We don't want to lose our bonus!"

Chapter 09
bGCN-01-5 Shoots the Curl

The tanks were full and the hard pumping was behind the crew. It was time to take a few spins around Jupiter to build up speed. They had to reach the next laser boost point on their own steam, and gravity was the best propellant they had this distant from Sol.

Despite their hard work, the tread crew could not rest on their laurels or even their haunches. Getting sucked into the tanks was hard enough on the clouds. Subjecting the mixture to more suffering was not productive and could reduce its quality and the crew's compensation. The captured clouds were stirred and mixed. Without movement, the molecules and living microbes would clash and suffer pain.

The clouds were in separate partitions so one group's trauma would not propagate beyond its section. The condensed Jovian clouds passed from the cold backside of the cylinder to the front, sublimating as they captured what little heat was available. Cloud to rain and back again, all the way to bGC's factory. There were always a few canines pulling duty on the treadmills, keeping the pumps moving and the gases stirred.

Captain Marjory saw Ganymede rising above the horizon and turned to her First Mate, "Let's shoot the curl."

Octopus looked at his sensors, then checked the sextant. He turned the wheel, plotting a new course. The plan was not to hit the rock but squeeze between Ganymede and the huge gas planet. The metallic sail was tightened and set at a 45-degree angle to the surface. The bioGel sensors kept the polarity pushing against Jupiter's cloud charge and Ganymede's magnetic field. Captain Marjory planned to streak between the energy patterns and shoot the slot, gaining speed.

Ganymede's gray, pock-marked surface started filling the portholes, blocking out the stars beginning to appear through Jupiter's cloud cover.

Paquito saw the path, "I'm not liking this, Captain."

The captain didn't answer, but stood, keeping watch on her route. Her bright red fur appeared to glow in the dancing Jupiter light.

Paquito's crew saw what was going down. The lead canine spoke up, "Did we sign up for this? I need to check the contract."

"I'm sure it will be fine. The captain knows what she's doing. There is no need to bring the Union into this."

Between crashing into Jupiter's moon or dealing with the Union, Paquito knew which he preferred.

"If you are worried, you can buckle in and put on a little helmet. I'll even supply the catnip." That shut down the argument. No dog wants be branded a scaredy-cat.

There was nothing but gray rock above and random flashes of lightning from the clouds below. The weak atmosphere played a goodbye song against the container's hull, rocking the ship, front to back. It began as a sympathetic wave beating against the magnetic flows, causing the ship to tremble in harmony as it sped along.

Everyone held on to any protuberances they could find, except the captain who stood, feet braced against the deck, riding out the waves. With prehensile feet and an enhanced grip, she reinforced her status as a tough, capable Jefe. Octopus wrapped another arm around the ship's wheel, a move noted by more than one crew member.

"Bring the ship to a parallel heading."

Octopus flashed acknowledgment, but his colors were lost against the reflection in the clouds.

"Is this normal?" asked one of the Chimps.

Paquito replied, "Sure, I've been through this dozens of times."

"Yes, I'm sure you have. This is not normal. I'm going to file a claim with the Union too."

"Sounds good. If we blow up, you can file it from this gas bag's core, if you get that far."

The ship passed the moon's shadow, accelerating as they headed up and out from the last pull of Jupiter's molecular debris field. Their speed increased as they picked up the gravity boost, Jupiter still covering the horizon.

Coming out from the shadow of Jupiter, the colors slashed across the hull like wild wraiths. The squeeze play with Ganymede quickly left the gas bag behind. They turned toward the nuclear-powered laser boost station on a planned course to Home Unity Belt.

They gained as much speed as they could from Captain Marjory's power move with the triangular mainsail sliding across the photon flow.

Acceleration was additive, the faster they were going, the faster they could go after the laser hit. Before taking advantage of the boost, they had to re-configure the sail to a spinnaker and attach the boost wings.

The two simians had little to do until now. They couldn't or wouldn't run on the treadmills, and their only assets were their arms, legs, fingers, and toes.

"Hey, you Chimps, suit-up and get those wings set."

Chimp #1 and Chimp #2 sealed the airlock and scurried aft. These two always stuck together, having teamed up at the Luna Academy. No one could tell them apart, so Chimp #1 and #2 became their handles. The moniker stuck. They seemed to like it.

This was no time for monkeyshines. They had to get the sails squared away, ready for the laser strike. They were rapidly approaching the boost laser, and it would fire off whether they were ready or not. This was their primary job. There was no excuse for messing up.

One took the port side, Two went starboard. There was no easy way to communicate once on the ship's hull and no need to with this team. In a coordinated dance, they unhooked the lines and passed them through the turnbuckles. Two ran up the mainsail, hand over foot over hand and disconnected the sail from the mast. He turned, face down, and ran to the base, unhooking the mast's connectors as he went. Each plasticene piece slid into the sleeve of the one below until it was no larger than a quarter-kiloliter drum.

One locked the sleeves down, and Two released the sail. Sol did its photonic magic and pushed the spinnaker out away from the gaseous mass behind them. They connected the turnbuckle to the ship's control gears hooked to the wheel. From then on Octopus controlled the pitch and angle of the sail.

Now came the hard part; remove the delicate metal sail, clamp it to frames and secure them to the wing sprockets.

One joined Two on what passed for a quarterdeck, the plasticine planks placed over the tank's surface. Helmet's touched, sounds exchanged, resembling words, "I'll set up the frame, bring the sail over, and we'll build the wings."

Two replied, "I ran the sails the last time. I'll work on the frame."

"No, I have seniority. You bring in the sail."

"Sorry, we are the same rank."

"OK, Asteroid/Sail/Knife on three. One. Two. Three!"

One threw out an asteroid, Two a sail. The work detail was decided.

Relegated to his job, One went aft and disconnected the lines holding the metallic sail, attaching each line to the winch.

Two knocked on the airlock and rapped out:

.... .- ..- .-.. / .- .-- .- -.--

Haul away

The runners on the treadmills started up, as the metallic sail, flat against the deck, wormed its way forward until aligned with the frame.

Jupiter was not ready to see its precious gases steal away unanswered. A shock wave from an exploding gas bubble fired up from the thermosphere gaining power and heat as it passed through the exosphere. The bioGel sensors noticed the flash of heat and pressure, lighting up an indicator on the First Mate's screen. Octopus saw the signal, raising a tentacle for the Captain's attention. Notification did little to alleviate the forces rapidly approaching the ship and the crew was already secure against the bucking forces of their Jovian exit.

The same couldn't be said for the chimps struggling to secure the metallic sails to their wing frames. There was no way to signal the paired simians and these two alpha males would ignore any warnings as trivial and unimportant.

The blast caught the spinnaker, raising the nose, pushing them further out of the weak planetary grip. Both chimps, One and Two rode the blast, grabbing nearby lines as the forces shook the ship. The back end of the blast dropped them into the vacuum behind the bubble. Chimp Two lost his grip as his half of the metallic sail began to rise with him.

Safety lines are required for outside work as a matter of course. Features which this pair of troglodytes chose to ignore. One reached out to Two as the wing and chimp drifted off into the remnants of Jupiter's upper atmosphere. It was a touching scene as Two mouthed *Help me* and hands reached out, missing the connection.

It looked bad for this furry pair, losing a wing meant a weakened boost from the laser, probably an unbalanced flight, and a serious loss of pay, status, equipment, and sentients.

Two reached to his belt and tossed his unused safety line to One. Locking his feet into a turnbuckle, he pulled his partner and wing back to safety.

One and Two hugged, helmets touched, and exchanged words in the old tongue, hooting and panting, finally switching to human languages, "Let's not mention this to the Captain."

Two said, "and especially to Octopus or Paquito. They don't need to know about this little issue."

"Agreed. Let's finish the job and get inside."

One was in control here as he attached the spar to the sail, then they both maneuvered the triangular wing into the guide and slid it down to connect with the control gears. A satisfying click echoed through the ship and reverberated on the deck. They repeated the job on the other side. They were done and ready to fly. Jumping into the airlock, the cycled the system and saluted as they entered the bridge.

Octopus flipped the control knobs on his panel and tested the wings through their permutations. He could move the wings parallel to the ship while the canine powered treadmills, connected to the gears and sprockets, could spin them around a full 360°.

Paquito barked out a command, "I needed a couple of you strong ones. The wings need adjustment."

No canine moved.

"I'm talking to you, Huskies, hop to it! "

The wings moved as the canines marched. Octopus flashed a green approval color. The chimps took it as praise for their work and bowed to the First Mate, who ignored their response.

The bulk carrier bGCN01-5 came along the boost laser with a final tack to point to where HuB Asteroid would be. Octopus had to calculate their current acceleration, the location of HuB in the future, and the ship's mass to determine the needed boost.

Captain Marjory turned to Two, "Line up the Morse code flasher for Octopus."

Chimp Two focused the signaling laser on the Boost array. Octopus sent a message requesting a path and power requirements. The Boost laser's crew sent confirmation and requested payment before getting the shot. Octopus quickly calculated the encryption color key containing the ship's ID and payment and tapped out the message to the boost cannon. The boost laser turned to the indicated heading, sending the bulk carrier on their way.

Chapter 10
Ben-i-five at HuB

bGCN-01-5 did not have a lot of acceleration after the Jupiter laser boost, even with the addition of the Jupiter/Ganymede gravity slingshot. They would stop and pick up a boost from HuB before the final leg to the bioGel Factory's transfer lasers.

It was not completely silent here in the void. Lines creaked, cogs turned, and the captured clouds bounced against their containers.

Muted high-pitched sounds echoed against the deck. It may have sounded spooky to some of the crew, hearing the cloud debris sliding and bouncing around the walls of the pressurized tanks. To the canines, the quiet screaming was either exciting or unnerving.

Paquito felt it was his job to keep the crew motivated, and he used his full-sized crew chief voice above the background noise. "We're heading for HuB. Do you know what it means?"

A look, a nod was the same as a yes. It was a serious request for anything new to discuss. Talk helped fend off the never-ending boredom of the ship moving through the darkness.

"They have the casino open again. There is a lot of fun things to do. I'll take you to the Box 'o Balls!"

Chimp #1 chimed in, "I heard they re-did the whole restaurant after the massive outbreak of saxitoxin poisoning from the algae jerky."

Chimp #2 "Good thing no one here likes jerky!"

Paquito and most of his running crew ignored the slight as the chimps stepped back from a few flashing teeth.

Gambling was ubiquitous throughout the heliosphere. Solar sail crews had an inexhaustible supply of free time between work duties. They honed their card skills in contests against their crewmates and the bioGel projected holographs. Crew members were known opponents, and after a while, predictable. BioGel holoplayers, traded or purchased at every port, prepared the sentients to wage card war at the distant casinos and hole-in-the-wall illegal card games. The illegal games seldom ended in death and destruction, but all games often yielded ΞStandards or the rare bankruptcy.

The crew's pockets, packed to the gills with bioGel chits, were practically screaming for attention. Bonuses for fast pumping had boosted some of the crew's take. ΞStandards were good for many things, but at this location, gambling was high on the list.

The Heliosphere Transport Union required the general crew to contribute to a managed account, which included the skim called Union Dues. Some would gamble their salaries away, chasing the mythical *BigWin*. The managed account guaranteed funds when they left the job, voluntarily or involuntarily.

HuB's casino was well known throughout the heliosphere. It did not meet the classy elegance of the core rocks but had an ambiance they could not duplicate. The peculiarities of ZeroG drove the games, uniquely different from those on Earth or low-gravity Luna. Everything was contained, and the cards were magnetic.

Gambling tables surround the central refreshment stand, floating suspended in a carved-out section of the asteroid. Super-cooled magnets kept the stand balanced as it gently moved when the air pumps kicked in. Chairs on sliders were spaced around the food ring, adjustable for all different sizes, with mesh seats, backs, and thigh clamps. There was a definite tilt when the gorilla crews sat together. Dust motes, and shall we say dandruff, from the all-too-common, all-too hairy sentients, sparkled as they touched magnetic force lines. It was an early warning against the powerful current if you were able to ignore the source. Jewelry could easily become part of the flow, ripped from or sometimes through the careless sentient.

The gravity-based casinos on Earth and Mars kept to the old standard games, there was no need to change, and the customers kept coming in and losing. Poker and related card games were a constant for all players. In addition, there were simple "guess the next card" games or complex performances requiring thinking, bluffing, and the often dreaded math skills.

The asteroids, either by design or the need to stand out from their Core cousins, developed different games for each species.

Math games were favored by the octopuses. One-on-One 3-D speed Chess was popular, as well as color cryptographic puzzles. The octopuses, as a species, did not gamble a lot, but they really seemed to enjoy pitting brains against brains for the glory.

Games of skill and stamina were popular with canines. Treadmill speed runs, chasing balls, and smell match searches were common.

The simians enjoyed simpler games: Their favorites were competitive weight lifting and full-body and arm-wrestling contests.

The match smell games for dogs were easy to play and popular with the novices. It was more of a carny game than a sophisticated gambling joust and interesting to only a few breeds. While smell games were unique for the canines, they were easily distracted and tempted to chase small moving objects. This reflex was buried deep within their genome and could not be ignored.

Drop ball games, driven by the always available vacuum, were variations of Plinko. They were usually a hit with any canine who wanted passive gambling amusements. Funnels fed into slots in a meter high colored cube. Each side radiated subtle colors as the ball bounced around the slowly spinning hexahedron. Even if the colors meant little to the canine bettors, watching a bouncy ball and flashing lights was entertaining.

One step up from Plinko was the ball pit, a cube filled, obviously, with balls; large, small, colored, and bright. It wasn't count the balls or game of pick-one, but capture the key ball. Sentients surrounded the ball pit, jostling for position, waiting to see who would be the next one to try their paw at the beeping "toy" chase. Speed was the name of this game, and the bet was against a count-down clock.

No simian would even consider diving into a box o' balls. The shades of green in a pick'n'match game was more to their taste. They purchased a randomized set of colors as the dealer shuffled and placed one card onto the table. Each card was only a 5 nm wavelength difference within the green range, giving them 17 matching colors. Only the exact wavelength match would win.

Human-originated poker-like games were also a skill the simians easily picked up. They could use the 4-suit numbering system or a card deck with the four green suits a few nanometers off the background. Invisible to anyone but a primate with forest genes. They had names for each color separation but could not easily verbalize them to other species.

Craps were not popular with the canines, they liked following the flying, bouncing die, but their Base - 4 counting always threw them off.

Roulette made it off the core worlds practically intact. It was easy to play and easy for the house to skim their cut on every spin of the wheel.

The wheel was transparent and covered; the ball, a diamond, nano-facets polished to a smooth cross-hatched grid. A red laser highlights the wheel's numbers, and a green beam picks up the ball, flashing yellow as each number echoes around the circle.

Players with diminished photoreceptor cones benefit from a tone-click where the ball and the number meet. The frequency was a simple 10 times the wheels' number starting at 20kHz. Easy for canines to decipher and out of range for most other sentients. Each strike of the clicker slowed down the wheel so it wouldn't spin for hours in the absence of gravity. Finally, a weak magnetic band wound around the wheel. In theory, the magnetic pull was equal at all points, and the ball would have the same random chance of dropping in any slot as the wheel slowed.

Card games are no different from anywhere else in the heliosphere. Only the names change. The cards, woven asteroid metal, tables magno-plastic, and chips plastic with metal threads indicating value. There was a satisfying click with each toss of a card and every chip tossed into the pot. The dealers are aces, sending a card flying to touch down and click directly in front of the patron.

Simians held cards in their hands. Octopuses suckered them close to their wet suit chest. Canines use standard poker harnesses, and each card is vacuumed into the apparatus by motor or paw pump.

Card-savvy canines and octopuses learned to hide their emotions, without wagging tails or flashing colors. Only the most skilled of these species would risk their ΞStandards against the card sharks playing HuB's tables.

The casino was not only a gambling house but catered to all of the vices and desires of its clientèle. The stores sold all the trinkets and *tchatchkes* a sentient would want. Jewelry was popular, rings, bracelets, and chains for the primates. The gorillas were especially fond of thick chains of exotic asteroid metal. Octopuses purchased shiny gems to decorate their sleeping caves and sucker rings. They were always on the lookout for upgrades to their wetsuits.

Dogs often purchased extra jerky to sustain them through the long, empty void. Collars, even if studded with precious metals, remind them of past subjugation and were seldom included in their shopping basket. They preferred Ear-ornaments, capes, hats, sunglasses, tools, and gambling backpacks.

All species liked tattoos, although the simians were often a bit hairy, and the effect was frequently lost.

Chapter 11
PnT to HuB

It was all hands-on deck for the *LunaBowling* nee *LunaCola,* repairing the damage done by the pirate's bola. Jack and Tang suited up and cut off the damaged fabric. They saved as much of the sail as they could, but the majority was crushed and contorted from the attack.

The Naval watch station, buried in the scrapyard asteroid, offered Captain Grace bolts of used and re-sewn sail material, at cost. The logistic officer was apologetic, "we would like to give you the sail since you're carrying cargo for the Armory, but our Jefes insist we make a profit or at least don't lose ΞStandards on every sale."

Captain Grace understood their requirements. "Fine. We all have to make profit. My Air is Your Air."

The PnT's tank-like transport slipped through the rocks and dust and dropped off the sail, disjointed and floating in the LiftShip's cargo hold.

Captain Grace never managed to improve her marginal sewing skills. Luckily, she had Tang and Octopus, the skilled tailors of the group, rapidly stitching the nano-spider fabric pieces to build a serviceable sail. Jack used his backpack tools to place rivets and eyelets along the edges.

The pirate ships continued circling, never approaching the scrapyard too closely. It was as if the Naval observatory was hidden in translucent dust, visible to all. They were flying a 3D grid, searching for their missing quarry, looking for revenge and booty.

Tang was the first to ask, "It's long way to Naval Armory and we don't have a big laser push."

"We can go back to Home Unity Belt. I'm sure we can purchase upgraded sails, and we can get our broken wing fixed. HuB's high-powered lasers will give us the speed to outrun our pirate shadows without too much risk of overheating the external wings."

At least two of the crew were big on the plan. Captain Grace would see if her family was still in port, and Tang was always ready for a trip to the casino, any casino, anywhere. Jack and Octopus didn't care where they were going. As long as Jack could find some jerky treats, he was good with the destination. What Octopus would do at port was anyone's guess, and probably wrong.

Tang had some other concerns. "Captain, do you think the bGC or the Navy will pay for the repairs? We could lose profit on this deal."

"I'm sure the Navy would rather pay for repairs than risk losing their new toys. I'll try to contact Herb and see what can be done."

"That would be good," offered Tang

"Maybe I can find a new sponsor. I really don't like the new name of the ship. *LunaBowling* seems a bit low class to me. It is not the image I want the ship to project. There are always companies looking to advertise on LiftShips, it won't be hard to get new signage."

Tang gave the Captain a quizzical look, "I did the best I could."

"Tang, the changes you made to the logo were perfect, under the circumstances, but if the pirates cross-check the name against the advertising registry, they will know it's fake."

Tang was not convinced, "We wouldn't be the first ship flying under false advertisements."

"You're right. I'm sorry. I really don't care for the *LunaBowling* logo and slogan. The sooner we can get a new sponsor, the better. I'm hoping we don't get penalized for abandoning the old logo before the contract ended."

Jack had to get his opinion in, "Me like *LunaCola* name. Maybe Tang can redraw?"

"Sorry Jack, the *LunaCola* is on the pirate's radar. We would never be left alone if we carried that name."

Captain Grace crafted a message to Herb explaining the situation and asked for an escort.

Before they left, the Naval station modified the ship registry database. They could not change the advertising database, but at least this would make the ship appear legal. The HSN (Heliosphere Ship Number) was updated to point from the *LunaCola* to *LunaBowling* and tweaked to delete any reference to the ship's old name. The change would eventually update throughout the solar networks. The message to Herb went out on the Navy's dedicated laser relay. It would quickly get directed to his ship, no matter where it was.

Octopus kept track of the pirate ships and, when they were at the far point of the search grid, moved *LunaBowling* into position. The Naval laser came out of the dusty asteroid and fired off, sending the ship, the crew, and cargo toward HuB.

If the first set of pirates knew about their cargo, others would certainly be able to figure it out. Gossip was one of the most important commodities in the void, and shifting truth from fiction was a great way to pass the time.

It would look suspicious if they were going in a straight line. The boost from the PnT would not give them the speed needed to squeeze past any attempted intercept. Captain Grace gave Octopus instructions to plot courses to keep then in the core of the asteroid belt, flitting from one protected shadow to another. She wanted to look like a simple trader, even with little to sell. The ship's cargo space was dedicated to the bioGel cassettes destined for the Naval Armory.

Captain Herb's naval rocket passed *LunaBowling* and contacted Captain Grace via the Morse code flasher. The message was clear. He would shadow the ship and make sure the pirates were kept at bay. Captain Herb would maneuver in the general area of *LunaBowling*'s path, close enough to let the pirates know they were around but not so close as to point out a target.

All the *LunaBowling* had to do was figure a way to reach HuB undetected from pirates.

Captain Grace knew the trick was to keep at least two pirates lengths away from their pursuers. On top of avoiding the pursuit, they had to appear as traders to the mining colonies, but without actually exchanging goods.

Octopus plotted a path passing a mining camp when the pirates were at the far end of their search grid. They would see the ship was doing something but would be too far away to resolve the fine details.

There was still the problem of what to do at the mining camps. The crew gathered on the bridge to discuss their plan. They all knew it was critical to keep the trading charade up and blend in with the other transports plying the sector.

Ideas starting flowing like cold tea, left outside the ship, which meant Jack had the deck.

"Me have no idea, Tang should know."

"Claim we have nothing but spoilt grains and moldy beer?"

Captain Grace seemed to have veto power at this table. "No. That would hurt our reputation."

Tang replied, "but the *LunaCola* doesn't exist anymore, and *LunaBowling* will soon go away once you get a new sponsor."

"I meant my reputation. I've worked too hard to throw it away. The option is off the table."

More ideas hit the now empty table.

"We're carrying nothing but clams?"

"Bones, lots of bones?"

"I know. Tell them we are carrying rocks. The mining camps won't buy rocks. It might confuse them, but I doubt if they'll care enough to make noise about it."

Their job was to get to the Naval Armory as fast as possible, and they were already behind schedule. The vote taken and the one vote that mattered approved, "Great idea, and we can take orders for the next time we are in the area. Even if we can't fill the orders, we could sell the lists to the other traders. Let them know what is in demand. It's bound to have some value!"

They signaled the mining camps, offering their services as they passed within range. Each camp was more than willing to give them a shopping list and seemed to accept that there was nothing to purchase.

This plan worked, and they had enough requests for two ships to carry. Each camp added to the store of gossip with their inventory list. It seems there was quite a bounty out for information on the *LunaCola*.

Tang had to comment, "Those pirates must be desperate. I didn't think this ship was worth that much."

"I'm sure the cargo is priceless," said Graciela. "We better continue keeping a low profile."

"Price-less? Me thought Navy was going to pay."

They were approaching Home Unity Belt, the only place they could get the laser boost and speed they needed to outrun opportunists and pirates. With its huge nuclear engine and spinning circumference of laser cannons, HuB was a hotbed of activity.

Chapter 12
LunaBowling at HuB

Home Unity Belt was visible in *LunaBowling* forward porthole. Photons, traveling from distant points of light, reflect off the solar sails buzzing around the asteroid. The ships extracted what solar power they could, maneuvering under the direction of the local Void Control Officers (VCO).

LunaBowling's speed boost had run its course as they made their final approach. It would only take a small laser brake to bring them into the asteroid's sphere of influence. As usual, it was busy, and they would be lucky to find a berth anywhere on the rock.

Octopus got on the Morse code flasher and began the negotiations for an insertion point into the swarm. There were two paths they could take on either side of the tightly spaced laser cannons circling HuB's circumference. Whichever circuit they were assigned to, they could not cross the cannon center line or risk a serious fine.

"Octopus, bring us around and pick up Sol's brake. I don't want to pay for any more of a laser hit than required."

Octopus grabbed his sextant, checked the periscope, and wrote his calculations on his work wall for all to see.

He had a path, sail position, and a plan. It took a moment more to signal the VCO and a little longer for permission. As long as the other ships kept on their trajectory, he would slip the ship in, cost-free.

Octopus used his suit's diaphragm controller to ensure there would be no miscommunication. Tang and the Captain are fine with Morse code, but Jack had to spell out each word and could not always keep up with the pace.

His tinny voice rang out, "fifteen degrees port."

Tang made the adjustments, pulling on the rope with his massive strength. A few EarthMinutes on the path and another tinny request echoed on the bridge.

"Five degrees starboard."

Jack barked out a warning, "We too close. Mort ship coming up."

Mort ships, the transports for boxed cellular remains of sentients, preferred dark colors for the ship and sails. The color scheme wasn't required for the job, but it matched their ethos. The void-black ship was virtually impossible to track. In the crowded HuB space, they were required to have running lights and they used the minimum required by law. The Mort ship had a single light on its mainmast and additional lights on the bow and stern. The flat blinking lights could barely be seen. Only the stars and galaxies disappearing behind the black shape gave away its position.

"Hard about! Tang, tighten up the lines; we need an angle here. Jack, get on the treadmill and pull the sail to port!"

Lines creaked, screws and nails strained as the ship twisted to avoid a collision.

"We gonna crash!"

Tang somehow decided this was the time for a joke, "At least it will be easy picking for the Mort-ship."

"That not funny."

The ships passed close enough touch. Captain Grace nodded to the Mort-ship's captain, dressed in fur with matching maroon eyes.

"Look like you, Tang."

"Remind me not to let those monsters use my pelt for a coat when I die. Toss me into a decaying Earthly orbit, and I'll quietly burn up over my homeland."

"That not legal, me think!"

"Don't worry, Tang, we'll make sure you don't become a Mort-Captain's coat."

Octopus followed this conversation intently. No one knew what the colors he displayed meant in this back and forth. It wasn't the expected primary colors they usually displayed when communicating with the crew, but gradations of strange mixtures. Flaming out in Earth's atmosphere was clearly not on his bucket list.

"Me not like being close to other ship!"

"Jack, it is no worse than when we pick up boost crews on Earth. 100 meters at the most. Are you questioning my skills?"

"No, No, it fine, let do it again!"

The *LunaBowling* skillfully dropped into an orbit on the assigned path, nowhere near another ship.

The crew passed the first test, but they couldn't orbit forever. Competition for docking space was intense. Captain Grace would need all of her bargaining skills to get a good berth. Octopus relayed a message from the Near-Space Control Officer (NSCO), who offered a spot at the far end of the asteroid's leading edge.

"Let them know we have a small stock of teas and fungi purchased at *SinensisPrime*. We can join them for a cup of tea when we land and discuss docking fees and taxes."

Octopus relayed the message. No response from the NSCO.

Captain Grace waited a full EarthMinute before instructing Octopus.

"Remind them we can bring the teas over faster if we are closer to the central area. I'm sure they wouldn't want us to get lost or waylaid along the way."

A berth quickly opened up.

"Captain, you love those teas, won't they take ΞStandards instead?

"Everyone has those, and it's illegal to offer bribes for landing rights. All I'm doing is offering a friendly sit down with fresh teas. We'll get some more tea. Most of these *meshuggener* ships are afraid to land on *SinensisPrime*. We can do it with our eyes closed."

"Now get to your stations. We need to land and repair the sail and wings."

Asteroid landing was relatively easy for this crew. Octopus lined the ship up parallel to their berth, then slowly descended using a solar brake until they were over the target. They held their position and waited for the asteroid to touch the landing skids. A clunk and rattle as the asteroid and ship joined, letting Tang know it was time to hit the casino.

There was no cargo to unload, so he dressed for the occasion. He took out his new Oshkosh™ blue and white striped overalls, purchased on his last trip to Las Vegas, Earth. Tang wasn't large for an orangutan, but the slimming stripes were a nice touch and could impress the other card players. With a deck of lucky cards in the left breast pocket and his green eye-shade in another pocket, he was ready for anything the rock could toss at him.

"Where you go Tang? We need wait for custom inspect."

"There is nothing to inspect, we are not trading anything. Isn't that right Captain?"

A message came over the communication 'gel before Grace needed to figure out an answer.

From: HuB Custom Department
To: Captain Graciela Lucerne, LunaBowlng
Please be advised that you may not remove cargo until after inspection.
There is a queue, and we will get to you in seven EarthDays

Captain Grace thought, *I wonder if Herb set this up? He seems to have some hidden strings he likes to pull.*

The crew assembled on the bridge as Captain Grace called a team meeting before shore leave.

"Hope not long. Me and Tang going to casino."

The captain glanced over at Jack, which closed out the conversation faster than a formal 'My Air is Your Air.'

"First of all, there is no need to continue the trading charade, bouncing from mining group to asteroid homes."

"Good, me not like going to miners, doing nothing. Me like to work!"

"We don't have to say we are trading rocks, but we can't let anyone know what our cargo is or our destination."

Grace looked around, waiting for everyone to signify acceptance of the new rules.

"Custom and Tax inspection is delayed, and I hope to be off and away before they try to come aboard."

"Won't they have to inspect us before we can use their laser boost?"

"Don't worry. We have a Naval angel who is smoothing our path."

"Herb? He not look like angel to me. Too big and furry!"

Captain Grace decided no reply was the best answer. Better to leave that question hanging.

She continued, "Once the wing is repaired, and we get some of the new high-tech sail I've heard about, we should be able to speed to the Armory in one blast."

Octopus flashed agreement and acknowledgment colors. He would have to plot a trajectory to a distant moving target, bending around gravity wells, avoiding solar flares, other rocks, dust, and debris, all at high speed. Happy time for the cephalopod.

"Any questions?"

Tang had some but kept it to himself. *Hope the acceleration is not as rough as the blast we got from the bioGel Factory. I'd hate to see the wings pop off, again.*

Octopus turned to his workstation and made a few notes on the glass wall, displaying spinning gray, iridescent blue, and black thinking colors.

"Tang, please drop off this small box of teas as a token of our appreciation. Hand it to the deck officer directly. They can brew the tea before we come over. Let them know if we miss the meeting, they'll have to stay with the left overs."

"Me join you with deliver, then we go to casino."

Chapter 13
HuB Casino

The crew of the bGCN-01-5 had a layover after leaving the Jupiter boost. They didn't have enough momentum nor power from the sun to transit to the outer fringes of the heliosphere in a reasonable amount of time.

HuB asteroid was the place to get a powerful photon push to the next leg of the journey, the bioGel Consortium's dedicated boost lasers. Then on to their destination at the edge of the heliosphere, close to the heliopause. HuB was the largest asteroid in the sector with dedicated boost lasers and a casino.

Paquito, Jefe for the running crew, sped ahead, stopping in front of a cube packed with hundreds of multi-sized, multi-colored balls, "Hey, Ben-i-five team, time for a little Chase-Ball? eh, guys?"

It only took a moment until Paquito reached the stand at the edge of the ball pit.

His crewmates start egging him on.

"You can do this, 4 seconds easy."

"I'll take that bet."

"I got 7 seconds."

"Never find it!"

Side bets rebounded from the crowd, recorded by the cubes' bioGel, each displayed as a colored square on the tote board. Paquito set the timer and placed his wager on the triple win line.

The noise and flashing lights drew a crowd to the game. An unlikely pair, wearing insignias from a LiftShip, stepped in for a closer view. The canine checked out the cube and stated, "Hey Tang, this look like fun game. Bet me win easy."

His simian partner looked at the tank, calculated the odds, "Okay, Jack. I'll wager on it." He failed to say if the bet would be for or against his crewmate.

"Quiet, everyone. Let the player hear the sound." The crowd settled down as best they could. Low murmurs and whines supplied the background rhythm to the game.

The barker held up a ball with alternating stripes and squeezed it, "Here is your ball and its tone. Remember the sound and the ball's pattern. You must grab it before the clock runs out."

The cube started rotating, mixing, bumping the balls around as the clock snapped and subtracted a full second, deducting Paquito's pick on the betting line.

The ball beeped as Paquito pushed off the edge and disappeared into the pit. One second into the search, the cube flashed, and the rest of the balls responded. The noise level increased from the cheering crowd and the blinking, chirping balls. A second passed, and every ball changed its tune. Each note, close to the key ball's frequency, pushed the odds toward the house. If a player forgot the correct frequency, it would be their loss.

The balls wiggled in the cube, seconds disappearing, humming, a millisecond a tick, as Paquito searched for that one beeping ball. His little paws pressed against the cube as he dove through the colored, tumbling ball box, again and again. The on-lookers shouted encouragement and disparagement, hoping for a win. A few milliseconds before the 5-second mark, the squeak of a caught ball called the game and the cube flashed bright green as another squeaker met its match.

Paquito jumped up, the ball in his mouth, doing a little victory dance.

"We have a winner! See, this is an easy game," as the barker paid off the bet.

BioGel's touched, exchanging ΞStandards. The crowd paid off their wagers, less the house vig.

"Okay, who's next?" the game's barker looked around. "You, Bleu-Aussie, you're new here. Why don't you give it a go?"

Jack looked around. There was no other canine who looked like him. He turned to his crewmate and said, "Here Tang, hold me cloak and pack," as he stepped out of his only garment and unbuckled his tool backpack.

Jack was considerably larger than the chihuahua and could barely fit on the launch pad. "How game work?" he asked the barker," This like roulettey?"

"You're new here. Let me explain. You pick a time, from 4 to 10 seconds. More time on the clock requires a larger bet to break even. Next, pick your payback, from 1 to 5. Every line above 2 takes another second off your time. Got It?"

Jack nodded, looked at his paws, counting the odds. "Me got it. Me bet on six seconds, three-time return."

Tang watched as the clock was set to six seconds. Only the player and the barker knew how much time would be subtracted. Despite the unknown time change, the bets from the surrounding players started around.

Most bets were against this new, untested player. Tang wanted that bet but figured he better support his crewmate. It was only a ΞStandard, and he could afford it.

The ball beeped, Jack jumped in, the clock jumped a second and started spinning down. He was large and quickly passed from side to side as his furry mass created wave after wave in the pit. The beeps became louder and louder, and the clock continued its inescapable countdown. Finally, a gong. The spinning cube stopped and flashed red. Jack poked his head up. "Did me win?"

"Sorry, buddy, you lost. Who's next?"

Jack stepped down, picked up his cape and backpack from his simian partner.

Tang lost a ΞStandard, Jack lost his bet, but the entertainment value was almost worth it.

"Me try again. Me got this figured out."

"You do that." Thinking, *and I'm done watching dogs floundering around, in public.* "I'll move on to my poker. You have fun in the pit."

"Maybe me go back to roulettey, it not so hard work."

No sentient jumped up to try the ball pit, and the audience started to melt away. Paquito, the leader of his band, announced, "didn't win much, but I'll treat to snacks. Anyone up for some jerky? I hear they even have real dried cow."

Some of his group nodded in agreement. Others drifted off, ready for more sophisticated types of entertainment, many with cards. Jack saw Tang heading for his favorite card game and mulled over the special, magic word, 'jerky.' He looked at Tang, his roulette games, and the leader of the jerky gang. It was obvious which direction he tended. "Hey, little doggy."

"My name is Paquito."

"Sorry, Mr. Paquito. Me Air is Your Air."

The apology and airy recognition seemed to work. Jack decided to move ahead with his goal of getting food, maybe even real cow.

"Me hear you know of good jerky?"

"For my crew, yes, but if you are interested in what we have to offer, we might be willing to share."

That was all Jack needed to hear. He could get some jerky, and he wouldn't have to use any of his stock of ΞStandards. As long as the offer was fair, Jack was game to listen and eat jerky. "This not not-legal, is it? Me don't want be stuck in jail again."

"Don't worry, blue. It is all on the up and up."

Jack did not know how it worked in ZeroG. It was all up and down at the same time. "K, me trust you. You can call me Jack. That me name."

"Okay, Jack, fall in with the rest of the crowd, and I'll show you a good, tasty time."

Jack looked around. "This look like fun group."

"Say, you look like you can run. Want a job?"

"Maybe. Me already on LiftShip. Where you go?"

"We're on the way to the bioGel factory to drop off a load of Jupiter clouds. Good pay and fast travel."

Jack thought, *me not like that place.* On the other paw, he didn't want to risk his free meal, "Me think about it, over jerky. Me stick with you. For a while."

Chapter 14
Jerky with Jack

Jack, Paquito, and his crew quickly found the cafe, their noses already tuned to track food.

Jack had a few questions for his host, "You ever have Moosey jerky? Or Deery? Hope this not algal jerky."

"No, Jack, the dispensers don't have Mussey, but lots of cow, algae, and even fish jerky."

"Me have Fishee jerky on Earth. It come from real river. You know about it, right?"

"I've heard it's heavy there, too heavy for me. I'm much more into the free-form ZeroG life."

"River is nice, tastes fresh. Water flows to ocean. You know about ocean too? Octopuses live there."

"That is interesting, I didn't know where the octopuses came from. Do they have houses in their ocean or rockets?"

"Me not know. Me heard they just float around, like in ZeroG but with gravity. And ocean is salty. Me try to drink it once. Never again."

"Me born on Earth and got to visit family with Captain Graciela. Luna nice too, has casino where me learn roulettey."

Paquito was having a bit of trouble keeping up with this stream of words and thought, *hope he can run as fast as he talks.* He replied, "that's different, my family has always lived and worked in the void. Asteroids, mining camps, even Luna, or so I've heard. My grand uncle went to Earth once. He didn't like it. Too hot and heavy. He didn't mention if he had jerky, but I'm sure he sampled some of the food."

"We're here," announced Paquito. "Time for some fine jerky treats."

Jack finally shut up. He wasn't rude and didn't want to talk with his mouth full of cow.

Dispensers, set up against a bulkhead, were locked down tight. Behind each display-window was a jerky treat, covered with nose prints as customers attempted to get a closer look and sniff. Paquito placed his bioGel wallet against the slot and hit a few buttons. Jerky, tasty and dry came out the chute. "Dig in crew, this is what we have in store after such a successful mission!"

Not a dog pile, but every canine pushed for the cow and fish, algae getting second shrift. They were polite as possible, with minimum flashing teeth and growls.

"See Jack, this is what happens when you sign up with the *Ben-i-five*. We are the largest and best Jovian gas carrier in the sector!"

"It not dangerous? Me heard Jupiter not happy when gases taken. Heat and fire monsters shoot at ships."

Paquito was in full recruitment mode. More paws on the treadmills made his job easier. He had to find what buttons to push to get this doggy into his pen.

"We can give you an easy shift to get started, no more than 10 km a day. And you'll earn extra jerky as you trot."

"Ask the crew. They will tell you. Right crew?"

The crew could always use another set of paws to help with the pumping. They knew what was expected of them.

"It pretty."

"Clouds whistle when you work."

"Food is good."

"Great Pay."

"We all Happy!"

Jack heard the litany and thought about the last time he was at the Heliopause. "Me been to 'gel factory before. It cold and dark. Sentients all in gray cloaks. It can be scary."

"I wouldn't worry, most of them are friendly, once you get to know them."

"Me not scared, but rest of me crew maybe a little afraid."

"Of course."

"Me not know anyone who works there. Me not think they have casino."

"No casino, but there are card games from time to time. My sister works in the Lab. I could introduce you."

"She look like you?"

"Better."

"K. Me think about it. The fast laser boosts were fun, but we broke a wing on the way back. Me not want to risk being stuck again."

"That's strange, we've never had that problem. Do you use two monkeys to set up the wings?"

"No, only one red monkey, an orangutan. He good poker player too. And he teach me 'gel programming and poker."

Paquito tried to look interested, thinking *maybe it would be better to leave this doggy in the dock. He sure likes to talk.*

"Really? Our captain is that type too. Maybe they know each other?"

"Me not know. Do all that type know each one?"

"That is a good question Jack. I don't know many red ones. I'll ask her. Her name is Captain Marjory. She went to captain school on Earth, near an ocean, I think."

"Me captain did that too. Me ask. We could party to celebrate the captains. Her name is Captain Graciela."

"I'll check. I don't think we have time for a party. Have you decided if you will jump to our ship?"

"Me need more jerky to help decide, so me not starve on me way to ships. Where you ship dock?"

"We're around 5km south of here. Not far at all."

"That a long way. Me need money for shuttle."

"You could run."

"K, me think about it."

Paquito sent some more strips of cow down the chute. "Be at the launch line, we leave in seven EarthHours. The BioGel Factory's cloud cargo will go bad if we don't deliver on time."

More treats, a few slurps of water, and Jack was ready to make a graceful exit, *Me really not want be running all time and bioGel factory scary.*

"Tell you what," said Paquito, "talk to your Captain and see if you can break your contract. meet us at the dock."

"K. Me check contract. Make sure no tiny print that would cost me. Then me talk to Captain, see if she let me break contract." Here was his out, the bulk carrier would have to leave without him.

"Thank for jerky and water. Me Air is Your Air." Jack had other plans, *me go look for Tangy, maybe play roulettey.*

Paquito called to his crew. "Be at the ship in six EarthHours, ready to run. If you miss the launch you won't get paid."

Chapter 15
Poker with Tang

While Jack was getting free treats, Tang surveyed the room and carefully picked a table for his game. He found one with three primates, one humans and two simians. They all had a fair amount of chips, but none of the piles seemed excessive. The humans had their poker faces on. It was harder to read the simian. This was his crowd, skilled but not professional players. Winning against this group would not be easy, but he relished the challenge.

Tang took out his green eyeshade and secured the chairs' thigh clamps. He sighed. *I've missed this on the ship. Cards with his crewmates and the hologame partners will never match playing in a casino with real live opponents.*

It's nice to finally get away from Jack and his bouncing balls. What a clown. Now, this is better, poker and primates; humans and simians. And not a dog in sight.

The simian was black and not too large, a chimp. Chimps weren't his favorite opponents, but they could hold their own in most games. The player at the end of the table was his height and looked sturdy, probably a dock worker. The other was tall, with grey hair and a funny-looking beard, small and pointed. He looked like someone he had met before, but space was large, as were the number of sentients on ships and rocks.

No matter, the game was more important than making random acquaintances.

To be honest, many humans looked the same to Tang and *vice versa.*

The drink cart came around, the server saying, "Capt. Hierro, your usual?"

Tang noticed and made the connection, "I'll buy one for my friend over here and I'll have a virgin banana daiquiri please."

"Have we met?"

"Do you remember the *LunaCola*?"

"I've seen so many ships it is hard to keep them straight."

"It was almost an EarthYear ago. We met when you and your crew came aboard. You looking for tea or something like that."

"That does sound familar. Who is the Captain?"

"Captain Graciela Lucerne, you must remember her."

"Oh yes! Isn't she Mykolas's daughter and the owner the *LunaCola*. You must be her deckhand, Tang, isn't it? Now I recall. Where is the rest of the crew?"

"They're around. I'll introduce you when they show up."

Tang did not bring up Captain Hierro's rapid escape when they heard the Navy was near, it could be a sore spot with the captain, and he could use that fact later if he needed to call in a chit.

The stocky one looked up, "Maybe you two should get a room. I came here to play cards."

Tang replied, "sorry. Let's play."

The game progressed as it always does; pots, bluffs, losses, and wins all around.

Jack meandered in from the jerky café to the main casino, looking for a game he could play and maybe win. Finding Tang at his poker table, he nods, waiting. Tang catches Jack out of the corner of his eye and returns the nod, allowing him into his private poker bubble. Jack knew his crewmate did not want any disturbances in the middle of a hand and waited a respectable distance before approaching him.

Tang addressed Jack as he looked at the human on his right, "Captain Hierro is here. You remember him, don't you?

Jack looked around at the humans at the table, "Where? Which one?"

"He and his crew visited the ship the last time we approached HuB. He wanted teas and fungi. They realized they had prior appointments soon after the Navy contacted our captain. You must remember!"

A twisting head, a few sniffs and Jack localizes the scent, "Oh that pirate. Now me remember!"

Wonder if he want hijack ship? Does Captain know?

"Hey, Mr. Pirate, you friend here too? Maybe I can get one of those neat beanies from him."

"Yah, I'm not a pirate. Just a simple trader like you."

Tang took it at face value, true or not.

"You mean Uri's yarmulke? Sorry, he is off at some sort of retreat. Something about a seasonal celebration, as if we have seasons in the void. I'll ask him when he gets back."

"How about you two? What brings you to this wonderful casino?"

Tang didn't want to tell this self-reformed pirate about the cargo or much detail of how or why they ended up at HuB.

"We had to put in for repairs. Our sail was torn in a dust storm."

Hierro had already tied into the asteroid's gossip string and knew about the pirate attack, but there was no information about the cargo he could bank on.

Tang thought, *no need to mention their encounter with the pirates or the secret bioGel power cassettes they were carrying for the Navy.*

"We're carrying rocks, lots of rocks, nothing more."

"Must be some special rocks. But I forgot my manners. Maybe you two and Captain Graciela can join me for ThirdMeal, to discuss old times? It's a bit lonely without my crew, off on their religious holidays. And the worst part is I can't even stop them from going. It's in their contracts."

"I'll talk to the Captain," said Tang. "I think she is hoping to tie up with her parents. They were staying at HuB the last time we came this way. We can all meet if they are here. I'm sure Captain Graciela would be happy to join you for a meal and chat about old times."

"Even better, I'd like to meet up with Mykolas and Pilar again too. Did you know Mykolas and I used to crew on the same ship? It would be nice to reminisce with that old pirate."

"I'll tell Captain Graciela, I'm sure she would enjoy joining the conversation," said Tang.

Captain Hierro replied, "I look forward to it. Please deal me out, I must run along, My Air is Your Air."

Chapter 16
Dinner with Grace

Captain Grace decided to stay with the ship as she considered her options. *I'm sure the Navy would pay for some security guards, but that's a pirate's invite. The best thing to do is lay low and blend in with the rest of the ships. We have time until the inspection is due to finish the repairs. Then we can leave this rock and complete our mission.*

Once alone, she double-checked the airlock and cargo doors.

She had some time to breathe and would start looking for sail and wing repairs after a few turns of the asteroid. Right now, she wanted to see if her parents were nearby. She could use their company. The first order of business was to search for the *BlackHornet*. With any luck, they would drop by HuB soon or maybe already be in port. Even if her parents followed the comings and goings of all the LiftShips in the sector, they would not find *LunaCola* or its registry number.

She started with the advertising database, but her parent's ship was not listed as docked at HuB.

Time to have the 'gel log on to the Heliosphere Ship Registry.

Nothing found. *Is it just me or did they block their signal? Typical.*

Captain Graciela was stuck. She could walk the docks, looking for the ship that might or might not be in port. Or she could talk with all the merchants to see if they had a lead, as long as it wouldn't draw too much attention to her ship and cargo.

This was going nowhere fast. Maybe if I search for a ship appearing in neither database?

A few pokes on the bioGel screen, some tweaks of the routines, and the goo set at it. The bioGel cranked along, longer than she would have expected, until a shortlist popped up.

"That narrows down the search. Only seven matches." Talking aloud to an empty room was a trick she learned at the Luna Academy. What sort of trick was anyone's guess.

Graciela pulled up the live feeds and started scanning the limited dataset the bioGel found. A few moments and *voilà,* there was the *BlackHornet,* blending into a dark corner, hidden from casual view.

Looks like my family may be keeping a low profile. Why?

Well, it was only a few kilometers to the ship. Time to take a walk, visit some shops and purchase a few gifts.

She dressed for the occasion; plain buttoned-down shirt, blue jeans, simple jewelry, and tied back hair. Her final piece was a H2LiftShip insignia proudly displayed on the lapel of her bomber jacket. She was set for shopping, visiting, or anything in between.

The shops lining the dock had all the wares a cargo ship might want, some they might need and a few which had no discernible use.

She needed to replenish the ship's store but could not purchase anything else to sell. Her ship was filled to the gunwales with the Navy's 'gel cassettes and had no room for more cargo. She wanted to surprise her parents and find some trinkets to use as a distraction to make the visit easier.

Graciela rounded a corner, stepped into the back of the dock, and saw her quarry. Hearing voices coming from the *BlackHornet,* she moved closer to check it out. She could recognize both her parents, but not the third person.

Nothing else to do but boldly enter, bearing gifts. A strong and confident "My Air is Your Air" announced her presence to the group.

Pilar looked up, "Hello Graciela. We were expecting you."

"You remember Captain Hierro? He told us you were in the area."

Grace thought, *Oh great, that pirate! It was bad enough he tried to hijack my ship, but now I have to make nice with him. So much for surprises.*

"Hierro, I seem to remember the name. Have we met?"

"Captain Hierro de la Zapatilla at your service."

There was no sign of recognition from the younger captain.

"I'm sure you remember. We came aboard your ship the last time you were in the area. We were looking for some tea."

"Oh yes, now I remember. I recall your ship tacking into the solar stream, scooting off to your next meeting. It seemed that you were in a hurry. As I recall, the Navy was nearby, and your crew decided to take a powder."

Hierro ignored the slight and explained himself. "I was at the poker table with one of your crew, Tang. Oh, and that goofy dog showed up too."

Well, he is an old friend of my family. So much for a surprise. What else would you expect from an old scallywag?

Before they could head down a possibly contentious path, a knock on the airlock brought dinner. The asteroid merchants had no problem finding gig workers to deliver hot meals on-demand. Her parents could afford it, and it was time to enjoy quality imported food.

There was no alcohol for this meal, although Captain Hierro seemed to wrinkle his nose at some of the liquid refreshments. Mykolas started with a toast, a bulb containing 100ml real Earth water, elegant to the last drop.

"Here's to family and old friends, may we journey in profit and peace. My Air is Your Air."

The ship's captains could spin fine tales. Discussions bordering on the absurd were common. Pilar sighed, "We are about out of tea. It is something I've gotten to savor once we gave up booze."

There was a silent pause.

"By the way, do you have any more of those fine *SinensisPrime* teas from your last trip?"

"Sorry, even my private stockpile is practically depleted."

Her father said, "We should all go there and buy some more. There is profit if we play it right."

"And not crack the ship's hull," interjected Pilar. Mykolas ignored the jibe. The less said about the experience, the better.

"I have an idea," Graciela said. "We can match orbits if we take a slow, indirect approach. This will lessen the need to use Jack's navigation skills."

"I thought he saved your ship the last time. He isn't good enough now?" Pilar asked.

Captain Hierro chimed in, "He seemed a bit goofy, not incompetent."

Better be careful. Don't want to insult the crew, especially if it gets back to him.

"No, he is fine, but anything we can do to make it easier will help."

Her mother sounded worried. "What about the *SinensisPrime* inquisitor? I heard he was asking about you and your ship. I thought you were not welcome there. Do they still want to throw you in jail?"

"Something like that, but the request from the inquisitor was for the *LunaCola*. They are no longer by sponsor."

Pilar looked up, "Wait, you lost your ship? What happened?"

"No, the ship is fine, only the name has changed. It's a long story."

That raised Pilar's interest. Captain Hierro was even more interested.

"On a related note, we need a new sponsor. Something simple. And legal."

"Okay, I know of a few merchants who could do with some cheap advertisements. Let me ask around, and I'll bring you a list."

"*Gracias*, it will help. We will be taking a direct route to the Core. No trading stops this time."

"What is your route? The ad will be worth more if they can see it on Earth and Luna."

That piqued Captain Hierro's curiosity, more than a name change. "What is so special you have to travel Solward without a trading stop?"

"Nothing much. A consignment from the outer reaches. We were delayed and will have to take a straight shot to meet the contract."

"Maybe I can help? My ship is empty at the moment, we can take the cargo, and you can get some more tea with your family."

"A nice offer, but I always live up to my obligations. Right, Dad?"

Graciela played her hole card, bringing her family into the discussion to trump the unwanted request.

Mykolas nodded, and Hierro decided to stop the line of questioning. *I may need to explore this. I bet there is more information I can gather, maybe profit.*

He picked up a different gossip thread, seeing if it could pull out a worm of data. "I heard from my friends there was a scuffle around the junkyard at the *PickNTrade* Asteroid. Word is out that a ship with a name similar to the *LunaCola* was carrying a rich cargo and attacked some innocent trading ships for no reason."

Graciela looked directly at Captain Hierro, "I hadn't heard about it."

Captain Hierro, undeterred, continued, "wasn't *LunaCola* the advertiser for your ship a while ago?"

"We don't work with that company anymore, and I hadn't heard about any attacks on innocent traders. Probably some other ship with the same logo. We're running as *LunaBowling*, a label we picked up a while ago.

Talk and food ran down, and Captain Hierro took his leave. "I must get back to my ship, happy to see you all so healthy and well. My Air is Your Air."

Family and friends left for the night. Ready for what the next cycle would bring.

Chapter 17
After Dinner

Dinner was fun, but now it was time to continue the trip and transfer the cargo to the Navy. The family and crew gathered on the *LunaBowling* to discuss options.

Captain Grace started the discussion, "We need to leave soon. Our client is expecting their shipment without delay."

"We like it here," Pilar said. "There's always a lot to do and our friends keep on popping by. The casino is only a few EarthMinutes away."

"I have an idea, said Graciela. "When we're finished with this job, we can all go back to *SinensisPrime* and trade for tea and fungi."

"That would be a profitable trip. If we can get past those flashing lights," said Mykolas.

Jack was ready with his ideas, "Ask they turn off solar cells?"

Pilar's experience at the asteroid made her cautious, "I don't think they can even do it. Let me work on getting past the lights. I know a guy."

"Of course you do."

"As I was saying, I know a guy who could make some interference glasses to neutralize the flashing. He knows how to tweak the 'gels so they are transparent and functional."

"So me not get to drive?" asked Jack.

"We may still need your help, Jack. I don't think Octopus would wear the glasses. He doesn't seem to like the bioGels and probably wouldn't like them on his face. And he seemed to enjoy the asteroid's color display a little too much."

"Me can do it. Me be backup. Me agree with Octopus, 'gel glasses not for me. But me not need special glasses, *SinensisPrime* colors not bother me."

"It would be great if we had some more of Earth's manure. They need it for their plants."

"Yes, everyone tries to trade the same goods. *SinensisPrime* is filled to the brim with the same Asteroid products. The exchange rate is horrible for cargo ships.

"Is there any way we can get some of the compost from HuB? I've heard they may be generating more than they can use. It could be almost as good as Earth cow poop."

"Let me check. I know a guy."

"Are they still composting dead sentients? It won't be as valuable if it is full of undigested bones."

"No, everyone uses the Mort ships now."

"Maybe you and Dad can follow the compost lead, unless you can meet us at the Core?"

"We were thinking of going to Earth, we've heard so much about it. But we're happy here for now."

"All that is missing for HuB to be perfect is the water thing you told us about…what is it…Oh yes, now I remember, an ocean. I wonder if we could get one built here."

Graciela decided the best response to that sort of inquiry was to say nothing.

There was a lot to do in a short time. Captain Graciela had not heard from Herb in the last few EarthDays. The new wing and replacement sails were due, and the merchants probably wanted payment before the ship left.

Graciela's reputation would cover the bill for a bit, but real ΞStandards would be better. Nothing to do but install the equipment and wait for the Navy to come through.

The replacement wing arrived, and the *LunaBowling* crew worked with the techs to install it. Octopus put the wings through their paces, changing from thinking gray to acceptance green as he twisted the wings in unison.

Pillar delivered a few boxes of supplies, one labeled "*SinensisPrime,*" the others unmarked, little surprises for the trip.

Herb checked in and sent Graciela a chit over a secure bioGel channel to cover the repairs of the wing and the cost of the new sail. The link was wiped after receipt, so there would be no tracking back to the Navy.

There was a little extra. Herb called it hazard pay.

"Do all us get HazPay?"

"We all took the risk, so I see no reason not to split it unless you want to go for a fancy new paint job?"

"Can't we keep the *LunaBowling?*" Tang asked. *"*It's a pretty good name."

"No way. An illegal name is a red flag. It has to go, and I'm not continuing one meter more with the *LunaBowling* logo. "

Jack jumped in, "Can me face be on it, like *Bina'sBeans*?"

"I'd rather have the money for gambling. Tell you what. I'll take your share and double the money, and then you can get the fancy picture," Tang said.

"Octopus?" A simple beige was his answer.

"So the consensus is that we split the extra pay equally and go about our regular duties," said Graciela.

Grace's mother was true to her word and found some new advertisers. Pilar sent her list to the main 'gel display, "Let's toss these out the airlock and see what comes back."

FowlFlyers© *From breakfast to dinner, in one simple package*™

"Me like chickens, they fun to travel with."

Grace vetoed the idea, "No chickens!"

FranklyMyDogs© *You'll care about these*™

It was Tang's turn to veto, "I don't know about that one. The algae *FranklyDogs* are Okay, except I prefer burritos. I've heard they use real and imaginary meat sometimes. That wouldn't do for me."

JanewayTransport© *Speedy freight, no side trips*™

Grace "No the logo would be a competitor. We can't advertise for someone who competes with us."

CeresGlacial Ice© *For your liquid requirements*™

Jack tossed his veto on the table, "Me not like Ceres, jail not as fun as me expected."

Asteroid Steel© *Helping workologists keep it up, everywhere*™

Grace's turn to veto, "It could work, but it doesn't seem quite right for the ship's ethos."

"Does ship have ethos?"

"My ethos, I don't like it!

LunaCompost© *Only the best stuff close to Earth*™

"No, we can't have 'Luna' in the ship's name. The pirates might make the connection."

CelsiusSensors© *We are far-in-height above the rest*™

"I've used those sensors, but their new logo is a horrible pun. Does anyone know of a sponsor who isn't essentially a rude joke or a bad pun?"

Pilar had to defend her list. "Those are the only ones I could find that paid a good rate without an onerous contract. You have to pick one."

"I guess we can't continue with an illegal advertisement. Celsius is probably the least bad of the group. Anyone disagree?"

Passive-aggressive questions always get the correct answer, and the H₂LiftShip *CelsiusSensors* was born.

Tang signed in on the name change, "It looks the best of a bad set of choices."

Captain Grace finalized the decision, "I do like their product. Let's do the deal."

"I know an artist who can paint the sail. For a good rate too," Pilar agreed.

"I'm sure you do. We need to check their design protocols."

Pilar offered, "Give me a list of your requirements and I'll check around and find the best price."

"No need. Let me talk to them. I'm thinking something exotic, a large bioGel tablet with a few probes jammed into the sides. It would be great if we could make the display interactive. I wonder if the Navy would pay for it?"

This me big chance, "Can me face be part of the advert? Me know it would help sell product."

It was Tang's turn to shut down Jack's line of reasoning. "Good idea, why don't you contact Celsius Sensors home office and ask for permission?"

"Me do that, where Celsius office?"

"Earth, you should get an answer in a few EarthWeeks."

"K, me tell painters to wait."

Tang worked a little harder and injected a bit of reality into the discussion, "You'll have to pay for the transmission and their reply. It will be a pretty ΞStandard."

"Pretty like me?"

"Pretty like a lot."

"K. Maybe next time."

It looks like Jack would be not get his doggy snout on the sail this time either.

.

Chapter 18
HuB to Naval Armory

It took more than a few cycles to install the replacement wing and sail. Graciela opted for new plasticine ropes and upgrades to the latest sail tech. It may not have been better than the old sails, but proved to be a nice background for the new logo. After all, the driving force for the ships was photons, not fabric. She knew the ship needed the latest, greatest tech after all it had been through. It was the least Graciela could do to improve their look, and she could afford it.

She didn't have the room or the need to take on new cargo, just supplies for the crew, including jerky for Jack and some high-end freeze-dried fruit for Tang. Octopus picked out his own food, and Grace found some extra-hot sauce to enhance her meals.

Everyone was ready to move on. Tang had his fill of poker. Jack was getting tired of brushings and spa time. Octopus was bored with nothing to do but eat and meet others of his species. Graciela was glad to spend time with her family, but it was starting to feel too much like home, and she needed to get away on her own.

It was time to book passage off this spinning rock.

Captain Grace checked into the nearest Launch Control office. There was an office at the four quadrants of the asteroid, some 50 meters from the laser cannon arrays. Each cannon was 20 meters high and 30 meters across. They stood off the asteroid rock on gimbals, allowing limited adjustments during a boost.

The deck officer was strapped into his seat behind the single desk in the room. BioGel tablets were strewn over the desk, given the appearance of a complex, busy job. He was not alone. Half-a-dozen ship captains stood around, checking out the new arrivals and gossiping as was customary.

"Good Air to You, Launch Master."

"What can we do for you, Captain?

"We need a launch window. We're heading to the Core planets."

"Certainly. Payment is required in advance. Today."

"Oh, and we need a full boost from every laser cannon."

"No one ever does that. Do you know how much it costs?"

Captain Grace placed the chit from Herb against the 'gel reader. "Will this cover it?"

"Of course, Admiral, we can supply what you request. My Air is Your Air."

"No. No, Captain is fine."

"This will cover boost fees and taxes. I see that Customs has already passed your ship and crew. You are all set."

An ancient printer started shaking and rattling, printing out a waybill.

"Here is your receipt and transit pass. Please check back three EarthHours before launch. The tug will take you out in ten EarthDays. Safe sailing, My Air is Your Air."

"I'm sorry, that is unacceptable. We need to leave this cycle."

"It's not possible. We are booked up and all the slots have been assigned. Ten EarthDays is the best I can do."

The hangers-on moved closer, the better to see the entertainment.

"You might be able to trade with one of the other ships for an earlier exit."

"Okay, give me the list of the captains, and I'll contact them."

"Sorry, I can't do that. It's restricted information."

Graciela was at an impasse. Flirting was not her style and could easily backfire. Their were few other options. Offering a bribe or threatening to beat up the officer would not guarantee a better slot.

One of the group stepped forward. "I couldn't help overhearing. I might be able to help you out of the conundrum, Captain Graciela."

"I've heard that voice before. Hello, Captain Hierro. I'm surprised to see you. I thought you were a permanent fixture on this rock, like my parents."

"It is fortunate for you that I'm here. I have the next position for a Core boost. I'd be happy to let you have it. We're almost family after all."

"Yes, it is fortunate and quite a coincidence. It's as if you knew I needed that slot."

"I agree. Fate is funny that way."

"Normally, I wouldn't accept this, even from *almost family*, but we need to leave. I will accept your offer with gratitude. How much?"

"No cost. Family doesn't charge."

"You are too kind, Captain. My Air is Your Air. I owe you one."

"No need, Captain, it is the least I could do, for family. My Air is Your Air."

"Almost family," Graciela corrected as she went back to her ship.

Her mother was hanging out with the crew. "We leave in Two EarthHours. Button everything up."

"You were able to get a launch window on such short notice?" Tang asked.

"Funny story about that. Captain Hierro was there, and he had the next Core launch. He offered it to us, at no cost."

Pilar turned, "Captain Hierro, you say? Beware of pointy-bearded sentients bearing gifts."

"I'm sure it's fine."

"Just because you didn't pay any ΞStandards doesn't mean there isn't a cost. You've been warned."

"You worry too much, Mom. We can meet at *SinensisPrime* after we drop off the cargo. I will send you a LaserMail to coordinate our arrival."

Pilar knew it was hopeless to argue with her daughter once her mind was made up. "I know you inherited that stubborn streak from your father. Don't let me get in your way. It was good seeing you and how well you are doing."

"Don't forget to open the present before we approach that tricky herbaceous asteroid. It is a little surprise to neutralize their irritating color scheme. It will make the landing easier."

"What that?" asked Jack.

"You'll see when you get there."

Bet it jerky. Every landing need jerky.

"Thank-you Mom. Please let Dad know we will see him on *SinensisPrime*. Tang, please order a tug and we'll get moving."

There were a few risky pressure points where they could lose their cargo to thieves and scammers. Captain Graciela wasn't worried. She knew there was help and resources if she needed it.

The encrypted payment from Herb contained messages and instructions and a bucket load of ΞStandards. Naval operatives would smooth the path and run interference as needed. Only Grace and Octopus knew of the hidden messages. Jack, Tang, and her family were better off not knowing the fine details.

The HuB-tug pulled the newly named *CelsiusSensors* up from the dock and dragged them some 3 km out to the launch path. They had to line up with the ring of red glass seemingly painted on the asteroid's circumference.

Jack checked out the view, "We sure we in the right place?"

Fortunately for the crew, the asteroid never stopped spinning in the short astronomical time the Solar-powered ships were in the area. It would be a few million years until it slowed down significantly or changed angles. As long as the local sentients needed the rock to face a particular direction and keep on spinning, there was little the rest of the universe could do to change it.

The tug pulled them tangentially to the laser's path and released the cable. Jack and Tang rigged the sail in its triangular lateen configuration. With the weak supply of photons coming in from Sol, they maneuvered into the cannon's path.

Octopus confirmed they were lined up with the laser ring and ready for the push to Core. Captain Grace had only nod to Tang and Jack as they went out the top airlock again to change the sail to a spinnaker.

Octopus got on the gears, extending the wings on either side of the hull. Captain Grace did not want to spend a lot of time building up speed on a slow acceleration and was willing to risk damaging the wings in exchange for a faster boost.

"Jack, Tang. Make sure everything is tied down. It could be a bumpy ride."

"Me not ready for this, can me cancel?"

"Get to work, Jack. We need to do as the Captain ordered."

"Captain, will the wings hold this time? I don't want to go spinning around the room like last time. I never replaced my burned-out work gloves. I'm worried. Can the new gear can handle the laser push?"

"I'm sure the high-tech sail and refurbished wings can take whatever HuB dishes out."

The *CelsiusSensors* drifted, facing their destination, as close to the lasers as feasible.

Chapter 19
Break the Laser

It didn't take much for the gossip stream to figure out that the '*Luna*' ship designation and the rumors of priceless, hidden cargo were somehow conjoined. The name change only altered the particulars, not the outcomes.

Grace knew that word was out about *CelsiusSensors*' high-value cargo, and there was no room for mistakes. Captain Grace and the crew checked and secured everything. Everything was tight, and there was no unexpected cargo on the ship.

They made it away from the dock without interference but were still not free and clear.

Jack was floating next to the rear porthole. Lookout duty came naturally to him and was one of his favorite jobs.

Octopus flashed a signal to Tang. He pulled on the massive handle, releasing the tug's line. A groan and chatter echoed through the ship as the quick release pin banged against the support plates.

"Tuggee is pulling away. We on our own."

"Thanks, Jack, Octopus, please slow-drift down the circumference and line us up, 12° north Core".

Octopus flashed, "*Aye, Captain,*" as he made two small equal opposing corrections on the wheel.

"Jack, Tang, go up top and tighten up the spinnaker. Keep an eye out for any visitors."

"Your family come wave bye?"

"No, I'm more concerned with their old friend, Captain Hierro and his crew of brigands."

"Good, maybe Uri back from vacation. Me can buy beany."

"Just let us know if anything comes close, Jack."

CelsiusSensors had no defensive weapons to speak of, and Grace knew they were sitting ducks until the lasers fired off.

The asteroid spun beneath them as Octopus kept them centered on the glass ribbon. BioGels were plugged into external sensors flagging anything else that might approach the ship. HuB security was responsible for their safety in near space, and Herb and the Navy were not far off either.

The main risk was an interception after leaving HuB. Pirates could lie in wait along their expected path, but Grace was not too concerned. As long as *CelsiusSensors* had a large initial boost, they would blow by those ships before they could react.

Of course, an attacker could take the next boost out, trying a boxing maneuver. It was unlikely a simple pirate could afford a full boost. Only the Navy or the bGC had enough ΞStandards for such an exorbitant photon display. Grace smiled, it looked like she had her bases covered, and it would be a fast, smooth trip to the Naval Armory after the initial bump.

The laser ring lit up as Jack and Tang entered the airlock.

"Lights pretty, but not look strong. Did pay enough?"

"Yeah, the Navy paid for a full boost. We're good to go," Tang said.

The first three cannons fired directly at the ship as the pressure slowly spun up. The ship groaned, strained, and shook as the sail and wings were pushed by the red photons. The laser forces increased exponentially, each cannon sending a more powerful photon stream than the other, pushing the ship faster.

Jack couldn't help needling his crewmate, "You gonna charge up 'gels? Me make bet with Octopus how many spins you have after they explode."

"I've learned my lesson, not more trying to charge up the cassettes. The wings are holding this time. Let's keep it that way."

"Well, Tang, I hope you didn't put any money on that bet. We need them charged up. They are safe. Let's connect and fill up a few."

"Are you sure? I was the one spinning around the cabin when the wing exploded. Let Jack do it this time."

Jack, as usual, was not paying close attention, "What you need? Me do it."

"The captain wants you to plug in the cassettes and charge them up from the laser cannons."

"No, not me job description. Let Octopus do it."

Octopus waived a dismissive tentacle. His job was to keep the ship lined up with the laser boost cannons, not handle hardware.

"Don't worry. I had some diode limiters built from a shop my Dad mentioned. The cassettes will disconnect once they meet the limit. We can pull them off and set them aside. I'm sure the Navy won't mind if we use a few of them for our protection."

"Both of you work on it. Let's start charging while we have the free power."

Orders were orders, and the two connected the cables from the wings to the interface box and the cassettes. The trapped 'gels started humming as they filled. Jack could hear them, not complaining this time but receptive, almost happy to receive the filtered power.

" 'gels not complain, how do that?" Jack asked.

Tang, always happy to go into explainer mode, began, "Gel batteries use the well-known atomic discrepancy principle. As the 'gels charge, every discrepant point stores photons and quantum bits, each one with the power of a molecular sun, a controlled fusion, wrapped in bioGel and Jupiter cloud matrix. If they aren't abused, they are happy to store the power."

Jack hummed along with the 'gels. He had no idea what Tang was talking about, but he liked the words flowing past his ears. They were reassuring. After a few moments, a sharp *ding* echoed throughout the bridge.

Jack jumped up, accelerating away from his work until he bounced against the bulkhead. The quick stop did not end his shock. "What that! Someone at door?"

"It's Okay Jack. The techs added a bell to signify when the cassette trays were full and could be disconnected."

Captain Grace laid out more sets, and they were well into the fifth group. Even as the power increased, the limiters kept things smooth. Jack even got used to the bells after a few false flights.

The asteroid kept spinning as it was wont to do, and the cannons fired as they lined up with the ship. Tang glanced back at the glowing ribbon centered on the asteroid. A spark, then a crack appeared in a cannon. There was no sound, but fragments spread out from the edges of the glass.

"Captain, look at the lasers!" Tang cried out.

The asteroid spun, with the red coherent photons emanating from the each nuclear-driven glass cell in turn and then, a hole.

"This isn't good.", said Tang.

The ship, bathed in darkness, no longer had the reassuring glow of laser lights to help it along its way.

Jack had his take on the situation, "Did we break it? Bet it cost a lot to fix. Hope we not get blamed."

They didn't stop, but dead laser-less space didn't add to the ship's acceleration. This could be serious. The lights and push continued after the blackout, but the missing photons could never be recovered. They had enough boost to get to the core planets but would need another unplanned boost somewhere along the line to reach the Armory. Whoever caused the explosion could well be on their tails.

The *CelsiusSensors* were on a straight shot to Core, or in this case, a curve. It would be easy for anyone else to plot their course and it looks like more than one group had it in mind.

"Octopus! What is that missing boost going to do?"

"We be chased by pirates?" asked Jack, "me not see them. They behind?"

"Captain, this doesn't look good. What if pirates get a bigger boost than we did? What if they have more sail? The broken laser would be moot, and they could be on our tail."

Captain Grace ignored Tang's plea and concentrated on moving forward, adjusting to deal with the change. "Octopus, what does this do to our trajectory?"

Octopus said nothing but kept at his calculations, writing furiously on his work-wall tank using three arms and brains.

None of the math helped.

Captain Graciela looked over the calculations. "Well, this doesn't look good. We need to find another way to gain some speed. I guess the plan to blow by any attempted interception has flown out the porthole."

Tang looked at the calculations, hoping for a different answer. "How about a gravity boost?"

"That could work. Octopus, plot a course to Mars. We'll see if the God of War can add some speed."

"What, we at war? How me not know this? Does Herb know? Me heard that Navy supposed to fight wars, not us."

"He can't help us. We were supposed to be undercover."

"Keep on the lookout for any ship on our tail or intercepting paths."

"Me not have much of a tail, Tang either."

Tang leaned over and whispered. "Better not ask about the Captain's. I've heard that *sapiens* are sensitive that way."

All they could do was ride out the boost and start tacking against the solar stream as they headed to Core. Speed was relative, and skill was the arbitrator of this race.

Chapter 20
Mar's Heat

The Red Planet was their touchstone, growing larger and pointing to their destination. "Captain, a ship is on an intercept course, coming around Mars. We don't have the speed to outrun it."

Octopus, on the periscope, tapped out

- .-- --- / ... .--. ... --..-- / .--. --- .-. - /
.- -. -.. / ... - .- .-. -... --- .- .-. -..

Two ships, port and starboard

Octopus spun the scope around,

.- -. -.. / .- / - .- .- .. .-..

And a tail

"They're trying to box us in, "exclaimed Graciela. "That's not going to happen!"

"How we get out this? Navy help?"

"No. Herb took off once the first laser fired. I'm afraid we're on our own here."

The pirates were too far away to board the ship, but they had other weapons at their disposal. They probably did not want to destroy their quarry, but disabling was easily in the mix.

A tube extending from the deck, as one of the pirate ships tacked across their path. A puff of gas, a tossed line wrapped in stones, a bola, spinning through the void. Octopus was ready. It took him a moment to plot the trajectory as he spun the wheel, tacking hard to port as the bola flew by. It might catch something, sometime in its never-ending journey, but the *CelsiusSensors* would not be wound up so easily.

The pirates had anticipated the first shot might not work, and another ship, outfitted with three huge solar sails, came up from below and ran toward *CelsiusSensors*.

"Octopus, dive toward Mars. Let's get a gravity boost."

Their tail kept with them and started closing.

Graciela had another trick up her sleeve. She passed over the tiny moonlet, Deimos, signaled Octopus, "Let's throw them off. Pull around Deimos and set a course for the equator of Mars."

Jack did not like where this was going. *Maybe me should have gone with Ben-i-five?*

Tang sees the moonlet pass above them, almost close enough to touch.

"Hard to Port. One more orbit then dive to the surface."

Mars' thin atmosphere, mostly CO_2 and a dab of Nitrogen started beating against the hull as they grazed the upper atmosphere.

"Drop the radiators. Let's see what this alleged God of War has to offer. Just let him try to stop us from stealing his hot molecules."

"Keep a temperature sensor active. Tell the bioGel to let us know when the temperature drops sharply."

A fine layer of dust and mist attached to the porthole. In a flash, it froze as they passed from the thermosphere to the mesosphere.

"Octopus, Pull up now! Try to angle off the atmosphere interface.

Grace wasn't done yet, after bouncing off the atmosphere, they circled back, heading straight to Deimos. The ship, puny compared to Mars but only tiny against its little moon, twisted around the weak orbit, speeding out the other side. The hot salt blocks added a small boost as they hurried toward the Armory.

As *CelsiusSensors* flipped around Deimos, Tang could almost wave to the pirate ship, on the wrong trajectory and too distant for a bola shot. The other two trailing ships were well away.

Tang sighed as the attackers fell behind, "I think that trick may have worked."

Grace nodded, "It's still touch and go. Two of the ships were eating our wake, and the one with three sails could be a problem."

Octopus plotted a new route to the Armory. Once they were in range of the guard asteroid, they would be safe.

"Tang! Do we have any left-over sail from the repair job?"

"You know I don't throw useful scraps away."

"Good, get down there with Jack and stitch up some more. We have Sol at our back and can use all the sail we can find."

Before they began sewing, Tang asked, "Captain, isn't Herb supposed to be around?"

Jack concurred, "Navy need protect cargo. They need help us!"

Tang suggested, "If the Navy isn't going to help, how about we build another 'gel laser cannon?'"

"Built 'gel cannons again! Me can do it."

"No, Jack. We can't go blowing up every ship that gets near us. It would be self-defeating."

Octopus looked up from his calculations, flashed a light green safe color and tapped out,

.-- . / .... .- ...- . / - .... . / . -.. --. . --..-- / ..-. --- .-. / -. --- .--

we have the edge for now

Physics, math, and the vagaries of the solar stream decided who would win this race. The farther out they got from the sun, the weaker the photon push and, more importantly, the peculiarities of solar sailing became. Given enough time, the ship behind gathers more energetic photons and could capture the lead ship. As they came up close to their quarry, they could easily cut off the sun and becalm their prey. Or at least slow its acceleration.

"Tang, do you have anything in your tool chest to help us contact Herb? If he isn't in bioGel cell range, he won't know the trouble we're in."

"I do have something that might work. Let me check my supplies."

Tang talked to himself as he rummaged through his special tool cabinet, resembling nothing more than a junk pile to the uninformed.

"Now, where is that piece of kit?"

"Here it is, my old single-sideband rig. My family said it once belonged to my great-great-grand-orangutang."

"I bet he'd be proud to know his old HAM radio would be in space! My troop insisted that I use it to keep in touch. They were under the impression that I could call home from the edges of the asteroid belt. Who knew it might come in handy?"

"Captain, I'm sure the Navy keeps tabs on transmissions and should pick up something as simple as this signal."

"I'll use the 'gel cassettes for power. I won't have to tap into the ship's supply."

"Good, now we'll see how well they work when they're not blowing something up."

"Me re-member that. Fun times."

Tang thought about the last attack. *I guess Jack forgot about the moaning and screaming emanating from the 'gels when they gave their direct current all to power the laser cannon.*

"You'll have to re-program the 'cassette 'gel to modulate the power."

"Right, I'll query the group and see which one is in charge, it should only take a few moments."

"Tang, you supposed show me how to program."

"This would not be a good time."

"But Tangy, you promise me."

Captain Grace looked at Jack. He knew what that look meant. "K, maybe next time."

The 'gels were still hopped-up on HuB's photons and were more than happy to build routines to export DC power. Tang found a probe, cut it open, spliced it into the transmitter, then stuck the 'gel with the needle end of the business.

The administrator 'gel displayed

<What this? Us never taught about this interface

"It's ancient. A transmitter before there were any bioGels."

<It make sense.

"Good, you'll probably enjoy checking out the ancient components. Let me finish the connections."

<Wait, what you mean? There is time before us?

Tang knew he was at a delicate section of the programming system. If he sent the 'gels down a rabbit hole, they would all but implode, and he would not get his power.

"No. You have always been around, in one form or another. We can talk about it later."

Not quite a lie, and almost a truth. This was not the time to teach a 'gel cosmology.

<K. What voltage you need?

Tang set the transmitter to hop from a half-dozen common frequencies. He didn't know what the Navy monitored but figured they would pick up at least one of them. The SSB HAM radio was a bit old school. No vacuum tubes but diodes, optical tuning, and physical memory chips. He flipped it on, and the rectangular, papaya-sized radio sprung to life. The bright touch-screen looked almost like a bioGel, but static.

Tang showed Captain Grace how to use it, "Record a message, they press the send button on the screen. It couldn't be easier, I've already programmed the transmitter, and the 'gel cassettes have agreed to power the device."

He made a final check of the transmitter, playing out the antenna line to the connector passing through the deck.

"I'll hook up a dipole antenna once I get topside. Give me five EarthMinutes."

Satisfied everything was working. He went off to connect the antennae and help Jack adjust the new sail material. The extra sail helped. It wasn't a lot of fabric. It gave them a slight edge from their pirate tail, and it may have been enough to outrun them for a while.

Captain Grace thought about what she wanted. *I need to generate a message asking for help but not scream wildly, desperately, begging for a handsome gorilla to come riding to the rescue.*

Mayday would be a bit extreme, but a shadow follow would come in handy.

"Captain Herbert Grauer of the Heliospheric Navy, this is Captain Graciela Lucerne of *CelsiusSensors*. We are coming in hot with your consignment. Please acknowledge."

The phrasing seemed like an innocuous informative message, not the cry for help they needed. Herb should be back from his detour, soonish, and would surely pick up on the meaning.

Solar Sail chases are not very exciting, only the inexplicable conclusion of physics and time. Nevertheless, everyone knew how the situation could develop, given solar constants and sail surfaces.

There was nothing else to do right now but ride out the photons.

Chapter 21
Pirate Compost

Everything that could be done to increase their speed was done. Only time or the addition of a discrepant would change the outcome. Octopus continued to scan for solar flares, wayward photons, or rocks to use to their advantage.

The rest of the sentients did what they do best in times of stress.

Captain Grace called a meeting.

"Octopus, how much time do we have?"

This was no time for Morse code. Spoken words ensured no confusion, "30 EarthMinutes, maybe less."

"Okay, keep an eye on that ship and let us know if it gets any closer."

Octopus signaled acceptance.

"We need a solution to this problem. The table is open to anything."

Tang started, "We're not hopeless. We've made weapons out of nothing before."

"Exactly, we need to find the best one. We will have one shot and need to get it right."

Tang threw out the first idea, for better or worse.

"Hit them with a conventional bola? It would give us a small speed boost at the cost of some precious gases. It worked before on Mykolas' ship."

"I don't think we can pull that off, they have a huge sail, and we'd have to hit it dead center even to begin to wrap it up. At worst, it would just rip a hole and not slow them down

"I guess a slingshot is out of the question too?"

Captain Grace thought about it before answering, "exactly, if a bola won't work, your little pea shooter is completely out of the question."

"So, no bola, no slingshot. I'm afraid projectiles are not something we want to try right now. There is too much chance of a miss, and they would strike back. They are professional pirates, after all, and have a lot more practice. They could easily destroy our sail."

Tang said, "Do they have gas cannons? They will probably try a bola when they are in range anyhow."

"Octopus, how close would they have to be for a bola shot?"

"2 kilometers, 10 EarthMinutes."

"Do we have any defense if they try to hit us with a bola?" asked Tang

"We could string up some rope, but we don't know how big a bola they might send our way. Even if we slow it down with ropes, it could still damage the sail."

Tang still had the floor. "We can't simply wait for a boarding party. We wouldn't be able to fend off the intruders."

"we could continue trying to outrun them, but we have no more solar fabric, said Captain Grace. "Octopus, how long until we're in range of the Naval Guard Laser?"

Octopus turned the periscope around, grabbed his sextant and began writing his calculations on the board. His tinny, sucker derived voice was loud. "Too long, we cannot make it."

"We could try a Hydrogen rocket boost, but that ups the ante for everyone, and blowing out gas for no good reason doesn't compute."

Jack had another idea, "We make another bioGel cannon?"

"No, Jack, I've already queried the 'gels. It seems HiveMother warned them about rapid, massive discharges. They are willing to charge laser bullets for the Navy, but not cannons."

"We short circuit them?"

"Did you forget how much pain they were in the last time we did that?"

"Oh. Now me remember. They not like it. Not good for me too."

Grace steered the conversation back their current predicament. "What to do? These garbage pirates are not our friends and we're coming up short on ideas. Any other suggestions?"

Tang spun his intellectual wheels. "That's it! Dump out garbage to clog the sails before the pirate gets in bola range!"

"Me like that, it like a vid me saw in me puppyhood."

Grace concurred, "let's try it. If we can slow them down a little bit, it will give us the edge and we can get away."

Game, set, and match, a plan is begun as Jack and Tang zipped down to the stern and started building a garbage bomb.

Tang, Jefe for this job, instructed Jack, "Pick up some dirt from the compost bins."

"K, Me get not-stinky stuff."

"No. Don't use the front bins. Those hold my good compost. Use some of the less processed material."

Using his backpack tools, Jack scooped the soft-dark, somewhat smelly matter into an osmotic water sac.

"No cowies around anyhow. They not need drink."

"Make sure it is good and wet. We need to spread this out, not tear a hole in the sail.

The pirates, running as the dogs of war, boosted by a Martian gravity sling, and assisted by fresher photons, slowly gained on *CelsiusSensors.*

Tang exited the airlock, carrying a small but mighty dirt and gunk bomb. He walked aft, checking out the view. *Good, the pirate is directly behind us, less than half a kilometer, from the looks of it.*

Tang unpacked the gift, aims and released it directly at the incoming ship. The bomb is dark against the void. It was unlikely the pirates knew it was coming.

"Alright, you dirty pirates, here's something to help you celebrate *'The Santa'* It's coming right down your stovepipe." Spoken words in his helmet in the void had no effect, but it worked for Tang to add a little zing to the shot.

The moist dirtball hit the void. Water crystallized into a tiny cloud around the tasty compost-filled center. No longer liquid, it still could pack a punch, with a soft mushy center. The pirate ship on their tail couldn't move. Any directional change, and they would lose the race. They were stuck nose-to-butt to their prey.

The compost bomb hit the ship's prow with a smush, and the poor ship stuttered from the impact. The aromatic, partially digested compost accumulation added insult to injury. Dirt and crystal-dirt spread up and out until they met their new favorite home, the ship's sail. A red splotch started expanding from the middle of the sail.

Grace, Octopus, and Jack peered intently at their foe. A sigh, maybe a small cheer, went up. It didn't look like much, but time and the cold void would tell.

"That me, me give tomato surprise! It rotten."

The compost bomb's microbial population recognized a new substrate and opportunity. The individuals, connected as clumps of colonies and tied together with slime, dove into their new nano-spidery home. They had a nice clean substrate, food, solar power, a scant bit of water, and no air. Other microbes have survived and thrived in worse conditions.

The shiny, nano-spider sail would have to adapt to its new friends. It had no choice. The powerful photons pushed out from the sun and reaching deep into the void are now shared with the microbe-infused sail. This did nothing for the pursuing ship's acceleration.

The pirates dropped back.

There were a million things the pirates could do to get back in the race.

Physics says, *nothing you have will work.*

Pirates listen and decided to look for easier prey.

Captain Graciela exclaimed. "We did it, gang! We shook those scumbags off our tail. They'll think twice before messing with *CelsiusSensors.* "

"And me tomato."

Chapter 22
Armory

Jack's tomato surprise, silent, but deadly, startled its recipient. The pursuit slowed as the pirate dropped back and the other ships caught up to them.

Tang was glued to the periscope, watching the action, "Look at their message flags. They seem angry."

"Good. Me glad they got idea and leave us alone."

"Oh, not to worry, they are more than angry, they are spitting dark photons," exclaimed Graciela.

"We're able to outrun them? Correct?" Tang asked.

Octopus tapped his voice diaphragm, "My calculations show they will not close on us."

It appeared that the navigators on the pirate ships could do math and read star charts as well as *CelsiusSensors'* First Mate.

"Look, Jack, they're turning."

"Good work everyone. I'm going to ask Herb for additional hazard pay. We're worth it," said Captain Graciela.

Octopus went back to his calculations and plotted a course to the Armory. With Sol at their back and Mars a distant memory, they headed toward a distant part of the Solar System. The Armory had no immediate neighbors and would not be friendly if approached. They were not the type to lend you a cup of sugar but more likely to fry your bacon with the guard lasers.

Tang stayed on the periscope as Octopus tracked their course. "It looks like we are approaching the outer protection ring of the Naval Armory." It was a tiny asteroid with a non-tiny laser cannon.

The bridge lit up with a pale red light as the tracking beam found them and focused.

"Octopus, please send the password to the guard station."

It took a few moments to ping the Navy's 'gel password server. A bit more to unencrypt and translate the color QR code, then generate a response.

Octopus sent the generated password using the Morse code flasher. The code response was a beep and short reply:

.. -. ...- .- .-.. .. -..
'Invalid'

The light intensified.
Then:

.-- --- / - .-.. .. . ... / .-.. . ..-. -
'Two tries left'

"They not cook us? We need more codes!"

Octopus, flicking through three 'gel tablets at once, seems frustrated. He used his diaphragm, addressing everyone, "that is the only one in the bioGel databases."

Captain Graciela looks at her FirstMate, "Octopus, didn't Herb send us the new codes? Where are they?"

Tang starts looking for the password in his private 'gel.

"Me fur hot. Let turn around. We sell 'gel cassettes to pirates! Where Herb?"

Captain Grace tried to take control of the situation, "he never checked in, not even to help us with the pirates."

"Tang, get on your single-side-band rig and see if you can raise the Military."

"It will take me a few minutes to negotiate with the cassette hive. They turned off the interface to my rig, something about disliking ancient tech. It seems a little rude. I wonder if the way we charged them up made them upset? You know, when I think about it, I think they are afraid of memory chips and diodes."

Captain Grace, always calm and collected with her crew, sang a different song. "Stow it! Connect to the ship's battery and turn on your ancient comm device at once."

The box lit up as Tang made the connections. Before Tang could send out another pitiful cry for help, the SSB speakers crackled, spit and whined. "Herb here."

Tang, "We hear you, 3x4."

"We need the passcode."

The crackling, spitting low resolution noise answered, "10-4. Will signal the guard station."

The heat from the guard laser started to dissipate.

Then shuts down.

"Don't we need to do that for the next one?"

"We not have passwordies."

Herb's rocket sped past them as they came into range of the 'gel's cellular communication array.

His deep sonorous gorilla tones came over the bioGels on the bridge "Sorry, we were on a difficult mission and could not answer your call. Looks like you were able to handle your guests, as I expected."

"It was an adventure! You owe us all a meal, we had to lose some of our compost."

"Will do. I know how much you SlowerSail ships love your home-made dirt."

Tang spoke, loud enough so the 'gels, and Herb, would hear him. "Do we need passwords for the other emplacement? I don't remember so many the last time we passed this way."

"You're good, everyone will give you a pass, although they may target-lock you for fun."

They bore ahead past the inner ring of naval protection. The rocket placements, lasers, drones and small attack ships, kept their cool and ignored *CelsiusSensors*.

The Naval base was the same as before, a spin-stabilized asteroid. There were no Solar cells, ammonia generators, Crookes radiometers or heat signature. It was flattened, with Quonset huts and tarmac landing zones on both sides.

Rockets stood out, most on a single narrow leg with a bulging body. Only a few, with their pointy noses, were designed for travel through atmospheres. They approached the cold piece of rock bristling with military gear and Marines shuffling along in formation.

Octopus was on the periscope, following Herb's ship to the landing zone. He made a few notes on his wall and stepped out to the wheel. A tinny voice ordered, "Bring in the spinnaker, tighten to a 37° pitch."

Herb's voice came over the SSB rig, "I figured I'd land on the sunny side, I know you solar sail types like that."

"Oh, you don't have to do that for us, Octopus can land light or dark!"

"Not what I've heard. Shiny *SinensisPrime* seemed to throw him for a loop."

"Do you snoop on every conversation? How did you know about it?"

"Don't worry, we never listen in. At least not on you. You do know that the only thing faster than light is gossip? I think Einstein explained that premise."

"Fine, you win. Are you ready to unload your cassettes?"

"Yes, my crew is standing by, once you set down."

Herb left his ship's bow flasher on, as a reminder, even if Octopus didn't need it. Octopus approached the ship, seemingly ready to hit the top of the rocket. A tweak of the sail, twist of the wheel and he flipped around the Naval rocket ship touching down neatly a few meters away from Herb.

Herb saluted, as he should, and Octopus waved back. Jack and Tang were soon on deck, bringing in the sail. The magno-plasticine covering the tarmac held the ship against any risk of an unexpected re-launch.

The two captains exchanged formal, airy greetings before Graciela stepped into a big gorilla hug.

"Captain Grace, good to see you again. Your crew can take a break. My sailors will unload our supplies."

"Captain Herb, your asteroid, your rules. Send them aboard."

"We're good to go. We can all meet in the cafeteria for ThirdMeal. The Admiral is waiting for us in his ready room."

Tang was ready. "That's good enough for me. I'm off to look around. I made a few friends the last time we were here, I'll look them up."

Herb whispers, "we have a poker game waiting for you, ask any sailor, they'll direct you."

"I guess my reputation has proceeded me. My Air is Your Air."

Octopus took a left at the bottom of the cargo door. He knew where his species liked to hang out. Time to share stories, snacks, colors, and math tricks. Laughing at the terrestrials was a bonus.

Jack tells everyone, "No spa here. Me explore and find jerky before dinner, for me snacks. Guess me go meself, others seem busy."

Chapter 23
Job Assignment

The two captains, Herb and Graciela met in the Admiral's ready room. It was sparsely decorated, like every other Quonset on the rock. The only indications it was special were the flags crossing the dais and the bulbs of real Earth water on the tables.

Herb saluted as the Admiral came into the room. Like everyone else, he wore his space suit with his helmet dangling off the belt, ready for any eventuality. Captain Graciela nodded and greeted Herb's Jefe, "My Air is Your Air, it's good to see you again Admiral Bristol."

"Welcome aboard, Captain Graciela, we heard that the delivery of the bioGel cassettes was uneventful."

"There was a little excitement, but nothing we couldn't handle."

"Herb mentioned you were the best crew we could find. The scuttlebutt of your exploits are famously repeated around the base.

"Thank you, Admiral, it's our pleasure to work with the Navy and quite a bit of fun."

"Well, we have a situation that might prove profitable for you."

"We are always ready to help the Navy, and of course, Herb." *And earn profit.*"

"I'm sure you and your crew are the right sentients for the job. The Navy's station at the apex of the Heliotails needs supplies. We want Herb to go with you to install some updated bioGel apartments at the bGC Port and Starboard factories."

"Well, that is interesting. I didn't know that there were other bioGel factories."

"They are small and isolated, but still part of the bioGel Consortium." said Admiral Bristol. "We can't initiate it for the better part of an EarthYear, when the belt spins around and HuB is facing the Heliotail. The Navy will pay for a full boost and you'll get additional boosts from our asteroid stations on your route."

"My crew will like that, they are quite fond of HuB's casino and my parents often use it as a base of operations."

"Perfect. The two bioGel Foundries at the end of the loops are getting out of synch with HiveMother. The hardware updates will let the Consortium monitor them better and includes a refresh of the software. Captain Grauer will be on board to monitor the apartments. I'm sure he will have no problems installing and rebooting the systems."

Graciela looked over at her old Academy compatriot. He had a stern, unsmiling look.

"Thank you Admiral, My Air is Your Air. We are honored you want to use *CelsiusSensors.*

Herb saluted and they left to join the others.

"Tang, Jack. I took a job to take 'gel apartments to the Heliotail for the Navy."

"What? Apartment buildings too big for cargo hold."

"No, Jack. They are 64 cross-linked bioGels. They call them apartment units, but they are not that big."

"K. Long as no spidey webs."

Herb looked at Grace, she shrugged."Don't worry, these are spider free."

Graciela turned to Herb, "are you really going to travel in a solar sail ship? I thought you hated our ships."

"It is not my favorite, but the Admiral insists I supervise the equipment and the installation."

"Why can't you take one of your fast rockets. I know you'd be happier."

"If only. The 'gel apartments are fragile and can't handle the acceleration or jostling. You are slow and smooth."

"I'll take that as a compliment. Let us know when the Belt aligns and we'll be ready."

"We'll ship supplies to HuB and send you a list of any other items they may need from the merchants before launch."

"It'll be fun to have you on my ship. It will be just like Academy days."

"Without rockets. It seems the Admiral wants me to broaden my horizons, even if they will be slow to appear."

"Come back to the ship, you can see where the apartments will be stored and you can let us know if we need any special equipment."

The crew, except Octopus, were in the galley. "Tang, how did your poker game go?"

Tang still had his poker face on, "you know, won a little, lost a little."

"Me find a little jerky, but not too tasty."

Tang decided this would be a good time to change the subject. "Herb, did Captain tell you we figured out how to charge up the cassettes from the sail wings? No nuclear power required."

"No. That's interesting. You need to talk to our scientists. I don't think they know about that."

"We have a few EarthDays before we're aligned with Core. Why don't you two find Octopus and show the Navy how to charge the cassettes with photons?" suggested Grace.

"I saw Octopus a few EarthHours ago. He was still with the other scientists, doing whatever they do."

"Go join him and you can teach the Navy a few things."

"Right, we're on our way. Octopus mentioned that some of the Navy 'Sparks' can tune up my HAM rig and boost the signal, without needing more power. I'll check that out too."

"Maybe science types have jerky, me check on that. Me sure they have snacks."

The reinforced doors to the lab sprung open as Tang and Jack approached.

"Must expect us. Me like this, it easy. Me ask Captain for auto doors too. Better than spinning airlock on ship."

"You do that."

The doors opened into a typical Quonset hut on the surface, there were was nothing resembling a lab in view. No machines, bioGels or fermentation tanks.

"This empty for lab. Me think it hard to get work done here. Wonder where science jerky stored?"

"Too bad Octopus isn't here. I thought he would be hanging here with his science buddies."

"Must be trick. Is it Fool Day today?"

Light shone from a hole in the floor, pointed the way down to the interior of the asteroid. "Jack, it looks like the Lab is down below. Let's check it out."

"K. You first."

"Of course."

The two intrepid explorers floated down to the lab proper.

"This is more like it. Look at all the bioGel terminals. I've never seen so many machines. And look at those flasks. What's in them?"

"Jerky, maybe?"

"And they have rifles, and more. What do they think is going to happen?"

It wasn't about food, so Jack had no answer to that rhetorical question.

Octopus strode over to his compatriots, reaching up to his speech diaphragm, "Welcome to the Navy's lab. You wouldn't believe the things they're working on."

"The lab is quite impressive. Octopus, do you have time to give us a half-a-ΞStandard tour?"

"Lot of science things," said Jack. "It look busy."

"Captain Grace wants to know if you told them about charging up the cassettes with the lasers and wings?"

The room was not soundproof, or large, and every word could be heard. A white-coated primate was listening intently.

"Wait. What?" The lead scientist exclaimed, "That isn't possible, the cassettes need a jolt of power that only a nuclear engine can product."

Jack whispered, "No wonder 'gels angry." *Uh oh, me think they got monkey explainer started.*

"On the contrary, we were able to harvest the power of the laser through the bGC's solar wings," said Tang.

"And we disappear a pirate sail!"

Octopus signaled affirmative.

They had the whole room's attention now, and Octopus's validation.

The lead scientist asked,"in that case, have at it, teach us what to do."

Tang was in intellectual heaven, Jack, bored but not enough to get into trouble, thinking*, me just wait till brainies get tired.*

He quickly spoke up,"Me let Tang help you, Me get coffee and jerky for everyone from cafe. Put it on Herb's account."

No one really acknowledged the offer, their attention was elsewhere.

It didn't take long until they had the new power source integrated with the cassettes.

"Mr. Tang, this is a huge advancement. My Air is Your Air."

"Maybe you can give me a few rifles in exchange? For research."

"I'll ask but it is up to the Admiral. No one outside the Navy knows about them and the jefes don't want to share, yet."

Jack ate the jerky purchased at the base canteen. No one seemed interested in the bulbs of coffee he delivered as connections and flashes of laser light outlined the scientists. Testing seem to settle down and it looked like a good time to interrupt. Jack brought the conversation back to his expertise, "it getting near ThirdMeal. We should go and get the ship ready."

Jack was right and there was nothing more Tang could teach at the moment. Tang nodded and asked Octopus, "do you want to stay here? It looks like a scientist dream."

"Don't tempt me, but I have a contract with Captain Grace, and I always honor agreements."

"I still have to talk with the 'Sparks' they have some ideas on improving the range of my HAM radio."

"K, Octopus and me meet you at ship."

Chapter 24
Goodbye CelsiusSensor

The *CelsiusSensor* received a boost from the Naval guard asteroid, sending them back to the Goldilocks core, HomeWorld, and its hanger-on, dead, gray Luna.

Captain Graciela preferred to have supplies to trade, but the Navy had nothing anyone else wanted. It isn't as if they didn't try, but the Navy were not farmers or miners. A platoon of Marines was not something anyone wanted to see come out of a cargo ship's airlock. In any case, they preferred to use the faster, more intimidating rockets for transport.

ΞStandards weren't the problem, Captain Graciela and her crew were well compensated for the 'gel cassettes. The hazard pay helped soothe their frazzled nerves and the embarrassment of traveling with empty holds.

They were flying into the sun, the photon stream pushing back. The laser push from the Naval base was starting to disperse, and they began tacking against the flow to maintain forward motion.

Luna, first appearing as a small round rock, was now filling the front portholes. This was the place to pick up cargo, do some low-gravity maintenance, and, for Tang, a trip to the Luna Casino.

Once they got in range, the A-mail 'gel refreshed, cycling the messages in the queue. This close to Earth, Tang, Jack and Octopus felt the need to let their friends and family know their whereabouts and catch up on the latest gossip. Their family groups wanted to hear the stories in detail. Many were living vicariously, as if they were out plying the void with their space-cousins.

Grace used the opportunity to send messages to her parents, proposing a meet-up at *SinensisPrime* on their way deeper into the Belt. She was hoping to find a supply of manure for the herb-growing asteroid, but Luna was not a great source of herbivore poop. The organic brownish crop would be expensive, if it was even available on this dry, dusty rock.

Tang fired up the HAM rig with the modified Yagi antenna and enhanced power his Naval 'Sparks' friends designed. He was able to punch through the ionosphere and talked with a few of the Earth and Luna wireless aficionados.

"Jack, this HAM radio is fun, I've made a few new friends, there must be more in the asteroids and mining camps, this will be a great way to pass the time. You should try it."

"That OK, me not good at the Morsey Code. Me fine with 'gelTxt."

The fresh A-mails were a pleasant diversion from the tedium of space travel. Captain Grace received the majority of the messages, telling her crew, "most of these are just advertisements from the warehouses, nothing exciting here."

An A-mail from the home office of Celsius Sensor's Corporate office flashed on the 'gel with a high priority flag.

To:
Captain Graciela Lucerne, H2LiftShip 'CelsiusSensor'
From: CS Home Office
We received notice from Heliosphere Flight Control that your ship
deviated from your approved flight path.
As per your contract, we will be terminating advertising
with your ship immediately.
Please remove all signage and references to our product at your next port of call.
My Air is Your Air.
Celsius Sensor, Advertising Division
We are far-in-height above the rest

Tang seemed to have the ability to see all of these unsavory messages as they appeared on the 'gel. He let Captain Grace know, "well, that is rude, just because we didn't fly in a straight line? Didn't they know we were being chased by pirates?"

"That may have been part of the problem, They may think my ship is unsavory."

"Me, talk to them, they not can do that, where is contract?"

Jack was a good choice for the contract review. Like most canines, he was compulsive when it was to his advantage and this little bony contract was something he could sink his teeth into.

"It too much words for me comm. Me need a full 'gel tablet."

"OK Jack, you can use one of the bridge's terminals, if Octopus doesn't mind."

Octopus flashed green on an extended tentacle.

The contract appeared on the indicated screen. "Thanks Captain. Me look it over. Let you know what me find."

Captain Grace had not sent the contract to the 'gel, but it made its way without sentient assistance. In a less stressful time, they might have made note of it, but the crew was distracted by the need for an advertising name change.

Octopus displayed a short query color, but he wasn't concerned if a 'gel was acting slightly out-of-bounds. He had his duties to attend to and those were more important than worrying about self-directed 'gels.

It took a while for Jack to paw through the document, but they had the time on the approach to Luna.

Jack reported back, "Captain, here on page 85 *Section 301.1, Miscellaneous*, contract say they can cancel for cause. Me guess pirates are cause?"

"I was afraid of that. Not to worry. I'm not sure I even want an advertising sponsor."

"I'm starting to think that this ship's advertising system may be cursed. Now the pirates are looking for *CelsiusSensor.*"

Tang thought, *great, now the captain is worried about curses. I should contact my cousin on Luna. He has close ties to our jungle troop and may know of a way to un-curse a ship.*

Grace continued her musing, out loud.

"Maybe I should do like my parents and go un-advertised?"

Tang could interject, but decided better of it. It was time to attend to his other duties. He let the captain have her thinking space.

The octopus really did not care what the air-breathers thought process was and rhetorical questions required no answer.

Graciela continued speaking to no one but herself, "That isn't a bad idea. Nothing says we have to have an advertisement agreement. I can call my ship whatever I want and switch logos at the float of a hat! We earned enough from the Navy job and do not need an advertiser."

"But now I have to find a name!"

"Oh well, it can wait until after we scrub off this cursed logo. We can go stealth! The more I think of it, the more I like it."

"With the bonus we received from the Navy, we should be able to purchase some high-resale cargo. This will be fun. And profitable."

This was not the time for the crew to put in their two ΞStandards worth and they wisely tended to their duties. Captain Grace turned to her crew, "I'd like to avoid going back to Earth on this run. It is colorful and entertaining but takes too much time and energy to find supplies at the right price and quality."

Jack nodded, "It heavy too."

Tang agreed, "I was hoping to visit family, but I can do it the next time we're near Earth. They move around a lot and the last time we 'gelTxted they were back in Sumatra. I can work with Octopus and find some ports you may like near my home when we are back this way again."

"Me too. Me promised me family trip to Luna. Still need save more ΞStandards. Me can wait."

Everyone looked at Captain Grace, waiting for confirmation.

"We'll aim for an Earth trip the next time we're in the area, and we can plan to explore the other side of the planet."

The landing routine on Luna was routine for this crew.

Octopus turned the wheel, pulling the lines controlling the sail until the ship lined up with the Luna laser. Jack and Tang re-configured the sail as a parachute, ready to catch braking photons. The ship skidded on the rough regolith as the Moon-tug hauled them to their berth.

"You can all take shore leave. I'll check on cargo we can re-sell."

"Me know you can sell jerky in Belt. Maybe me help pick it out?"

"I'll call you if I find any. You all need to take some time off."

This was fine with Tang. He could just spend more time at the casino, especially if he could shake his canine shadow.

"I've uploaded 25% of your salary to your 'gelWallets, spend it wisely."

Tang smiled and nodded. He knew that he would easily double his money at the tables.

"Me get a brushing and food, you coming Tang?"

"Sure, then I'm off to my game."

"Should we ask Octopus to come along?"

Octopus flashed a negative color and tapped out

-. .- .--. / ...-. .. .-. ... - --..-- / - .... . -. /
... . --- .-. . / .-.. . .- ...- . / ...-. --- .-. / -- .

Nap first, then shore leave for me

"Don't forget, we still need to replace most of the plasticine ropes. They took quite a beating this last trip. I'll order an electrostatic cleaning team to wipe the sail. I want it clean and shiny for the next trip."

"Any questions?"

Tang always seemed to have at least one more question "Any idea where we will go?"

"I'll ask around and see what the needs are and where we can get the best return. We'll start the maintenance in Seven EarthDays, I should have the cargo and supplies lined up by then."

Chapter 25
Another Name

Captain Grace had some work to do before she could take a break. They had successfully fended off the pirate attack and delivered the cargo; a little late, but intact. She had to straighten out the paperwork and register the ship with Luna Docking Control before she could take on new cargo. At least there were no taxes to pay and only the usual docking fees. It was unusual for a solar sail cargo ship to be on Luna with nothing to sell, which might raise some questions with Control.

All she had to do was claim that she had sold everything, although an explanation should be at the ready to explain why they purchased nothing. At least she could ignore the raised eyebrows of her peers if she wanted. Or pay for a round of liquids to change the subject.

The ΞStandards in her wallet would cover any embarrassment. Good thing she didn't need to party and brag like most of the other captains. She knew being a transporter for the Navy could have some downsides to those who wanted to believe the void was free of government interference.

Jack and Tang had already left for food, spa time, brushings, and entertainment. Octopus was well into his nap inside his cave.

Grace was happy to have her ship to herself and set about coordinating the new name and checking the 'gels for supplies. This was her entertainment, being in charge of every detail.

"First to get rid of the cursed *CelsiusSensor* logo. No need to make it easy for pirates and dubious merchants to find us."

The ship's advertising name and logo was scrubbed off by the workolgists hired by Celsius Sensor's corporate office. This was nice in one way, bad in another. Captain Grace had a blank palette, but the transition to an un-advertised vessel was a bit of a shock.

Solar Sail advertising had been part of her life since she was a small child. It was the ships' identity and a source of pride, for the most part. This was a new experience and was a bit unnerving and risky.

Even if she wanted to go advertised, it could take a lot of time to find a new sponsor. The constant name changing and piracy issues were probably not to the ship's advantage. It was time for Captain Graciela Lucerne, formerly of the *LunaCola,* the *LunaBowling* and the *CelsiusSensor* to discuss options, out loud to her empty ship.

"Forget it! I'm done representing these capitalist slimeballs, telling me where I can fly and what cargo I can carry! I'm going sponsorless. We'll be free and clear! All I need now is a new name."

Multiple ships could use the same name, but for the un-advertised, it was considered gauche to have a name claimed by another. Captain Grace could not simply pick a name out of a hat. And she didn't have a hat.

"I guess I better fire up a research 'gel and see what is available, or at least what isn't used already. I certainly don't want something pointing out my ship's somewhat confusing history. I need something new and exciting."

"Think! What did I learn in the Academy? It needs to relate to solar ships, with an emphasis on power and mystery."

There was no ship naming course at the Luna Academy or Earth's Solar Captain's school. It wasn't an oversight since that question almost never came up and was a bit unusual, at best.

"It's times like this when my mother's skills would really help, but she isn't here, and it is up to me."

"At least Jack and Tang are off on shore leave. Their suggestions can be quite unrealistic. Jack always wants his face on the sail, and that isn't something I need to hear right now. Tang would probably want a deck of cards, which is no better. I don't know what Octopus would like, he probably doesn't care one way or the other."

Fingers poked at the 'gel in QWERTY patterns as names flew out, spun around the bridge, and died in an ignoble martyrdom of bad phrasing. A few raised their little wordy heads, looking for reprieve or mercy, but very few made it off the deck.

"Solar, solar, what says solar and mystery? I need to look deeper than a photon. There must be a quantum particle who wants to join the ship."

Octopus had woken up from his nap at the start of this soliloquy and observed everything in the safety of his watery workstation. Grace did not see him watching the proceedings but he heard every word and judged with simple color schemes.

Bosons, tiny and energetic, started spinning their way up the pile of discarded phrases. A signal, the slightest beckoning, a wave, caught Graciela's attention.

"*BosonsWave!*"

Bosons, excited, flew around the room and Octopus flashed a firm agreement color.

"Octopus, I didn't realize you were there. How long have you been listening to me prattling on?"

Octopus signaled a noncommittal answer, he was the epitome of politeness.

"What do you think? Shall we become *BosonsWave?*"

Octopus flashed agreement and tapped out:

.. - / .. ... / .- / --. --- --- -.. --..-- / ... - .-. --- -. --. / -. .- -- .

It is a good, strong name

"Great. It's unanimous, I'll register the name and get an artist to paint the sail and prow."

Octopus tapped on his suit's diaphragm, "I'll leave you to your work, I'm off to the ponds for some fresh, live food."

"Sure, enjoy. I can take it from here, My Air is Your Air."

Now where are those workologists? I have a job for them.

Graciela got on the comm line and contacted the Artologist Union. Her ideas were exciting and engaging. The artists were more than willing to do the work. Their quote was a bit high, even if she had the ΞStandards to cover it.

"Maybe I need to scale back the art work, their quote is a bit pricey for paint." Octopus had long gone fishing, there was no one to bounce her ideas and concerns against.

The captain, artologists and workologists came to an agreement. Gold paint for the prow, with a quantum particle, larger than life, flashing across the sail.

She examined the work from the tarmac, using the helmet's telescope to check it out at different levels.

"This will work, it is simple, not too expensive, and I can always add to it in the future."

The critical re-naming and labeling was completed, *BosonsWave* was ready for its first cargo and a flight to the far reaches of the heliosphere.

I should get a tattoo. This is a historic occasion! My dad would be proud.

I hope the crew can find the ship when they get back. Jack is easily confused and Tang always over-thinks everything. I better send them a 'gelTxt!

The naming was over and Graciela had to start ordering supplies before she could take on new cargo and return to her home, the void and the asteroids.

"No sense in running around this moon, searching every nook and cranny for equipment, I'll just put out the requests to the merchants and let them bid on the price. That will be fun too."

> To: Luna Brokers
> Please send bids to BosonsWave within 6 EarthHours for the following:
> 300 meters of plasticene rope 8mm.
> 300 meters of plasticene rope 4mm.
> Standard food, water and air supplies for human, simian, canine
> and octopus crew (one each)
> We are also taking bids for compost and herbivore manure,
> Earth origin preferred.
>
> Note: We request samples before accepting bids.
>
> Captain Graciela Lucerne, BosonsWave
> My Air is Your Air

"The first order for the newly named ship. Feels good. Let's see who responds."

Chapter 26
Cargo on Luna

Ship re-painted, re-named, and re-registered. Everything was buttoned up and Grace was ready to find interesting cargo for the asteroid settlements.

The 'gelTxt was moderately successful. She got the rope, nutrients, and some leads on fresh manure and grains. It was time to hit the regolith and search for some more supplies and tasty snacks for the long journey ahead.

Captain Grace was in her element, picking out products to re-sell, for a serious profit. She was looking for bargains and kept away from the central storehouses.

Anything relatively inexpensive with high resale value was checked and a bid offered. Grace was looking for completed, certified bioGels tablets, imported grains and seeds, and interesting trinkets. Mining equipment would always sell, but new tools were too expensive, and the mark-up would barely cover costs. Wet and dry chemicals imported from Earth were always in demand, although the cost was high and the profit margin too small to justify the risk and expense.

Refurbished equipment was a better bet and always in demand. She had no lead on the needed manure, but would ask around and see if it was available. This was one time she could really use Jack's nose. He would have easily directed her in the right direction.

The plan to meet her parents on *SinensisPrime* was still an option. The growers could use grains and maybe updated seed stock but they really wanted manure. There were few ungulates on the Moon and imported poop was rare, expensive, and odorous. She could have gone to Earth and picked up an unlimited supply of the rich, smelly supplements, but a trip to ground was not in the cards this time. Whatever it cost, it would give them access to the herbs and fungi on *SinsensisPrime* and was worth the expense.

Everything seemed to cost more than last time. It seemed to be a constant in this commercial environment. Even with a pocket full of bioGel chits, she wanted every ΞStandard to count.

Luna had no home-grown products for sale. Small rocks and dust didn't seem to have a lot of demand on the dusty, rocky asteroids. Ice, mined from deep craters, was always profitable, but it was illegal to export. There was an excess of urea from the waste plants, but most established asteroids had enough of their own to convert to ammonia. It could sell at the smaller asteroid mines, but it was not rare enough to justify tying up cargo space.

She was looking for foodstuffs that would be stable on the long trip to the belt. A few barrels of quality Earth compost and even recently processed cow manure were easy to sell if the price was right. She could have picked up nuclear pellets, but Tang had begun to have a strong aversion to the product anywhere near his cabin. There was no place on the ship far enough away to make him happy, and she had to respect his worries to keep the ship safe.

She made her way topside to the warehouses which couldn't afford the steep rents of the commissaries below the surface. She was hoping to get better prices at these marginal shops. The Quonset huts at the far end of the Lunar tarmac were split into tiny warehouse spaces. Each space appeared more unattractive and run down than the next, but prices were sure to be better.

The sign over the airlock said it all, "Luna Exports-Best Material/Best Prices" and the tag line 'We have it all.' The purveyor of the shop looked up as his new customer passed through the security airlock doors. His red fur flecked with gray reflected off the lunar light shining through the hut's portholes. He walked up to Captain Grace and began the introductions, ready to deal, "My Air is Your Air, Captain. What can we do for you this fine Luna day?"

"We are heading to the inner asteroid belt. These grain bins look interesting. What's their history?"

"This is some of the best you'll find on all of Luna, imported from Earth. It is certified and comes directly from the wheat fields of the Northern hemisphere. We can offer you an excellent price."

This was Grace's gambling trip. She got a rush from every barter and the give and take of the deal. "It depends on the product. Let's see what the bioGel says."

BioGels attached to containers monitor temperature, humidity, and gas levels. Ideally, the bins would be dry, but not bone dry, and the temperature stable. Anything out of range should raise a flag on the bioGel. Buyers seldom requested opening the bins. They did not want responsibility for any loose particles escaping into the ambient air. The 'gels reported all the information they needed and were trusted as accurate.

"This 'gel was attached at the point of origin and certified when it was sealed. We've kept the product cool with a dry vacuum and a touch of Lunar oxygen to ensure it's stable."

Grace examined the 'gel. The tablet's surface was not the smooth gray of young 'gels' but mottled with splotches of white. "The bioGel seems a bit worse for wear. Are you sure it is up to snuff?"

"The bioGel is an older model but still serviceable. It will have no problem tracking the grain's status. And we updated the software. They are protected from the MalGell-02 virus and related variants."

"And you guarantee their functionality?"

"Don't worry, it looks old, but it has a long and successful history. I validated its provenance all the way back to a bioGel Consortium factory."

"Look, to be honest, this shipment has been sitting here longer than I like. Don't get me wrong. It's a fine bin of grain, grown on Earth and first-rate. I prefer faster turnaround and this bin is starting to give me a bad reputation. I can give you a discount if you buy it today. The bioGel says the grain is in good shape and should fetch a good return."

No good deal should be ignored, Grace took out her comm and plugged it into the bin's 'gel. "There are some variations in the output. How about another 10% discount."

"I don't normally do this, but you look like an honest captain and the bin is taking up a lot of room."

"So 10%?"

"It's a deal, make sure to get it out of here within an EarthHour."

"I'll arrange for a transport crew to pick it up right away."

Grace shook the orangutan's hand, sealing the purchase with a serious "My Air is Your Air."

"By the way, do you know who is selling Earth herbivore manure?"

The orangutan looked out the porthole, "Yes, the hut, way over there will have some."

This was the deal she was looking for, grains, straight from the farm and at a surprisingly good price. The manure was in her grasp, and she would have enough in her budget to pick up some high-end products, maybe even some classy Earth-wine. Liquids, even with 12% alcohol is bulky but an easy sell with a good mark-up in the outer fringes.

Grace ran through the scenario, smiling to herself.

There were an unlimited number of settlements who would buy the whole grain bin. With the discount, she could pick up a good amount of manure and make another killing at *SinensisPrime*. Then take those teas and fungi for an even bigger profit. That little trip to the Naval Armory is turning out to be a real money maker. *Wait until Tang hears about this.*

Chapter 27
Meet the new Ship
Same as the old.

Duty called as Tang and Jack met in the transport tube leading out to the dock.

"Me do good on roulettey. How 'bout you?"

"Poker was good to me. It's been a nice SevenDay holiday, but I guess it's time for work."

"That fine, me got tired of spa. Jerky good, though. And me smell good too. "Me went to Luna Museum. Have you been there?"

"No, I always seem to have more important things to do. What did you see?"

"Lots of rocks. And old metal ships. Is it true rockets burned oil in before-days to fly to Luna?"

"Almost, a lot of oxygenated kerosene at first, it was a big mess. They finally figured out the H2LiftShips and everything has turned out great."

"They dragged old probes to museum. Me looked inside, no human, monkey or dog bones. Just bunch of weird wires and electronic stuff. Some had tools like me backpack, but not as good."

Tang gave a grunt, neither a yes or no.

"You should go. Me sure you like different launch systems: Sail Drag, Luna ski jump, laser boost and rocket ship."

"Sorry, I'm not a big fan of ancient history."

"Even had pictures of failed launches, broken rockets and busted tools. Me know you would like to see!"

"No. That is the last thing I want to think about."

"Look what me got. Me honor Laika."

"What's that? A fried potato?"

"No. Like me. You know. Us first in space! Lakia first to orbit."

"You mean canines?"

"No dog. Laika."

"OK, I suppose so. Where's the bling?"

"Not bling, EarToo. Look."

"I'm not touching your ear."

Jack answered with a flick showing a black and white mutt, wearing a helmet, tattooed on the inside of his ear.

"She cute too."

"Very nice. Looks painful."

Jack grimaced and winced a bit, "little, but worth it."

"So, what brought this on? It because we escaped the pirates?"

"Yes, with me tomato bomb. Me want to celebrate me heritage. You helped too. Maybe get space-monkey tattoo?"

And the moment is gone.

Tang checked the 'gel on the outside of the warehouse. Living in outer space meant that verification of the next room was always wise. Breathable air and a little heat filled the space. He spun the airlock door, and they both stepped in.

Food, brushings, and gambling were amusing, but fun could only keep them entertained for so long. They both spent some time shopping and brought a few bins to add to their personnel supplies. "Me brought bin of jerky. It good price. You find fruits?"

"Yes, I've found some nano-stabilized fresh fruit. Two bins, one for me, the other to trade on the way. Better than Ξstandards."

"Me only have enough jerky for me. Nothing to trade."

Captain Grace heard the airlock open, and she was waiting on the cargo bay ramp, ready to see the reactions to the new name and fancy paint.

"Where *CelsiusSensor*? Tang. Ship leave without us." exclaimed Jack. "Captain did you sell ship? We fired? That rude. Better get me chess set back, it family heirloom. Antique."

"Calm down, Jack. It's the same ship. Only the logo has changed. Didn't you get the 'gelTxt?"

"Me heard comm ding but forgot to look."

Captain Grace pointed at the sail, "Welcome back. How do you like the new logo?"

"What it say? That not same sign."

"Captain, it is beautiful, although I would have thought you would wait for our input. We have to live with the logo too."

"Don't worry, the artist who designed it and paintologists liked it."

"Captain, you know we will all be known by that name wherever we go? Did you check the cultural dictionaries to make sure we aren't insulting some group? Are we allowed to use that name? I have more questions."

"Don't worry, I did my due diligence and I'm pretty sure we are safe with this name. You weren't here when the workologists finished removing the old logo. I had to decide quickly while the contract with the union was still live. Nice, right?"

"It not me face, but it look nice."

"Octopus thought the name was strong. You don't like it?"

"It's fine. Fine, Captain."

"Great, it's a consensus. Welcome to your new ship, *BosonsWave*."

Tang still had more questions and wanted more information, "I've never heard of that product. Who is the advertising sponsor?"

"You won't believe it, but I'm going un-advertised. This is the name I picked for my ship."

You could hear a pin drop, slowly, in Luna's weak gravity.

Tang waited for the beat to hit, "Is that wise? Don't we need to be advertised? Won't the merchants expect it?"

Captain Grace took a while, another pin drop, before responding. "No. That is just a myth promoted by the companies to keep us hard-working sailors under their thumb. We don't need them."

"Still, shouldn't we consider an advertisement? It would be prudent."

"Sorry Tang, the decision's been made. We are now *BosonsWave*, un-advertised and free of corporate control!"

"You don't even have a tagline. How can anyone identify our ship?"

"Fine, you all work here, let's hear a tag."

Tang had a lot of ideas:

> '*BosonsWave*, you won't see us coming'
> '*BosonsWave*, we're around a photon'
> '*BosonsWave*, only the best particles'

"Enough. Let's just table this discussion."

"But we can get a regular, paying advertisement later if we want to?"

"Drop it. The decision's been made, and we are all going to be fine."

Octopus flashed agreement. Jack had no dog in this hunt. Once he found out his face wasn't on the sail, he lost interest in the whole naming process. And yet, he still shared one opinion, "we should celebrate. With jerky. You should order some for a party."

"Good idea Jack. Tang, will you join us?"

"Not with dried meat. I'll bring some more nuts to the party."

"Great, I'll order some party supplies and I'll chip in for the salt and bread, and tea, no vodka."

"Me not want salt-vodka-bread. Ruskies let Laika die, me not follow their celebrates."

"What does that mean?"

"Something about a tattoo. Don't get him started."

Tang decided to end the discussions, "Captain Grace, I think I speak for the whole crew. We are proud to be part of your newly named independent ship.

This was a dangerous point for Captain Graciela Lucerne of the newly named *BosonsWave,* even if she didn't know it.

It was not simply a name change but invalidation of all crew obligations. Union rules were specific and contracts were written for the ship and its name. With any name change the crew could leave without risking penalties or repercussions. This fact was buried deep in the Solar Ship rules of the void.

Not everyone was familiar with the fine detail, although any Union rep would be sure to bring it up. Jack wasn't the shop steward, but he had read the contracts in his spare time and knew the details. He was happy on the ship and with his captain, be it *LunaCola, LunaBowling, CelsiusSensors* or now, *BosonsWave.* Octopus understood the permutations, but it meant nothing to him. His contract was the same no matter who or where the ship was.

This was time for re-negotiation. By the same rule book, contracts were set once the ship made its first sale.

Tang knew about this clause in the name change rules. He didn't bring it up during the earlier changes since the advertising contract overrode the individual changes. This one was different. There was no advertiser to supplement their salaries.

Fortunately for the Captain, Tang had no plan to re-negotiate. His salary was good. Even if he got a new title, he would be doing the same work. The job was the same, and titles or ΞStandards didn't change anything.

Bonuses at the end of the jobs were shared based on seniority, and he certainly didn't want to start over at level 1-A. He was happy with his share level.

The only thing more important than the ship was his troop on Earth and in the asteroid belt. He kept up to date exchanging 'gelTxts and sent gifts to all his nieces and nephews on their birth dates. They all loved their space-traveling Tio Tang. It didn't mean that he wasn't going to milk the name change for all the benefits he could get.

"Captain, to celebrate the new name and the new contracts, I'd like to ask for a laser launch, just this one time."

"OK, Tang, I think we can afford it, and it would speed us on our journey. I'll set it up with Luna Launch Control."

"Time to store the cargo. Everything is stacked in the warehouse, ready to go. You can distribute the load evenly for laser lift."

"You'll have to replace any worn lines before we launch. The spools of plasticene rope are in cargo bay number one."

"Why not painter do that? They worked on sail."

"Because I pay you, let's move."

Tang was overjoyed. No ski lift launch, no drag across the crater floor, no risking death in exchange for acceleration. It almost made the name change worth it.

Chapter 28
Rats! Rattus rattus

BosonsWave is well away from Luna. The laser launch was just what Tang had hoped for. A gentle lift beyond Luna's horizon, then flipping the sail to a lateen configuration and tacking against the solar stream. First, a gravity sling around Earth, then out to the boost laser at the L4 Lagrangian point.

Captain Grace filled the holds with everything they could sell at the asteroids and isolated mine camps. She found a source for Earth manure. Not a lot of volume, but a lot of cost and significant stench. Good herbivore shit wasn't cheap at any distance from Earth, but it had a high resale value, which made it a worthwhile cargo. Even if they didn't get back to *SinensisPrime*, every asteroid farm was a market for the product.

The usual items filled the holds; grains, wine, Earth and Luna fashion items, tools, new and refurbished bioGels, and anything else of value. Anything organic monitored by the bioGels and tracked for changes that might indicate unexpected fermentation or decomposition.

It was Tang's turn to check the cargo. The 'gels transmitted a continuous data flow, but regular quality control checks were prudent. It was a job that gave the crew time to move around and broke up the routine.

Captain Grace reviewed the last readings. "The bioGel network is reporting an anomaly. One of the 'gel reports is looking funny. Tang, take Jack with you and double-check the grain bins in cargo bay number one."

Tang grabbed a few probes and a tablet and dropped down to the cargo area. "You coming, Jack?"

"Why me?"

"Because the Captain ordered it."

"K, me not hear that. Was thinking 'bout jerky."

Unplug the probe from a bin, plug in his probe, tweak the controls for the sample types, record and repeat. Boring, repetitive, but it's a different boring and always an improvement.

The last bin in the bay was against the bulkhead, just a few centimeters from the ceaseless void.

"This gel looks the worse for wear. And the readings are a bit strange."

"It look tired."

"Look at these readings. Oxygen is way down, CO_2 high, nitrogen seems okay, but why is there methane?"

"Is that bad? Want me sniff?"

"No, my probes are fine. I thought the Captain would have flushed the bin with nitrogen, but I guess it was too expensive."

"The signature is unusual. This 'gel doesn't seem standard. The QR lines say its origin is the heliotail. Look, it has holes and dark and light spots. It may be hacked. I wonder if it even logged onto the 'gelNet correctly? I bet our 'gels treat it badly. You know they don't like foreign 'gels."

Tang opened a speaker tube, "Captain, I found a container with a bad-looking gel. The bin seems to have some gases that don't belong."

"Roger. You and Jack can open it and see what is going on. Don't let any grain get out."

"Jack, I need you to hold the net over the bin in case any grains float loose."

"K."

Tang unclipped the cover, and lifted it. They both jumped back as a swarm of four legged vermin float out. They are a bit groggy and seem unsure of what this world is all about. Tang has his screwdriver, hammer, and spanner, but they make poor defensive weapons. "What in the name of all bad fruit are they? They look angry!"

"They rats, me know about them!"

"Jack, we need to stop these from getting out!"

Jack's primal instinct kicks off. He's not a cat, but he could herd rats.

The rats were in some sort of hibernation hangover. The lights and fresher air brought them to a semi-conscious confused state. They had known Earth and Luna's gravity. ZeroG was not in these rats' wheelhouse.

A few minutes of bouncing around and Jack is able to force the little fomites against the bulkhead.

"Let's go! You have them corned."

They both jump for the door and seal the vermin onslaught tightly behind them.

The two adrenalin-driven crewmembers make it to the bridge in record time.

'Captain Graciela, Ma'am, we are overwhelmed with four-legged grain-eaters."

"What does that mean?"

"Me know. Had in barn where born. Rats!"

"Are the sealed up tight?"

"Yeah, Jack pinned them against a bulkhead, and we locked the bin down so no more can escape."

"And you are sure none got out of the cargo hold?"

"Aye, Captain."

There was only one thing to do in a situation like this.

Captain Graciela called a general staff meeting.

"We obviously have a problem here."

Jack asked, "Captain School not teach how to handle?"

"No Jack, it was not in the books."

"Suggestions?"

"We kill vermin friends?"

"That is what we're trying to decide, Jack."

"Me know! Us drop them off in bin. Let new owners deal with it."

"Sorry, Jack, no one wants rats. They have little value and only destroy other sentient's food."

"Unless you want to take care of them and share your food and air?"

"No. No. Me not want that, me only have food and air for me."

Tang had a more practical outlook, "We can't sell vermin infected grain."

"No, it would be unfair and bad for business. We can't give our customers live rats. I could lose my reputation and my license."

"Toss the bin out the airlock?"

"Sorry, No. We are in well-traveled space lanes. Some other ship would probably spot it and try to pick it up. Those miner ships are always checking for metal and loose debris."

"That be fun when they open it!"

"Remove Air?"

"That is a bit tricky. If the cargo bay's door leaks, we could lose our air."

"Tang, when was the last time the seals were checked?"

"Let me think, it was before the first trip to the bioGel Consortium, now when was that?

"Too long. I'm not sure we can trust the seals."

Tang said, "We need to ask for your money back."

"Unlikely. It was a cash, ΞStandards up-front deal. Even if they lie, cheat, and used a hacked, foreign bioGel, there is little we can do."

Tang offered, "I wonder what the bGC would say if they learned about one of their 'gels getting hacked? Maybe I'll tell them. Let's track the history of the bin and see if we can find the culprit.

"How get foreign 'gel?

"Tang, did you check the QR code?"

"Of course, it was made in the heliotail, at one of the bGC sister factories. They work fine, most of the time, but break down a lot."

"So, rat friends have to die?"

"I'm afraid so. I can't ask any of you to do it. I'll pump out the air from the hold and deal with the consequences. Tang, you will have to monitor the seals to ensure they don't leak."

"At least they are in a sealed cargo bay. Before we commit to murder, there is one other option I want to check. I'll contact the Zoo on Vesta and see if their snakes would like some live rats."

"Tang, Jack, go re-check the cargo bins. We don't know if the other 'gels are infected and giving wrong readings. And re-calibrate all those gels against our good probes."

Tang grabbed a few probes and a spare 'gel, *Hope 'gel doesn't squirm when it's connected. I really hate the wiggling.*

Tang turns to Jack on their way out, "you're in charge of other animals. Why do I have to go?"

"You 'gel expert."

"Right, and don't forget it."

Tang bled off as much air as was safe and plugged his scope in the cargo bay's fiber-optic line. "I see floating rats, but they're not moving. It's safe to go in."

"Captain said lock rats in bin."

"Right, pick them up and stuff in the grain bin."

"What if they bite?"

"They won't bite. They can barely breathe."

Tang equalized the cargo bay and cracked the entrance hatch. He peeked it, "It's safe. They are still knocked out. Quickly. Let's grab and stuff."

"K. This be fun."

The boys bounced around collecting rats.

"Hey, this one moving, try to bite me!"

"It's fine. You've had your rabies shot."

"Right, of course. Still me better check me vacc card."

"Good, let's finish up."

Tang neglected to remind Jack that rats don't carry rabies. They were both vaccinated for all known bugs, and having Jack worry about a non-issue was not productive.

"Me not see any."

"Right, these rats can't escape from us! Seal the bin, and lets go."

Tang and Jack returned to the bridge to report to Captain Grace.

"All the bins are cleared, the only one with vermin is locked tight. They all are back in their grain bin."

"Okay. Go back down and lower the air in that bay. It will keep them asleep."

"Jack, keep an eye on the door seals. If they start leaking, bring the pressure back up immediately."

"Aye, Captain."

Chapter 29
Lilly gets a name

"Thanks, team, you handled that well. Now we have to figure out what to do with a bin full of grainy rats."

"The table is open to any idea. We need a plan that can work. Jack, let's hear yours first."

"Good idea, Captain. We can hear his plan and get it out of the way."

Jack, in fact, didn't have a plan, but exclaimed, "Tangy, your fur moving funny."

"What do you mean?"

"Fur has ears."

"What?"

"And eyes."

Captain Grace came over, "Let me see."

"Tangy, it have huge red ears!"

Eyes look back, ears flick from one sentient to another as Grace starts a detailed inspection.

"I know what this is!"

"It rat?"

"No, it's not a rat. I saw one of these on Earth at Rocky's place in the forest. He had puppy-hood friend named 'Peanuts'. I think it is called a squirrel."

Tang did not seem happy even with a not-rat identification.

"What do you think, Tang? Rocky's little squirrel was friendly, and this one seems to be the same." said Graciela.

"Well, I guess there is no need to murder him, if he is friendly, but everyone has to share in its upkeep."

"Tang, congratulations. It looks like you have a new friend. We will all pitch in to feed and aerate him, and at least it isn't a rat. We need to give it a name."

Jack checked out eyes and ears, called out a name. "Peanuts?"

Eyes narrowed, ears back, not the response he wanted.

Tang asked, "Is him a him?"

"Me know how to tell."

Squirrel friend started chittering as Jack got closer. There was no way he would be able to peek under the hood.

"K, me can do sniff-ID, have all me need from here."

"Him is her."

"Okay, maybe she will respond to a specific name?"

"Hello, Lilly," asked Graciela.

Squirrel lifted an ear, cocked her head.

Tang said, "Looks like this little fomite has a first name, at least."

"Color like you Tang. Is red? Right? How bout Lilly Red?"

Still no approval from the furry little girl.

"She isn't as dark as Tang. Hello Lilly Rose?"Grace offered.

Lilly Rose flicked an ear at the Captain, accepting her name, and her new home, which seemed to be Tang's shoulder.

"This little rodent isn't going to live on my fur. Jack, you're the animal wrangler. Find some place for her to live that isn't me."

"Lilly look good on you. Maybe we leave her there?" offered Jack.

Tang answered with his eyes.

"K, me have small box for chickens, me can fix it up as her home."

"Yes, do that. Right away."

"Lilly Rose, nice name. Wonder if related to me friend 'Ellgi'?"

"The malamute?

"Yes."

"No."

Grace decided to end the session. The discussions were falling off the beam. "OK. Let's take a break. Get everything settled, and we'll continue the meeting after FirstMeal."

"Fine with me, this has been a stressful day. And I'm not so sure about this rodent hanging on my fur. I'm not her mother!"

"That be funny. Me ask Lilly what she think."

Tang offered, "I should update my resume. Is rat herding a skill? Not that I want to chase down rats ever again."

"Me should update me resume too. Rats not nice like Lilly. They mean and bitey. Oh, me forgot. Me better check me records for Rabies shot."

"You do that, no one wants you foaming at the mouth, biting everyone."

"Like in horror vid me saw. It had humans biting humans. No dogs or red apes. So not too real."

Lilly Rose settled into her new home, the modified chicken nesting box. She rapidly adapted to this new ZeroG life, zooming around, bouncing off bulkheads, a flying squirrel in the best sense.

Tang and Lilly came to an understanding. He would allow her to nestle on his shoulder when flying, food, and other duties were completed.

After FirstMeal the crew gathered again to discuss the rat problem. Captain Grace started the discussion. "We have to find a home for the rats."

Octopus, with his tinny sucker-generated voice, announced, "Let me take care of it, please."

"I appreciate the offer, but we have to give them a fighting chance. I've heard that the Vesta zoo herpetarium ran an export business. They are selling snakes to miners and asteroids for vermin control. If they want the rats, they could become meals for reptiles and raptors."

"Me agree with Octopus. They still be food."

Lilly became a bit agitated, it seemed that 'snake' was a word she knew.

Tang dug deep to find a relevant comment. "Octopus. I don't think your digestive system is setup for fur. I'm certainly not going to skin the little beasts for you."

Octopus, using his sucker voice, "I can skin them, I can use kitchen tools. Easy to learn."

"Are you sure you want to have sharp knives around your wet suit? Are the rats that tasty?"

He tapped back.

.. / ... . . / -.-- --- ..- .-. / .--. --- .. -. -
I see your point

"Good, we've come to an agreement. We omnivores and carnivores are not desperate enough to eat rats. Right, Jack?"

"Now me wonder how taste too."

Captain Graciela raised an eyebrow, looking directly at Jack. The message was clear.

"Me mean no. Or yes. What was question?"

"Octopus, do you agree with the decision?"

Octopus began rapidly tapping against the glass partition.

"Taping too fast. Me not know pusses' code."

They all strained to hear the words, and after a moment the random dots and dashes switched to understandable Morse code.

.. / .- -.-. -.-. . ,--. - / -.-- --- ..- .-. / .-. ..- .-.. . ...

I accept your rules

Lilly settled down, buried a bit deeper in her humongous protector.

Captain Grace extended her prerogative, "At least at the zoo they might have a fighting chance. We're going with that option. No additional votes or discussions required."

"Tang, We better check the 'gel and confirm Vesta's Zoo snake-rearing project. I'm more than certain they would be interested in fresh Earth-born food for their predators."

It took a quick mini-EarthMinute for Tang to report, "the database says the breeding program is successful and they have put out a request for food for their hungry serpents."

Captain Grace nodded, "Then it's a go. I'll send them a 'gelTxt and let them know we may have a solution to their problem."

"Hope snakeys not too hungry. Maybe we not have enough rats?"

"Not to worry, Jack, they will be satisfied with any rats we have. No one else wants them, I'm sure."

Tang offered, "we should trade a few rats and get us a pet snake for the ship."

LillyRose, hanging out on Tang's shoulder, starts chittering and dancing.

"That's not funny Tang. Don't you know Lilly would be put in danger?"

"Sorry, it was just a joke."

"Hope ratties okay in bin. We still not at Vesta."

"You're right. Please check up on them, make sure they are healthy."

"K. They just like chickens. Me can do that."

"And make sure they don't get out, use the 'gel sensors to monitor their oxygen level. You can bleed out any noxious gases too."

Wonder if taste like chicken? Maybe me and Octopus can check?

Chapter 30
Rat for Dinner

The ship drew closer to its target. It was time to trade some merchandise, stretch their legs, maybe a bit of gambling, and sell rats.

"Octopus, ask Vesta Dock Control if they have a berth near the zoo. I don't want a long ride with a bin of rats."

BosonsWave stood off Vesta in a stationary orbit. A tug sidled over, attached a cable, and dragged them down to their assigned dock, adjacent to the warehouses and only a few kilometers from the zoo.

"Tang, query the asteroid's inventory and see what they might need. Don't forget to use a six-EarthMonth regressive analysis for pricing trends. We can part with a little of our manure and compost, but I want to save most of it for *SinensisPrime*."

Grace reviewed Tang's search results and sent her inventory lists to the merchants. The selling prices looked good, but it only worked if someone purchased the stock. Everyone waited for the onslaught of orders. There would be no shore leave until the requests were paid and delivered.

"How long till reply? Me want go to spa."

The wait was a little longer than she expected. Jack's trip to the spa and Tang's card games were in limbo. Finally, a single reply pinged the comm' gel. There were no bids at the prices she was offering.

Tang reviewed the list, "Are these merchants for real? Look at those low bids."

"This is disappointing. We may have to visit each merchant and try to make a sale in person."

Tang disagreed, "that is a lot of work. How about we sell the rats and go somewhere else?

"You might have a point. I'm afraid our cargo is not that different from any other merchant ship. There are too many ships trading the same goods. We can't stay here much longer. All we're doing is paying dock fees and not making sales. We don't even generate money for the tax wardens."

"But then, that's okay. Right?" said Tang.

"If it wasn't for those rats, this leg of the trip would be a complete loss. At least we don't have to pay taxes on the rats. For some reason, they're not on the tax charts."

Tang replied, "I'm sure they will make that change by the time we get here again."

"Let not pay tax and let rats out."

Tang explained, "Not the best plan, Jack, I don't think that will work in the long run."

"I'm still disappointed in the lack of sales. It's not like we went back to Earth and picked from their horn of plenty. I'm afraid it is the same cargo everywhere. We have nothing different, except for the rats."

"Me know! We get more rats and sell them."

"No, Jack, I don't think that would be profitable, and it is way too risky."

The discussion ran out of topics without a viable conclusion or direction. The Vesta bioGel mail server filled up the comm with the usual advertisements, but no more offers for the ship's cargo.

"At least we know the manure will sell for a premium on the shiny herbal rock. I don't want to sell Vesta any of our manure if they're not interested in the rest of the cargo. Let them get their own poop."

There was a note from her mother buried in the mass of pleadings.

"Alright, crew, my family confirmed it. Our next stop is *SinensisPrime.*"

"Once we pick up teas and spices, we'll have products no one else has. Enough of this Core-designed junk."

"We can charge a premium for the teas. I bet the asteroid teas are better than Earth. The air is regulated, and no floating dirt or viruses infect the plants. We'll make a killing on *SinensisPrime*.

"Captain, I'm sure we can sell our stock to those herbal nuts. Hardly anyone stops there. No one likes to risk a crash to make a sale."

"Exactly, and we have enough ΞStandards from our last job to fill the ship with all the aromatic teas and fungi that will fit."

The crew still had to deal with the small problem of rats. The zoo offered to buy the rat-bin and the bonus grain they called home. The deal was for ΞStandards on delivery, at the front door. It was time to become movers.

Graciela rented a cheap little scooter and trailer. The bin hung out the back a meter or so. It was ZeroG, easy on, easy off.

"Tang, secure all the straps. We don't want to give away any rats for free."

"Aye, Captain. It is tied down and secure. Nothing is going to shake that bin loose. If you don't mind, I'll stay behind this trip. The rodents stress me out."

For Tang, the rats brought back memories of his youth in the jungle. His troop taught him that rats were the enemy of primates. The rats were unrelenting, omnivorous, fast-breeding, long-toothed destroyers. They make great garbage collectors but easily get out of hand. If it wasn't for the occasional zoonotic plague, the rats could become a real plague.

Grace handled the scooter as the trained Captain she was. The overloaded, extended bin did not know about her driving skills. The tail started wiggling, setting up a harmonic wave from the back to front, side to side across the road.

Sitting on the front of the bin, Jack told Captain Grace, "Someone pushing on back, go faster."

The obvious happened, the bin tipped, sliding down the road, still attached to the trailer.

The inertia of a 5km/E-hour scooter isn't that bad, even when scraping along a tunnel wall at slightly more than ZeroG. Plasticine bins don't break very often, and there were no sparks, just smoky chemicals. Somehow Grace kept the scooter upright and hit the brakes.

Jack jumped off the front as friction did its work.

"It Okay. Ratties still asleep."

"Tang did say it was secure, and he was right about that."

Jack took out his speed tape and patched the little, barely rat-sized hole. *Me sure all inside.*

"Check the bin and help me turn it upright before the local Gendarmes notice."

"Jack, are they any breaks? Did the rats escape?"

"Me got it!"

"Are they all in there?"

"It fine. Me not know, not count."

Snakes probably catch them. Me just keep quiet

Jack looked up at the directional sign, "Captain, exit one kilometer. On right."

"Got it. We'll be there shortly."

The little scooter, cart and sentients, rats and grains, all sped along to the exit at 3km/E-hour this time.

A tootle of the horn, and the zoo gates opened wide for their prize.

"Welcome back to our zoo. I hear you have a special delivery for us."

"Ratties and grain."

"Jack's right, as I explained in the 'gelTxt. The bin was infected with rats from Earth. I'm sure your snakes will enjoy the fresh food."

"It will be a thrill for them. We've updated your comm with the agreed-upon payment. My crew will take it from here. My Air is Your Air."

"We're happy to be of service. My Air is Your Air."

Jack, under his breath, "Goodbye rats, for good."

"Are you interested in purchasing any of our extra stock? A snake, for instance."

"No, we're good. We didn't have a lot of sales here and don't need any more cargo. We'll pass on the offer for a snake too. One of my crew has a serious issue with those animals."

"Me not afraid of snakes. Tang not afraid snakes. Is Octopus?"

"Lilly."

"Oh. Right."

Graciela and Jack took their leave, sans rats or snakes.

Chapter 31
Sinensis Prime

"I confirmed with my parents. They are ready for a cargo run to *SinensisPrime*."

"It didn't go so well last time. It was a tricky landing."

"Me did it good, me can do it again!"

"Not to worry, I've got some special glasses my Dad ordered for this occasion. These should neutralize the flashing lights."

Tang had to ask, "Should? Have they ever been tested?"

"It will be fine. We can neutralize the flashing lights."

"I'm not convinced."

"Me take care of it, Tang. Me landed ship last time."

"True. I guess we have a backup system, a short furry one."

"Wait, we can't go back to *SinensisPrime*. Didn't they accuse you of being a thief?" asked Tang.

"Can me not go? Me still not want be in jail. Again. Drop me off at HuB, they have good jerky."

"You do know we are a few million kilometers away from HuB?"

"Oh."

"And we're going in the wrong direction for your jerky?"

"Tang, you shouldn't worry. We are no longer the *LunaCola*. They will be looking for its captain, not its crew. There should be no issues."

"And that isn't a problem? They might recognize you."

"Got it covered. Tang, do you want to be Captain for a cycle?"

"Really? I've never thought I would be Captain. Of course, I'll do it."

"How bout me? Me know how to land there. Me could be Captain."

"The temporary captain will have to talk to all of the farmers and negotiate for the best trades."

"K. Maybe next time. Me not like talking to them. They dress funny."

"Jack, don't worry, we still may need your navigation talents, which is more important than a title."

"K, but me could be Captain too. If Tang can talk plants me can too."

"No, navigation is too important. We don't want you distracted with Captain duties."

"Me guess it fair." *But me not call Tangy Captain. Me keep quiet.*

SinensisPrime's sparkling, flashing colors, bounced off the bridge and seeped through the portholes. Octopus was already at his periscope, seemly distracted from his navigation duties. Colors were running up and down his arms to his mantle.

Jack thought, *Puss disabled, too much colors. Me color sense better!*

Grace unpacked the two special bioGel-connected glasses. Jack didn't need them, and Octopus was already out of the loop.

The glasses had a single wire down to a bioGel tablet tied into the sensor array, analyzing and canceling the colors across the spectrum. They weren't elegant, more improvised than professional, but suitable for the job. This time, newly appointed First Mate Graciela would not be mesmerized by the flashing colors. It was white, black, and a pleasant gray for the landing zone.

Captain Tang put on the color-correcting contraption, "I can see the tarmac, bathed in simple gray lights. These lenses really do the trick. No headache this time, I bet."

Other Captain Graciela said, "It is all yours Captain Tang. Make the ship proud."

Tang tacked into the sun, slowed, and gave the orders to reef the sail. Ex-Captain Grace released the catches as Jack started on the treadmill pulling the sail down the mast.

The asteroid continued spinning, as space rocks do, lightly connecting with *BosonsWave* at the landing zone.

Tang exuded all the confidence of a first-timer as he surveyed his domain.

A loud clunk echoed through the bridge. Tang let out a quiet sigh, "Please bring your meal trays to an upright position and unfasten your seat belts."

"Me not wear seat belt and had no food. Now me hungry."

Ex-Captain Grace smiled. "Excellent landing. You did well. Thank you for taking such good care of my ship."

"Thank you Captain, it was an honor."

Another loud clunk, outside the ship, and the sound of skids dragging across the tarmac.

"Guess my family is here too."

"Let's get ready to meet our hosts."

"Tang, I'll need you as acting-Captain a while longer as we negotiate with these herbal rubes. I'll be standing by as part of your loyal crew. My Air is Your Air."

"Let's go out and meet up with my parents. We'll present a strong team to the locals."

Mykolas and Pilar waited in the tent area leading to the village proper. Both dressed in their finest fancy clothes; blue jeans and bomber jackets. Certainly drab by local standards.

Tang was shirtless in his best overalls with a jaunty cap, and silver-tipped cane. His fine red fur was all the color he needed on this shiny rock.

Jack was wearing his blue cape, hat, and doggles. His blue merle fur completed his colorful ensemble.

Ex-Captain Grace had the same tie-dyed shirt she wore the last time she was here, this time turned inside out. *No need to wear something new. The local yokels will never know it's the same shirt.* Blue jeans were required and complemented the shirt's pattern.

The crew of the *BlackHornet* joined Grace's family on the tarmac.

"Glad your landing was uneventful." said Graciela.

"Right. It is easy when the colors are neutralized."

"I agree. Those glasses worked great. We couldn't even see those irritating, flashing colors. Thanks for coming up with this trick, Dad."

Pilar and Mykolas were thrilled to make it to the meeting, their first time trading with their daughter as equals. Still, her mother had to bring up another obvious point. "I see you have another name for your ship. This is getting a bit much."

"Don't worry. I'm going un-advertised. Like you and Dad. What do you think of the name?"

"It certainly is attractive. Let's see if you can keep it for a while."

It was time to change the subject, a bit of misdirection away from her mother's passive-aggressive inquiries.

Jack turned and asked, "Captain Grace, why not family dress fancy? We not want insult locals."

"This is fancy dress for those two. Those are Earth jeans, antiques, I bet. They'll be fine."

Pilar overheard Jack's comments, "What do you mean, these are real Levi's® jeans, straight from the Gap. Made with real cotton. If they don't like the subtle blue colors, they can turn the other way."

The assembled crew walked out to meet the Jefe and Assistant Jefe. They left the bioGel glasses on the ships. Those would look a little weird, even for a LiftShip crew.

Pilar reached into her bag, "Here, put on these polarizing sunglasses. They will help you deal with the color onslaught."

Grace looked at Tang, "You look good in those fancy shades."

"As do you."

Jack kept his doggles on, safe within his limited color sense.

The ship's two octopuses would not miss this expedition for anything. Dressed in their transparent reverse wet suits, photophores matching the ever-changing background color-for-color. They strode off, tentacle in tentacle, enjoying every color change.

"I see our hosts waiting in the anteroom airlock. They are as badly dressed as the last time!"

"Agreed, I don't know what it is about this asteroid, but they sure know how to abuse colors."

"Look okay to me. What is problem?"

Tang replied, "There are so many colors, and look over there. I haven't seen so many shades of green since I left the jungle. And yet, they are still able to make it look overdone."

Pilar spoke to Grace, "before we meet our hosts, you need a better disguise. Your face is probably too well known. I have a big, floppy hat you can use."

"Thanks. Do we have a game plan?"

"Me know, sell high buy low!"

"Aside from Jack's suggestion, anyone else?"

"We know they want Earth manure, so it will be our bargaining chip. Captain Tang, you should probably lead on this. My mother will help and I'll stand in the background, keeping out of the way."

"Captain Tang? So, you lost your ship's name and now your title? What else is happening?

"Mother, it is just a ruse, don't worry, I'm still in charge."

"If nothing for me to do, me go look for jerky, me not interested in leaves and twigs."

"Good plan, Jack, and maybe you can nose around and see what else they may have we can re-sell."

"He does have the nose for it!"

"Be nice, Tang. You are supposed to be Captain."

"Fine. Let's go meet our hosts."

Chapter 32
Jefes prime

In the plasticine air bubble surrounding the landing port, the two bureaucrats discussed the arrival of the cargo ships.

Jefe was dressed in his official uniform, a flowing coat reflecting the ever-changing lights of the spinning solar-cell/Crookes radiometers. The tiny power generators stood as tall welcoming flags for any visitor. His tricorne hat, with gold highlights, was a sign of rank. Two real Earth feathers adorning the hat swayed gently in the circulating air.

Asst. Jefe, dressed similarly, silver trim and one feather, stood by his side. "Do you remember the time we got the fine cow manure from a LiftShip? We sure could use some more. They claimed it was from Earth, but I still don't believe it."

"I read the waybill and don't doubt it was quality Earth poop. The documentation is hard to fake and it was some good stuff. We won't see that this time, I'm afraid. After reviewing the first ship's manifest, it's only regular Asteroid supplies and a little excess compost from HuB."

"Do you remember when we hired an Ag inspector? He really helped our yields. Too bad he was a thief."

"Yes, that was a real mess. Didn't he buy his way onto a LiftShip? It was called 'Luna' something."

"*LunaCola*"

"Right, that's it."

"I heard he was a bit of a grifter along with his other talents. Maybe he was able to sweet-talk the captain into a free voyage."

"Do you think they were in on it too?"

"We never did figure out how he got those plants onto the ship. Virtually everyone has been brought in for questioning, and we have nothing."

Asst. Jefe nodded.

"I even sent the captain an order to come back for sentencing under 'First-Class Grand Theft Seed' rules, but they never replied."

"Sounds guilty to me."

"Sooner or later, I'll find them and let them know we cannot be trifled with."

Asst. Jefe stopped and asked, "Wait, first ship? Do you mean we'll see more than one?

"Correct. A convoy of sorts. The other ship is coming from the Core rocks, but I don't have information on their cargo."

"You know, Jefe, this can work to our advantage."

"Exactly. We have a bumper crop of herbs and fungi from the last Earth poop boost. If we can sell to these two ships, we'll be able to turn away others for a couple of seasons. We can stash our products and drive up the prices!"

"Agreed. It would be great to limit how many merchants we'll have to deal with. Jefe, the ships are getting closer. Should we lock the radiometers down so they won't have a hard time landing?"

"Nah, we have never had a reason to do it. If word gets out that it's easy to land here, we'll be overrun with outsiders. We need to concentrate on our needs, not those of the rest of the heliosphere."

"You are right again, Jefe. If we have too many strangers running around, we'll risk losing our unique position as purveyors of herbs, good and spicy."

"Look, here comes the LiftShip. It seems on the right approach. I guess they aren't having any problems with the flashing lights."

"Too bad, it is always fun to see them struggle."

"As long as they don't take out any of our power towers."

The approach of the ships is flawless.

The two ships, a LiftShip and one decked out as an intra-asteroid carrier, blocked out the sun as they approached the tiny landing pad.

BonsonsWave drifted to the landing platform. The sail was angled into the sun, holding it virtually steady against the turning rock.

It was almost as if they had done this before. The *BlackHornet* followed *BosonsWave* on its track to a smooth, almost bumpless landing.

The settlement, wrapped in its clear plasticine bubble, was filled with oxygen supplemented by the flora, keeping everyone happy and respiring as it pushed out against the void.

An accordion tunnel wormed its way out to the ships, expanding to encompass both airlocks in its cavernous maw. There were no tremors as the ground crew secured the tent to the front of the ships. The two bosses,

Jefe and Assistant Jefe stood by the airlock to the village, waiting for the crew's arrival.

Jefe stepped up as the team approached, "Welcome to *SinensisPrime*. It's so unusual to have two ships at the same time. We look forward to trading our fine wares."

"Thank you, Jefe. Please meet my two deckhands, Grace and Jack, and of course, our First Mate, Octopus."

Jack had to suppress his little tail, *Me same as me Captain!*

Asst. Jefe asked, "You know, the last time we had a LiftShip coming from Core, they delivered manure. By any chance, do you have any? We miss it."

Captain Tang played his introductory card, to get their attention, "We have some compost and herbivore manure we purchased on Luna. It is directly from Earth and only the best quality. We have commitments for it further down the line, but we can part with some."

Asst Jefe moved closer, showing a little too much concern.

Jefe looked at Asst Jefe, hiding a smile, "We'd have to check our stock, but we may want to trade for some, if the rate is right."

"If you need more, *BlackHornet* is carrying compost from HuB. They seem to have more compostable material going down the chute than they can use locally. We can throw that in the pile, at market rates."

Asst. Jefe ignored the offer, still stuck in his ruminations about herbivore manure. "I was wondering. Have any of you heard about a ship called *LunaCola?* We are hoping to talk to them about some of our viable seeds they may have taken with them."

No one in this crew had any intention of letting the truth out.

"Don't all the LiftShip captains know each other? You must know about the ship."

Tang was able to let his intellectual spirit fly, "Sorry, there are a lot of LiftShips, and their advertising names change from time to time. We've all seen ships by that name. The Luna Cola brand is a particularly common advertiser.

"If you want to find the ship, you can check the Heliosphere Ship Number registry and cross-reference it with the Ad-Directory."

"I'm not familiar with those tools."

"If you don't have the equipment, we would be glad to offer our services. For a fair price."

A pause to let the options sink in, then, "Training would be extra."

"I'll ask my Jefe."

Asst. Jefe continued, "They must have been pretty smart to pull off the heist."

Jefe spoke directly to Captain Tang, "Your crew looks familiar. Don't I know you?"

Grace smiled, thinking *this discussion is not going in the right direction. I should head this conversation off before it gets out of hand.* "Have you been to HuB? Might we have met there?"

"No, everything we need is already here on *SinensisPrime*. I have no desire or need to visit any less colorful rock."

Jack chimed in. "You should visit Earth. It colorful, Me born there and visit family while ago."

"Never been there. I've heard it was heavy."

"Yes, we LiftShipers keep fit and strong. Me have no problem with Earthy weight."

Grace thought, *leave it to Jack to send the conversation in a different direction. This time for the better!*

"Liftship crews do seem to look alike. Sorry for the intrusion. I must have been mistaken. Please make your way to the warehouse. My Air is Your Air."

Asst. Jefe, unwilling to let the subject end, turned to Pilar and Mykolas. "Perhaps you know the captain of the *LunaCola?* They stole some valuable plants and seeds, and we have lost contact with them. The captain was Human, female, I think, simple dresser, thin, dark long hair, not too bright."

Pilar shook her head answering in the negative.

"You sort of look like her."

"Sorry. Never met anyone meeting that exact description."

Chapter 33
Prime Shopping

Captain Tang had never been to the warehouse or anywhere else on this herbal-infused asteroid. The last time they visited, he was bedridden with a cold compress to block out the lights. Now with his sunglasses, he could deal with the overly bright flashing, spinning illuminations.

Octopus joined his compadre from the *BlackHornet*, and they wandered off to communicate and play with the colors.

Maybe me follow Octopus. Not find any jerky in plant house last time. Might have better luck with more arms. "Wait for me, Octopusis!"

Tang and Grace can dicker for leafs and moldies. Not me.

It was a short stroll to the warehouse with the four captains in their color-deadening sunglasses.

Pilar whispered, "How do these sentients handle all the flashing colors?"

"We should check their eyes. Bet they have tinted contacts."

"Probably just a lot of aspirin or something stronger."

"Right."

Asst Jefe held the door open for the party, Jefe in the lead. It was a conference room adorned with flowers, leaves, sticks, and fungi. Grace whispered to Tang, "Same setup as last time."

Tang seemed lost in the display, even with his sunglasses on. The delirious, complex, exciting odors drew him back to his jungle-filled youth.

Grace nudged Tang. He ordered, "Sailor, please record these samples in your 'gel's database."

"Aye, aye, Captain."

One-feather Jefe spoke first, "Please join us. We are delighted with your visit and wish to honor you with samples of our local bread, salt, and tea."

Captains Tang and Pilar lifted a cup to the Jefe and Assistant Jefe.

Graciela had a job to do. *At least this time, I don't need Octopus to re-order the list. I'll combine the data with the last set.*

A quick capture by a bioGel probe passed to the old database, and she was ready to move on to the next one. The 'gel displayed the biochemical traits and prices bought and sold.

At the front table, tea-drinking, salt-and-bread eating continued as the work of identification continued.

The ceremonies were over by the time Grace was done recording.

Captain Tang reviewed the list and knew what the stock was worth and what he could bid. Time to discuss pricing.

Mykolas spent his time sampling teas and a few special fungi. "I should go check on octopuses and Jack."

"Yes dear, don't miss our launch window, although this rock looks better than the last one you were stuck on."

The reference was not lost on Mykolas, but the fungi reduced his reply to a nod as he took off to look at the lights.

"Hope that old man remembers where the ship is, or that he is even on one."

Pilar sent her in-trade inventory to the Jefe's 'gel, who shared it with his group of growers. She poured Tang another bulb of tea and offered a drink to his deckhand, "Here, dear, it looks like you can use a some tea too. It is quite fragrant. I hope a rough-and-tumble sailor like youtself can appreciate it."

"Yes, ma'am - I mean Captain."

The discussion circle broke open, "We're sorry, we don't need most of your products. We get the same goods from every other cargo ship."

Graciela nodded to Tang and sent the list of *BosonsWave*'s inventory to the Jefe.

"Now, the list from the other ship has a few interesting items. We need a lot more manure than you are bringing. It is hardly worth it to be burdened with the other supplies for that little bit of poop."

Tang said, "That is all we could get on short notice. If you still need some, we can be sure to pick it up the next time we swing by here."

"Sailor, please make a note of it."

"Aye, Captain."

"How big a deposit will you be putting down?"

Jefe replied, "we will have to take that under advisement with the growers. And we need written guarantees and timelines."

Pilar joined the negotiations. It was her favorite part of the job. "We require 25% down before we'll commit to bringing the product. Likewise, we need to take the contract under advisement."

"Our fiscal team doesn't meet for six revolutions, about two EarthDays in common time."

Grace would have joined in, but she was just a lowly deckhand. Pilar continued, "If our ships return with a full load of manure, you will need to show your commitment. You'll need to purchase our stock. From both ships today."

"This is not something we can do. We don't need those products, and we can purchase the same items from a different ship."

"The whole heliosphere knows how badly you treat merchants and how difficult you make it for anyone to visit."

"We do like our special little world. We consider it exclusive."

"Well, if you want our exclusive Earth manure, you'll agree to our offer. Most ships will avoid even coming close to your over-illuminated dirt patch."

"We are quite willing to pay, in ΞStandards, for your crop and go find some other asteroid that can use our little pile of manure," said Pilar.

"We can speed up the process. I can let you know after our daily meeting, in two cycles."

"That is a bit longer than we wanted to wait. We leave as soon as we get loaded. We are very busy and have other clients we need to visit. You can send us the deposit by A-mail if you can't come to a decision soon."

"Sailor, make a note of that," Tang ordered.

"Aye."

Better tone down the commands. This may come back to haunt me.

The back-and-forth negotiations didn't take long before they reached a consensus.

Jefes, large and small, smiled. They negotiated for the supply of herbaceous poop, accepted supplies from the *BlackHornet* and a promise of Earth poop in a future delivery. It was worth a celebration.

Tang stepped up and bowed slightly, saying, "My Air is Your Air."

Jefe did not respond with the expected answer but "What is wrong with your fur? It is wiggling."

"And it has eyes!"

Tang was not alone in his decision-making. Aside from his deckhand, his new buddy LillyRose was along for the ride.

"Oh no. No. No. We don't allow rodents on our asteroid. How did it get here?"

"What, there is nothing here. What are you talking about?"

"On your shoulder! Two eyes, ears. I've heard about those. It's a rat!"

"Oh. LillyRose? She is a squirrel, not a rat."

"Take it away. The deal is off!"

"I think not. Do you want to know about our bin of real rats? They were fast asleep the last time I checked."

Grace gave Tang a look. He shrugged.

"Is that a threat? We don't respond to threats."

"Not a threat at all, but they are a little hungry, after being in hibernation for so long."

The Jefes stepped back and transformed into a discussion circle, complete with dirty looks and narrow eyes.

Tang, Graciela, and Pilar went to the table, poured some fresh tea, had a bite of bread, and waited.

Grace whispered, "We don't have any more live rats, do we?"

"No, but we did, and I never said they were on board right now, so not completely a lie."

The Jefes circle came apart as Jefe bowed, his two feathers leaning with him and said, "We will honor the deal, as long as that rat stays where it is. The material will be on the dock within an EarthHour. Please do the same with your supplies."

Grace got on the comm. "Jack, Octopus, Mykolas, we're loading up and taking off. Back to work!"

Only Jack had to do physical work, the octopuses went back to their charting, and Mykolas went in for a laydown.

"Captain Grace, I turn your ship back to you. My Air is Your Air."

"Tang, I accept the ship and its command. Thank you for taking such good care of it. My Air is Your Air."

That was fun. Maybe I should try for that job?

"Tangy, was it hard to be captain? Me get to be captain next time!"

"You'll have to take that up with the regular captain. Not my decision."

"Good idea. Me talk to Captain Grace."

"Let me know when you do this, I want to be there."

"To help?"

"Something like that."

Before Jack could get himself into any trouble, work called.

"Everyone to your stations, we bought a full 50mw boost, and we're heading back to HuB to sell some leaves and fungi. Tang, please verify the cargo before we launch."

They had full cargo holds, but there was little mass. A promise to return with Earth-herbivore poop and compost weighed nothing. Captain Grace saluted the Jefes as they made their way to the boost laser.

On the tarmac, Asst Jefe turned to Jefe for one more try, "You know, I'm sure I've seen that crew before. It looked just like the *LunaCola* we've been trying to find. But on that ship, the monkey wasn't the captain."

Chapter 34
Leaving Prime

"Graciela, we're going back to HuB. The haul from this trade will let us sit around, selling herbs and drinking tea for quite a while."

"You sound like a bunch of old retired sentients!"

"And that's bad?"

"No, it's fantastic. I hope you enjoy your time off."

"We've made a lot of friends there, and they love our teas and herbs, especially the ones that help their overworked livers after years of hard drinking. Your dad really likes the Burdock and Milk Thistle teas. I know his liver is happy to get healthy liquids for a change."

"This trip worked out quite well, thanks to the interference goggles you found. I'm glad you could dispose all of your cargo to those crazy plant merchants."

Jack broke in, "You not travel with family? That sad. Me would like have me family here."

Tang had a suggestion, "my cousin is successful with his Mort Tee-Shirt shop on Luna. You could do the same with the teas. Some of my troop are on HuB and could help you open a tea shop."

"Oh no. That is too much like work. We'll host our friends on the *BlackHornet*. It is just like having a shop, but no overhead or employees. We get to set our hours, and we don't have to serve anyone we don't like."

"And no taxes, too, I bet," said Tang.

"That thought has crossed my mind. What the tax wardens don't know about, they can't tax. As far as they are concerned, we are just a place for our friends to visit. And we have a lot of friends."

"We'll have to catch you there next time. We're heading toward Earth to meet Herb on a job he wants us to do for the Navy. We'll sell our stock as we go, although I'm keeping a good supply of teas for my use this time. No telling when we'll be back this way again, and those shiny herb merchants are not the easiest to deal with."

"I think you have them running, especially with your Captain Tang and his pet squirrel at your side."

"A point of clarification," said Tang, "Lilly Rose is not my pet. She is a stowaway."

Lilly Rose couldn't speak for herself but looked at Tang and tweaked an ear. The meaning was clear.

"You helped give her a name. That sounds pretty friendly to me."

Jack changed the subject back to the most important team member, himself, "Next time we come to plant rock, me get to be Captain. Tang be me crew."

Tang rolled his eyes and tweaked an ear. Not necessarily doglish, but Grace understood.

Grace answered directly, "Jack, we will give that a try. You would have to negotiate with the Herbal Jefes. Are you up for the job?"

"Tang do it, me can too!"

"Fine, we'll start your training on the flowers, herbs, sticks, and powders you will need to know about."

"Did Tang do that?"

"He grew up in the jungle. He already knew about plants. The pictures, prices, and descriptions are in the 'gel, but you will need to learn their scientific names to sound knowledgeable to the farmers."

"K."

Tang added, "Do you know Latin? Most of the names are based on that dead language."

"Tang, can you key up the taxonomy reference books Jack will need?"

"Books? More than one? What is dead words? Do they smell bad?"

"Don't worry Jack, the reference books are less than a pawfull, I think. It won't take long for you to memorize. There are only a few hundred plants that are important."

"Hundred? That a lot. Even sail classes not have that many memorizers."

"Sorry, it would be required."

"K. Maybe me be captain when we go jerky asteroid instead? That be better. Me know all about carne!"

Captain Grace tried to lead the conversation to a conclusion. "Good idea. We'll use your expertise. Let's work toward that."

"Me ask Octopus to plot path to jerky rock."

Pilar watched the conversation like a tennis match. She called in an audible, cutting off discussions. "Why don't you take the first boost,

142

dear? You have a longer trip. I think it takes at least an EarthDay to recharge their laser."

"What are you going to do while the laser recharges?"

"Don't worry about us. I have lots of new teas to try, and your father seems to like the fungi. He'll probably wander off and look at the light show."

"That sounds like Dad. We'll finish securing the cargo and get on the catapult. My Air is Your Air, Mom, Dad."

Pilar and Mykolas replied simultaneously, "Our Air is Your Air. Safe journeys."

Captain Graciela turned to her crew, "Herb will meet us near Earth's L2 point."

Tang asked, "So we can drop by Luna? It's near L2. I could use a recharge after being captain."

"What we recharge? Batteries low?"

"My recharge. Shore leave."

"Sorry, Tang. It looks like there is no chance to hit the casino until after we meet with Herb. We are on a tight schedule this time."

"Captain, don't misunderstand me. I don't always look for casinos. I'm here to work for you and the ship."

Jack added. "Me too."

Octopus had nothing to add. As long as he had his salary, math, sextant, and a few live clams, he was content.

"Good. You all know where we have to go, anyone have a preference on a trading route?"

"Can get some jerky on way?"

"I don't think there are any bits of rock that have a lot of jerky."

"Know can make from cow. Not hard."

"Not a lot of cows out here. You'll have to wait until we get to Core, maybe even back to Earth."

"Good thing me have lot jerky in me bins."

"So you don't need to stop and refill?"

"Not have 'nough to share. Barely 'nough for me."

"Well, you can check a 'gel and see if there something on our route that meets your criteria. Otherwise, you'll have to make do with what you have."

"We may have to get another boost along the way. Octopus, can you see who might be in our path with a working laser?"

.- -.-- . / -.-. .- .--. - .- .. -. --..
.. / ..... .- ...- . / .- / ..-. . .-- / .. -. / -- .. -. -..

Aye Captain I have a few in mind

Octopus reported back, sending route information to Grace's tablet.

"There are a few promising colonies. We can do a mail drop on the smaller asteroids. There seems to be only one rock with a large, working boost laser. It isn't clear what they do, but they are probably a central clearinghouse for the surrounding area. We'll stop there and do some serious trading."

"Our stock from *SinensisPrime* will be valuable and an easy trade, although I don't want to use it unless there is no way out of it. We sold all of the manure and a little of the regular cargo. I let my mother have most of the trades. At least now we have a lot more to sell. We can get better prices at the smaller asteroids and mining colonies."

The ground tug pulled *BosonsWave* to the catapult. Once the asteroid aligned with their planned route, Octopus signaled, and they were tossed out into the void, then boosted toward Core.

The laser did all the work, filling the spinnaker with its powerful red synchronous photons. They had some time before the push wore out or any course corrections were needed.

Chapter 35
Anarchy and Steel

Octopus guided them to a moderately large asteroid deep within a small field of metallic rocks.

Jack was the lookout, his nose almost touching a forward porthole. "Can see bright lights from rock."

Tang stepped up, "The smelter looks busy, and there is a strange dust cloud. I thought they trapped all the waste products."

Captain Grace added, "No matter, it still looks like a good chance to pick up some metal at a fair trade price."

Tang could make out more of the detail as they got closer. "Should the smelter be glowing like the sun? I hope it will not be a problem."

"You could be right. They may have a leak. We better not get too close. Octopus, bring us around to the rear, as far from the smelter as possible."

"Tang, you better plug in the ion sensors. Have the 'gels report directly to the bridge."

Tang, always ready to bring worry to another level, "Hope the nuclear engine doesn't go critical. It will be hard to get back up to speed without power for a laser push."

"We ride explosion instead of laser. Be fun!"

Tang responded, "Jack, this is not a vid. Real life doesn't work that way."

"Let's not go down that road. A nuclear explosion is nothing to joke about."

"Still think it work, vids maybe not wrong."

As they slid along to the backside, they saw the guts of the rock and its exposed nuclear engine and boost laser.

"It looks like the laser is adequate for the job, and look at the size of the nuclear power plant!"

The asteroid appeared to be a cross between a free-floating miner camp and a solid piece of rock. Equipment was attached, cross-linked, and bolted on with little concern for organization.

Captain Grace added, "The nuclear engine seems like it was plopped down and connected to the superstructure's grid. I wonder where it came from?"

She answered her own question, "It doesn't look like it was imported from Earth, more likely cobbled together on the spot."

"We don't want to stay here too long." offered Tang.

This group ran the smelter directly off nuclear fuel instead of the normal coal-fired plant. It was efficient but not safe. Oxygen-free smelting was *de rigueur* out here. There were no molecules in space to contaminate the metal as it cooled. The problem with nuclear smelting was the risk of impregnating the product with hot ions. There were ways around the problem, some better than others.

Lead was still the best shield but was a rare and expensive commodity. Lead, famously dense, was more abundant and easier to find on Earth than in the asteroids. The gravity transport penalty could be overbearing, and lead balloons were not a thing. The alchemists of old tried to turn lead into gold, but in the asteroids, lead had far more value.

Nuclear contamination was a risk, and every piece of metal was checked with a Geiger 'gel probe before purchase. *BosonsWave* had the advantage here, as very few cargo ships visited this unnamed accumulation and they had more steel than food. Even if the inhabitants were desperate and able to offer a low price, Captain Graciela would have problems selling glowing steel.

Negotiations began before landfall. A Morse code message and a reply was received to start the discussions.

The asteroid was looking for basic foodstuff, re-furbished tools, and updated 'gels. They did not seem interested in teas, but ΞStandards were readily transferable.

There was nothing special about the tarmac. One asteroid platform was pretty much like any other. Although on this one, the nuclear smelter glowed, sun-like lighting up the area.

"Tang, can you get a reading on the background radiation?"

"Please. Me want have puppies someday. Me heard hot stuff not good for baby making."

"In your case, it would probably cause a mutation, although it might be a little too late for you."

"What that mean?"

"Can it you two. Look sharp. The Jefes are approaching."

Every isolated place and every government seemed to evolve the same: A leader, an assistant, and a virtually unlimited supply of minions running around. The minions try to please the Jefes and plot to rise up in the ranks. In sort, this asteroid was perfectly normal, only the names changed.

The two Jefes wore robes befitting their ranks. No hats and feathers as on the herbal asteroid, but subtle piping along the edges of the robes indicated some sort of rank.

Tang whispered, "this group is just like *SinensisPrime's* Jefes. Although it looks like the two Jefes are the same rank. Do we know the type of government?"

"I'm not sure, but it looks a bit loose. They don't seem to have a Chamber of Commerce, and the 'gel historical references aren't clear," replied Graciela.

"Does this place even have a name or at least a number?" Tang asked. "I'll even take a QR code, if that is all they can do."

"Nothing that I've been able to find. Maybe they will let the name drop during the introductions."

The Jefes and minions approached the ship, "Welcome to our little asteroid. Our Air is Your Air."

"We understand you have supplies and will need a boost. We will be happy to trade. We have steel we can exchange for your cargo, and we would be willing to take ΞStandards to cover the boost cost."

"That can work, although we have to be sure there is no residue radioactivity buried in the metal. None of our customers will accept hot steel."

"Our products are routinely listed as Double-A on Luna. We take care not to contaminate our products."

"That must be difficult. Your nuclear engine is huge."

"Thank you. We acquired it a while ago, and it has worked out well."

"Acquired? Do you mean it wasn't installed when you set up the smelter?" asked Graciela.

"We started with a coal-fired smelter but had problems with delivery and quality. The nuclear engine works better for us."

"It must have been an expensive proposition."

"Well, it sort of fell into our hands. But enough of our history, I'm sure you want some refreshments before we begin trading."

"You have jerky? We like jerky snacks."

Gold Piping offered, "We'll find some jerky for you, I'm sure, but please join us for bread, salt and vodka."

"We'll have tea if you don't mind."

"We don't drink that beverage here. Is it better than alcohol?" Silver Jefe asked.

"I think you'll like it. We'll brew up a pot for you."

Silver Piping, a large simian sniffed the tea. "This is quite tasty. I'm not a fan of liquor, it doesn't agree with my tender tummy, and I do like this beverage. Around here, fermentation and distillation liquids are all we seen to get."

Gold Piping saw his assistant enjoying the brew, picked up his bulb, and chugged the drink. Choking, gagging, and spitting out, "This is real tasty. However, it may take some getting used to. It doesn't taste like beer and not much of a kick, but I could drink it."

Captain Graciela knew a sale when she saw it. "We have a limited supply of teas we could sell, for the right price."

The two Jefe's stepped back, whispering, loudly. Silver Piping spoke first. "We need to buy this tea stuff at any price."

"We can't afford it. We need tools and food, not leaves. I have to veto the order."

"I disagree. We have to purchase products to keep the workers happy."

"Workers? Or you?"

"All of the workers will like a change of pace from the booze you push. I'm going to veto your veto."

"What! You can't do that. I'm in charge."

"Now, wait a minute. Our rules say we change every 20 rotations, and my count says I'm now in charge. It is my turn to be Jefe."

"Wrong. I still have 1/4 of a rotation. I'm in charge!" Gold Piping opened his cloak, "And this little simian sticker agrees with me."

Silver Piping bared his teeth, displaying his two long fangs, "Don't threaten me with that little chimp poker!"

Captain Graciela stared, waited, and finally broke in before blood started flowing. "I don't care who is in charge. If you want the quality goods in our holds, you have to pay. We will take payment in ΞStandards or high-quality metals. And a boost."

"And it better be a full-power boost," Tang interjected.

Jefe looked at Assistant Jefe. The asteroid spun. Assistant Jefe looked at Jefe.

"Look, I'll throw in a free box of our tea and fungi samplers if we clinch the deal in the next three EarthMinutes."

Silver Piping stepped up, "Deal. My Air is Your Air."

Gold Piping let his cloak close and said nothing.

BosonsWave got the boost they needed, clean steel to re-sell, and lost a sampler box of tea and fungi.

Tang congratulated the Captain. "That was some classy deal-making." Graciela smiled, "It was worth it. Just wait until they try the fungi."

Chapter 36
To>Heliotail via Luna

It took a while, but *BosonsWave* and its crew made their way back to the Sol's Goldilocks rocks. Luna was their goal, where a meet-up with Herb was in the works.

Graciela was able to trade the rest of her goods for steel from the unnamed smelting asteroid. Her private stock of teas and fungi was not something she would easily share. It was priceless in the near-empty void she called home.

The first order of business was to sell the steel and pick up supplies from Luna. There was no need to land at the Luna base. The Earth/Luna transport ships would deliver supplies to her clients.

"Octopus, plot a course to orbit Luna. We'll want to use its gravity to decelerate before we meet Herb."

"So we not land on Luna?" asked Jack.

Tang listened intently for the response. Captain Graciela had stated there would be no time on that grey rock and its fine casino, but things change. Maybe there would be some low-gravity free time?

"Me low on jerky. We should get more on Luna?"

"Sorry, Jack, we will off-load the steel and meet Herb near the L2 boost lasers. He has arranged for supplies he wants us to bring, so I assume we are on a re-stocking run for some distant Naval stations. It should be good money for little effort. We'll spend time on Luna on the way back, I promise."

"You can put in your orders and the Earth-Luna Jumpers will bring it on their next run out here."

Octopus tapped his diaphragm "Three orbits, no more."

Jack quickly got on his comm and started building his supply list.

"You want stuff, Tang? We can join order, get better price."

"Not jerky, but I'll draw up my list."

Graciela joined the fray, "We can send in a single request. I'll order snacks and supplies for the Naval asteroids. The little extras will be good sellers out in the neverlands where the Navy is parked."

"Anything you want to add, Octopus?"

Octopus flashed an appreciation color and posted a list to the Captain's tablet.

My usual clams and crabs is all I need.

The little transport ships followed *BosonsWave* orbit, transferring steel and cargo as the ship slowed down in the gravity well surrounding the two spinning rocks.

"Look Tang, me ordered fishee jerky, salmon from aqua farms, dried in the sun and vacuum. Just like Earth."

"That's nice." Tang decided not to mention that there was no readily available vacuum on Earth to process the fish. The fact would confuse the issue and not lead anywhere.

"What you get?"

"The usual, nano-stabilized fruit and nuts."

"Sound yummy." Jack was doing his best to be agreeable, for a change.

"Do you want some?"

"No, me fine with jerky."

Transfers completed as Octopus pulled out of orbit and set a course to the L2 **Lagrange** Point.

"That Herb Ship?"

A large, white oblong loomed in front of *BosonsWave*.

"Look like tick me mommy pulled off me. It hurt. It not give back me blood when we ask."

Captain Grace said, "Enough blood-sucking reminiscing. We will need the spinnaker set. Herb will be giving us a laser brake."

A wide-beam laser burst slowed the ship down to match the Naval rocket's trajectory.

Luna Academy graduates, Herb and Graciela, Rocket and LiftShip hung in space, safely in the static gravity hold around Earth.

The two ships came into 'gel comm range. Grace took the initiative, "Why don't you come over to my ship, Herb? We have more room. I bet you are cramped on that little tin can."

"Tempting, but I have better food on this 'tin can'."

Jack joined the discussion, "Me want to see rockety toy. And food."

"Great! It is unanimous. I have jerky, carne, and algae burritos, greens, fruit and live clams."

"What are you? A Naval ship or a flying buffet."

"Hey, be nice. The military travels on their stomach."

"Don't forget to wait for 20 minutes. Can your navy space-sentients even swim?"

"Well, the octopuses can."

The crew of *BosonsWave* suited up and drifted over to Captain Herb's rocket. It was standard Naval issue, roughly egg shaped, around 500 meters tall. Designed for intra-heliospheric travel, never having the need or ability to pass through thick atmospheres. The business end of the ship extended an additional 200 meters to the rear, flaring out at the tail.

"Welcome to the best ship in the Heliospheric Navy, HN07-5T. My Air is Your Air."

"You can leave your space suits in the lockers. We don't leak!"

"Captain Herb, My Air is Your Air. We finally get to see what is in these tin cans. This is quite an eventful trip."

"Better not say that too loud. The crew is sensitive."

"Oh, we don't want to offend your sailors!"

With his uncanny situational awareness, Jack changed the subject before it got out of paw. "This different from our ship. Not too roomy. Where is buffet?"

"Before we eat, let me show you the bridge. I think you'll be impressed."

The bridge was filled with bioGel screens and a hemisphere of portholes. Octopus navigators had their work areas on either end of the bridge. A dozen assorted sentients milled around the instruments, doing Navy things.

Tang noticed the displays, some apparently mapping out the local space with lights that seemed to match ships in transit.

"Where is the 'gel that snoops on us? Can we listen in on other ships?"

Herb did not answer the question but changed the subject.

"We have ThirdMeal all set up. Some of the Marines have never met solar sailors. They'd love to chat with your crew."

The mess hall was laid out like any other food dispensary, with long tables and buffet selections.

The usual assortment of sentients were in the mess, all dressed in uniforms indicating their ranks and sections. The Marines in drab tight-fitting garb, doubling as space suit shells, ready for action. Medical staff in blue, officers in white, and the expected red-shirted engineers.

BosonsWave's crew stood out from the professional Navy. Captain Graciela wore her best LeviStrauss® blue jeans and bomber jacket, indicating her independent standing. Jack wore his cape, and Tan stood out with his ever-present overalls and no shirt. Octopus was in his reverse, transparent wetsuit, like every other member of his species. The signet ring on his tentacle indicated his ship and status.

"You'll find carne and tortillas over there and fresh greens and fruits for the taking. Real Earth-Water, coffee, flavored beverages, and tea dispensers are against the bulkhead."

"Captain, can we eat like this too?"

"Of course. Join the Navy."

"Herb, this meal is wonderful, and we'll accept it as payment for not helping us with that little pirate issue."

"Deal."

"Until the next time. But why did you bring us here? What is this special job?"

"It secret mission? It dangerous? It explode?" queried Jack.

"No, Jack, it is quite mundane. We need a ship to re-stock the Naval bases in the heliotail and drop off a few apartment blocks of bioGels."

Tang was a bit leery, "How big are the apartments? Are the 'gels awake?"

"They are just regular 64 'gel apartment groupings, freshly programmed by HiveMother. She put them in stasis before they left the Heliopause. They are simply software updates for the tails."

"Why use solar ship? Take Navy ship, they faster.

"That's the problem. These are special 'gels and are too fragile for our powerful rockets. They have to be carefully handled without shocks or jolts. Even gravity can cause problems with their programming."

"So, you want us to take the apartments?

"Yes"

Tang broke in, "for Ξ Standards?"

"Don't worry, you and the ship will be well compensated for the cargo."

Graciela supported Tang's concerns, "Profit is always good, and it's a run to a part of the heliosphere I've never seen."

"Exactly. One more thing. The Admiral insists that I shepherd these blocks of goo all the way to the Heliotail."

"On our ship?"

"Yes."

"Me heard you hated solar ship?"

"Don't worry, Jack, he will learn to love it. Right Herb?"

Herb quickly turned, "Oh, look, desert is on the buffet line!"

Desert met everyone's expectations and then some. For Herb, it changed the conversation, and for the rest, there were treats they haven't seen for ages and a few beyond their wildest fantasy food dreams.

Chapter 37
Manifest Pirate

"Did you like the ship? What else can I show you?" Herb asked.

"Where your jerky supplies? Nice flavors at ThirdMeal. Me might join Navy."

"I'm sure there is more than jerky to look forward to on a Naval ship. I've not a meat eater, but we have lots of carnivores here. They work hard too."

"Me can work."

The sailor sitting next to Jack started a conversation. "So, what do you do on your ship? I've heard that you have to use ropes and pulleys to fly forward."

"Yes, it be hard sometime, be we tough."

"And you have to stand on the ship's shell? Out in the cold void?"

"It not bad, we have spacee suits."

"That sounds difficult. All we have to do is ask a bioGel to change course."

"That sound easy. We should do it too. Me ask Captain if we do that too."

"What do you do when the 'gels stop working?" Tang asked.

"What do you mean? Our 'gels always work. We keep them oxygenated, fed, and clean. There is no reason they wouldn't work."

Tang thought, *he sounds a bit sensitive. I guess they have a better quality of 'gels than we can find.*

"Sure, I just thought you Navy types had to plan for every possible scenario."

"Of course, we train to work without 'gels, but that is an outlandish idea. The Navy would never let us be without the 'gels. Can you imagine working on our engines without the little brainy goo to control and diagnose the machines?"

Tang saw an opening. He had a thirst for new knowledge or maybe tidbits to wow his friends and family. "Exactly. Maybe you can teach us a little? What powers your engines?"

"Sorry, I'm not authorized to give out that information."

Jack added to the inquiry, attempting to worm out some information for his crewmate. "Me bet Herb know. Me ask him. He a captain."

The sailor did not take the bait and Jack would have to search for another fish. Before Jack could continue his line of inquiry, Herb called everyone together as the tour and dinner came to an end. They had no more excuses to sit around. It was time for work.

The Navy readied the two 'gel apartments, a bin full of Herb's personal gear and supplies for the Naval outposts.

Tang checked the manifest. "That's a lot of stuff, good thing we have room."

"Right. It been two EarthYears since the last supply drop, and they are a little anxious."

"Now I see why your little tin cans aren't being used to re-supply your troops." Grace said.

"It isn't only the amount of cargo, but the fuel requirements. At least you get to use Sol to push the ship along for a substantial part of the journey. Our ships have incredible acceleration but a finite fuel supply. Your solar sails can magnify the Sun's power in a constant curve."

"So you admit the Navy needs our ships? The truth comes out!"

"Why Navy not have own SolarShipees?"

"I'll tell you why Jack," Grace interrupted. "They are too proud! They want to present a tough sentient image to the heliosphere. Right, Herb?"

"No, that isn't it."

"So, what is it?"

"I'll get back to you."

"That's what I thought."

A few awkward moments passed; less than an EarthMinute, if anyone was counting.

"I have to go supervise the cargo. The 'gel apartments are fragile."

"Tang, Jack, please help Herb secure the cargo. We don't want anything shifting around. His admiral wouldn't appreciate it."

Herb addressed his new helpers, "Jack, the 'gel labels on the bins are self-defining. You probably haven't seen this version. Tap the corner, and they will figure out where they need to be and flash their suggested load order."

"K, will follow 'gel directions."

ZeroG loading was fast and easy with the new active labeling system.

"Captain Herb, there are five bins that are unlabeled. Where do you want them?"

"Let me look." The first two bins were Herb's dress uniform and snacks. He popped the lid on the third bin, and shiny new 'gel cassette-powered laser rifles were there for all to see. Herb checked the other bins. No more rifles, but stacks and stacks of 'gel cassettes. "Everything seems to be here. You can put them in my cabin."

"Herb, I'm not against weapons, but what sort of conflict are you expecting?"

"Nothing really, but the Navy likes to be prepared. We've heard about your cassette cannon, so I know you can handle these."

"Exactly, so long as mutiny isn't part of the package."

"Now, Grace, you know I'd never support that sort of interaction. The Navy knows you are the best for the job."

"My instructions are to drop off supplies to Naval Asteroids on our way to the tail. We can pick up a boost at each one. You can return to HuB on the way back or any direction of your choice."

"How will you get back to your ship if we don't go to Luna?"

"Not to worry, when we get close, my second-in-command will pick me up."

"Do the heliotails have anything we can re-sell, or will this be another empty return trip?"

"There isn't much in the tails, but you might be able to trade for the special bioGels from their factories."

Tang asked, "are the tailGels different enough to be worth more than the regular 'gels?"

"Don't worry." said Herb. "I know the tails' special 'gels are easily sold to select audiences."

Grace wasn't impressed, "so limited volume and limited possible sales. Just what ever trader wants to hear."

She continued trolling for information and sales, "I've heard that there are small groups of sentients flitting around. Does the Navy have any information on them?"

"Not pirates, me hope"

"Don't worry, Jack, our Naval base keeps things in ship-shape, although there is little detailed information on the tail inhabitants."

"I've heard that they don't get a lot of cargo ships." said Tang. "But they have a shopping list bouncing around Core and the Belt. There is profit if we can bring the right supplies."

"Sounds good. The Navy isn't using up all your cargo space. You can bring anything else you think might sell."

"What they want?"

Tang asked the key question, "And can they pay?"

"The Navy can't answer those questions. We work differently than you traders."

"Are there any other possible customers? So far, it looks like it is just the Naval supplies and maybe some small groups we can trade with."

"There are some rumors of independent contractors who support the tail factories. I'm not sure what they do."

Tang started checking the 'gel, "It says here they are ion chasers, but doesn't explain too much. Could be fake?"

"We'll do some more research," Grace said. "And see if there is any sort of market out there.

"You shouldn't worry. The Navy will cover all the expenses and pay you a handsome bounty when the cargo is delivered and installed, just like last time. And the Navy is paying for the boosts, so *BosonsWave* incurs little penalty for extra mass."

"Thanks, Herb. The payment was great, but we're a cargo ship, not a bank. And I miss the fun of trading."

"The tail factory 'gels could be profitable. You can drop them off at Luna for final assembly. Otherwise, we can off-load them to local transports for delivery." said Herb.

"No, we can take them all the way to Luna. Tang promised to show us his home on Earth."

"You're lucky. I kinda miss visiting that muggy green jungle and hanging with my buddies."

"You can join us."

"Sorry, the Navy comes first, for now."

"Herb, how long can we sit at L2? I'll buy cargo that won't spoil in case we only find ghost trades."

Jack's ears pricked up. "Like Mort Asteroid? Me not like ghosts. Maybe me stay at Luna."

"No, Jack, I'm talking about different ghosts, not the smell-talk ghosts of the Mort asteroids. These would be non-existent customers, not deceased sentients."

"K. Me still not like ghosts."

The crew finished loading the Heliopause 'gel apartments into the cargo bay and secured them in their racks.

"These look like 'gels me saw on pirate ship. Hope they not have spiders."

Herb looked up from securing the last set, "You were a pirate? You don't look like one. Did you have an eye-patch?"

"No me. Me just crew on ship. It me first ship after training school. Captain was pirate, not me."

"I haven't heard any of this. Please tell us at the next story-time session!"

"Me not proud of pirate time. Me embarrassed being in jail. It not fun. Gig work hard to find after jail. Tang gave me job and here me am."

"I do want to hear this story. It sounds fascinating. You should write a book about your journeys."

Chapter 38
Navy Supplies

Captain Grace needed speed for this trip and circled Earth a few times before catching the boost from the Eastern Lagrangian lasers, speeding toward HuB. Acceleration was additive, and the station followed their orders, ramping up carefully and slowly, leaving the fragile bioGels sleeping in their berths.

Their path was similar to the last time they ran to the Heliopause but without a chance to stop at HuB's stores or renowned gambling hall. Of course, they were going in the opposite direction this time, but planets, dust, and gravity were still moving in their paths.

They swooped in close to HuB as Octopus lined up with the circle of lasers, the Navy paying a full boost.

"I'm sorry, Tang, we'll stop here on the way back."

"It's okay, captain. Work first, then play."

"My parents are still parked here, but we're going so fast, I only have a few moments to contact them on the comm."

"I can set up a HAM link. It will give you more time to talk."

"Thanks, Tang, but I'm not sure I want my conversations blasted over the airways, as good as your HAM friends are."

Herb was busy on this leg of the journey. He had to shepherd the two 64-slot 'apartment' blocks of bioGels, one for each lobe of the heliotail-gel factories. They were in stasis but not stagnant. He checked their oxygen and nutrient levels and ensured that any waste products were handled. Normally his techs did all the work, but this solar ship ran lean and didn't need any extra sentients wandering about, doing little except breathing, eating, and excreting.

They had a full load of supplies for the Naval Asteroids and Tail-gel factory. Herb had arranged to pick up a couple of Marines at the last boost asteroid to help with the installation.

It was normal to send software updates from HiveMother every couple of EarthYears. They needed special software routines to help the 'gels mature, and even with HiveMother's help, the 'gels had a high error rate.

HiveMother was known to keep 'gels that didn't make the cut, often adding them to her supply of workers. She had no idea how the HelioTail Hive Sisters handled their high failure rate. It wasn't bad nurturing on their part, but a tough, environment causing the problems. There was nothing they could do about their surroundings, and the software fixes would only smooth out the edges.

Herb was done with the daily apartment checkup and met Jack and Tang in the galley.

"Herb, you want snack? Jerky maybe?"

"No thanks, Jack, I have some dry leaves. I'll pass on the cow."

"Captain Herb, you special 'gels okay?"

"Thanks for asking, Jack. They are doing fine."

"So, you expert on 'gels?"

"Well, I did have advanced 'gel training, but I'm no expert."

"Better than Tang?"

"I wouldn't say that, but I do alright."

"So, you teach me how 'gel program?"

Tang smiled.

"I'll see what I can do. My Jefes gave me specific duties and I may not have the time."

Jack's tail drooped, "K. No one want teach me. Me been reading manuals me got at PickNTrade. Me can do it."

"I'm sure I can sneak some instructional time it. I'll let you know."

Tail un-drooped, but not a wag. "Okay. Me be ready."

The response was not missed by Tang. *I guess I should help the little four-legged beast. He really seems to want to learn programming.*

Tang spoke first at their weekly meeting, "We still have a long way to go. Can we spin around a few planets to earn a gravity bump?

"That would be nice, but it would probably slow us down. We're going too fast and we'd pop right through their magnetic fields before we could turn."

"I knew it would be slower than a rocket, but this is getting a bit ridiculous. Can't you go any faster?"

"Patience Herb. We'll be speeding along once we get the first boost. By the way, I was going to ask you, what is the propulsion system used by your rockets?"

"Oh, you know, nuclear and stuff."

"Stuff?"

"Yes, we use every type of stuff."

"So you're not going to tell me, or you don't know?"

"Yes."

Captain Grace called out, "Tang, Jack, go out and check the lines. We'll be picking up speed shortly. Bring in the spinnaker a bit, I want a nice tight target."

"Captain, aren't we going to stop, maybe spend some time visiting?" asked Tang.

"No, we will do a mail drop. I don't want to lose any momentum. We need all the speed we can get."

"Herb, are they ready to give us a boost?"

"They were ready the last time they were inspected. I'll let them know we need a boost."

"Tang. Can you line up the Morse code flasher for Herb?"

"Captain Herb, you can use my HAM radio if you'd rather."

"Thanks, but there is too much ionizing noise here. The laser flasher is more reliable."

Messages flew at the speed of light, straight and true with only a small dusty signal loss.

Octopus did his calculations, and bins were directed on a track to orbit the asteroid. Magno-plasticine covers slow the packages down on each pass, helping the small Naval rocket ships gather their supplies.

"Hold onto your hat, Captain Herb. We are about to get that boost you want."

They passed the centerline of the rock, and the Navy's boost laser fired off, bathing the ship in wonderful, linear red photons.

True to her word, the flaming red photons hit *BosonsWave*, flashing around the metallic graphic the artologists had designed. The ship looked like a wraith flying the flags of a quantum particle.

The ship's speed increased exponentially, but not enough to add any gravity to the situation. They still had to protect the fragile apartment 'gels and busting them out of their containers would not be productive or for Captain Graciela, profitable.

Herb's hat stayed on, but acceleration was persuasive. "This fast enough for you, Herb?"

"Yes, quite exhilarating.

Grace nodded

"Captain Graciela, don't forget, we need to pick up the replacement crew for the tail at the next outpost."

Once the bins were on their way, Jack and Tang had nothing else to do. There were no supplies from the asteroid they could pick up and re-sell. This was a fully paid-for Naval job.

Chapter 39
About the HelioTail

Nothing is static in the void as the solar system spins through the local galaxy. Heat and magnetic power define direction and speed. It takes all of Sol's energy to travel its path in this accumulation of stars, dust and darkness.

Sol, with its spinning rocks and debris, keeps far away from the galaxy's distant black hole. Set in motion by an ancient singularity, the galaxy's core patiently waits to consume the heart and soul of Sol's heliosphere in the balance of time.

The heliotail lobes don't have a lot of help from their toasty sun to push interstellar gases away. They are, after all, the wagging tail of a magnetic bubble. The tail lobes move around, tossed by galactic winds and solar burps. The bioGel factories are tiny compared to HiveMother's and can only handle a few hundred growth chambers.

The distant factories started as experiments. No one expected them to be successful and after showing up their nay-saying administrators, they set off on paths of their own. After EarthYears of struggle, they are now established as distinct entities. The bGC and HiveMother thought growing bioGels at the tail was an interesting idea and failure was not unexpected. Success meant that the Consortium found it was both interesting and profitable.

The two factories, nestled on spin-stabilized asteroids, manage the young growing bioGels. On one side, the nuclear engine surrounds the asteroid's tail, bulging like a wart. The huge nuclear engine turns the asteroid into a mobile factory, moving around the heliotail, chasing the edges, looking for the best ions for bioGel growth.

With the active buffeting of the solar stream mixing with the galactic void, the waste stream from the nuclear engine has little effect on the surrounding mix of ions, photons, and blackness. These hot atoms simply blend into the background, mix and swirl around with the foreign cosmic rays.

HiveMother has been getting a lot of complaints about the quality of the heliotail bioGels. There was no direct communication between the two ends of the heliosphere. The distances were too great. The only way she knew about the problems were the complaints she received. Everyone blamed HiveMother, because it was simpler and more direct than finding the Sisters.

HiveMother accepted the lumps and black inclusions of the heliotail 'gels from the unusual cosmic rays as normal features. It could be subjective with this group on what is a defect and what is a feature, but the complaints were starting to impinge on her reputation.

The Hive Sisters considered none of their 'gels as defective, no matter how they appeared. To them, the design was part of the charm of the 'gels, and they were coveted by scientists throughout the heliosphere.

In spite of the rough look, there were a lot of non-working products in the last few batches. The factory administrators blamed it on excessive wiggling of the tail from solar disturbances.

Accusing the source of their product for their problems did not go over well with HiveMother or the administrators of the bioGel Consortium. HiveMother had a solution, but it wasn't one the Sisters would necessarily agree with; a complete re-write and takeover of their systems. The sisters would become clones of HiveMother, whether they agreed to it or not.

The facts were clear. The two ends of the heliosphere were completely different environments, and divergence of the bioGels should be expected.

There are no nutritious clouds nearby to merge with the proto-gel DNA produced at the heliotail factories. The tail-factories had a few cloud ships dropping off tasty 'gel food, but not often and never enough. The cloud contractors were paid more at the Heliopause and that factor influenced their routes.

The tail-bioGel factories did not let the lack of Consortium-approved ingredients get in their way. If they didn't have the cloud nutrients, they found other ways to make a ΞStandard.

The tails contained all the gunk flowing off Sol and its rocks combined with interstellar cosmic rays. Where the port and starboard heliotails crossed, the energy signatures were transformed into substances that mimicked Jupiter cloud swarms. It didn't contain any living organisms but acted as such when combined with the proto-gel DNA in the fermentation tanks.

It wasn't possible for the lumbering 'gel asteroids to capture all of the transmuted ionic particles they needed. A symbiotic relationship developed between the asteroids and a host of small, fast ion chasers flitting around the neighborhood.

Each little ship supplemented its nuclear rocket with a modified solar sail, funnel-shaped, acting as an ion capture array. These fast little beasts chased the tail, harvesting the complex cosmic ions produced at the spinning intersections.

Many tried to calculate where and when the best ion interfaces would exist, but math had a hard time dealing with divergent complex equations. Not only Heisenberg's Uncertainty Principle but deep quantum interactions skewing the numbers up, down, and sideways. Location, luck, and random chance were critical to a successful run.

The ion ships skirt along the junction's interface, grabbing what they can find, before moving back to the Hive factories to deliver their scrapings.

Just like their brethren in the Heliopause, the bioGel tablets required activation by cosmic radiation. The intertwined heliotails spun the cosmic rays, changing paths and natures. These complex ionic hits did not immediately pass through the proto-gels as they do at the heliopause but bounced around in the DNA 'gel mixture. The final bioGels were not the perfect gray tablets of HiveMother but had a rough matte finish with dark singularity holes.

Nevertheless, there was a hot market for these special accumulations. Tail-grown bioGels are beloved by physics and mathematicians working with universes within universes. The twists and turns needed to handle the math were best managed by these unusual 'gels.

Chapter 40
And Herb Makes Four

The second outpost on their route was coming up fast.

"Octopus, please calculate the mail drop points. Jack, Tang, the cargo is labeled and ready to go. We are going to pick up a few Marines to help Herb install the bioGel apartments."

Tang asked Herb, "so, we'll stop to pick up your Plus-ones? I thought we needed more speed, not less."

"No need. The Navy and Marines drilled on this. It is no different than boarding an enemy rocket."

"Wait, you have enemies? And they have rockets?"

"Simulation, I forgot to say *simulation*."

"We call this fast-train boarding. If you can attach a cargo net to a long line, the Marines will take care of the rest. We need at least a kilometer."

"They have trains here? That strange."

"Jack, we don't have trains. It is just a description from the before times."

"K, cause me not hear horn!"

"Funny, very funny." The crew jumped to their stations. Dropping the cargo bins on the First Mate's command. The released bins followed their ordained paths connecting with the Naval team on the asteroid.

True to Herb's scenario, a rocket ship from the Naval boost station caught and paced *BosonsWave*. On the outside, a gaggle of space suits clung to the superstructure. As the ships matched speed, the spacesuits peeled off the rocket and sped toward the net.

Tang followed the trip intently. He had never seen this operation and wasn't sure how it would work.

Two of the Marines quickly connected with the cargo net. The third Marine backpack started sputtering as one of the jet nozzles sent him for a ride, away from the ship.

"Captain, we need to turn for that Marine." Said Herb.

"This isn't one of your machines with unlimited power, we're not changing direction or slowing down. Signal the rocket ship they came in on to pick him up."

"I need a full complement of staff to finish my assignment. Slow down and pick him up!"

"No can do, but we have another kilometer of rope. Give Tang a hand and tie those two ropes together."

"What? How? I don't know how to tie knots," said Herb.

"Com'on, you're in the Navy, didn't they teach you basic rope handling?

"Just an EarthMinute. We're on metal ships, and we're not Boy Scouts."

"That's for sure, talk about Never Prepared. I'll do it myself."

Graciela grabbed the ends of the rope and tied a perfect Carrick knot.

"Tang. Send this rope out. You aren't Navy, so I know you won't forget to hold onto the tail end."

"That be funny," said Jack." But not for lonely Marine. Me can't tell, is it canine or primate? Maybe octopus? Hope not lost doggy."

The rope was now slack. The two Marines, holding onto the cargo net powered up and flew toward their misplaced compadre.

It took some maneuvering for the three lost Marines to connect. Tang observed "They must have practiced. I bet that is hard trick to pull off."

"Hey, look, Tang, you caught a bunch of little fishies."

"See there was no problem," exlaimed Herb.

Herb's comm lit up, and a thin voice came out of the speaker, "Request permission to come aboard, sir."

"Captain, we sure not pirates?"

"Jack, these are Navy, like Herb."

"Captain Graciela?"

A nod to the question, and Herb replied, "Permission granted."

"Tang, what happen if Captain not give permission?"

"Jack, that's not an option, don't worry about it."

"Tang, reel in the net. Our visitors are ready to come aboard."

Three sentients exited the airlock and removed their helmets. Each carried a bin with their tools and supplies. A human, canine, and small primate presented their credentials. "Captain Graciela, Captain Herb, I am Master Sergeant Nico, along with Corporal Aero and Technician First Class Lorraine. Request permission to join your crew."

Jack whispered, "Tang, did they bring food? Me not have enough jerky to share."

Tang touched his lucky cards in his overall's pocket and checked to make sure his green eyeshade was in his left pocket, thinking *there could be some great poker games. Hope they have enough Ξ Standards to lose. I'll have to see if the canine can play. Maybe he can borrow Jack's card rig? Jack sure doesn't use it.*

Captain Graciela took control, "Welcome aboard the H2LiftShip, *BosonsWave*. Please stow your gear and join us for SecondMeal in two EarthHours."

"Jack will show you to your cabins."

"Sergeant Nico, you cabin across from me. Corporal and Tech here."

Jack spent a little time introducing himself to the canine. Or, in this case, spewing questions in a constant stream.

"Corporal Aero, you know about Lakia? Me have Eartoo honor her. No like Ruskies. You know they murder that poor puppy?"

"Where you from? Me from Earth. Me home a barn in the mountains."

"How like Navy? It fun? You play dog chess? Me almost Dog Master Level."

And finally, the most important question.

"You bring jerky?"

Corporal Aero waited for Jack to take a breath. He had a choice of what to answer and, as any good military-sentient would, carefully picked his way through the mine-field of words.

"Chess sounds like a good option. Does anyone play poker?"

"Tang good at the poker, Octopus not so much, the two captains seem okay. It not me best game."

"That's good to know. We'll have lots of time to discover our skill levels."

"You can borrow me poker rig if not have one. Me watch and give you pointers."

"I look forward to some games of chance. I couldn't bring my gaming harness and would be happy to share yours. We only had room for a few personnel items, and jerky was more important."

Jack thought, *A dog after me own heart, me think me get along with him.*

"Maybe when done with the poker, we can play chess. For jerky!"

Chapter 41
Algae Rockets

The new crew members spent a few EarthDays getting acclimated to the ship, its pacing, air, and food. They each had to spend some time on the compressors, keeping the air moving. Tech Lorraine helped Tang in the garden and took lead on managing the airflow.

Sol receded, and the boost asteroid was a moving target they couldn't see.

Herb had the bridge.

Octopus spent his time checking out the surroundings as the rest of the crew were on a break or in the galley.

Octopus flashed a notification pattern and tapped out:

.- .-.. --. .- .-.. / ... .-. / --- ..-. ..-. / .-. --- .-. - / -... --- .--
Algal ship off port bow

The ship was in front on the same heading, moving well, but not as fast as *BosonsWave*.

"What in the name of all rotten fruit is that green thing? Is it a rocket ship?" asked Herb.

Grace came in from the galley as Herb exclaimed, "I've never seen anything like that!"

"We've dealt with them before. You can't tell me the Navy doesn't know about the algal ships?"

The green blob pushed out a sail, twisting in the weak solar stream. The course change put it on a parallel path to *BosonsWave*.

It wasn't as large as their ship, if you counted their one-kilometer wide solar sail. Otherwise, they were around the same size. *BosonsWave* was flattened, saucer-like, able to gain lift as it transited through Earth's atmosphere. The algae ship had no such need to land and was simply a ball of seething cells.

Tang had his telescope out, inspecting every centimeter of their visitor. "I don't see a cockpit. I bet those black spots are photosensors."

"You could be right, Tang," offered Grace. "I wonder how we could find out."

"Did you recall if the one we shadowed at the comet had the same structures?"

"No, I was too busy trying to scare it away, but this one seems a bit more friendly, or at least not on an attack vector."

Herb was still confused, "No one ever mentioned anything like those green monsters to me. What are they?"

"It's complicated. I guess you never met Ponos. He rented out my mother's old ship, the *Bina'sBeans*."

Herb was getting a little desperate, "What does that have to do with this monstrous green thing?"

"Let me explain. He had a job scraping algae off a farming asteroid and had a story about the algae escaping the farm, floating off and merging."

"I still don't see where this story is going."

"He heard stories about the mess becoming algal ships."

"Stories don't make it real."

"Well, we almost crashed into one of them a while back and that was real. You can't deny the reality of the one here."

"Interesting. I'll have to talk to the scientists when I get back to base. I'm sure they would be excited to study something as unusual as a green rocket."

"We figured they were following the strongest light source and would burn up in the Sun, but I guess they had other plans. I'm pretty sure they aren't sentient. Still, we need to keep out of their path."

"We scare them away before. Bet we do again!"

"I think this is a little different, Jack. We were able to throw a shadow, and they didn't like it."

"Right, they afraid of shadow. We do same now."

Tang, the explainer, said, "I don't think that would work here. I don't think we can even cast a shadow. They wouldn't even notice our weak attempt of darkness."

"Herb, shouldn't the green ships show up on your snoopy 'gels?" asked Tang.

"They may be too different. We would have to recalibrate our sensors. Anyhow, we don't check every piece of the heliosphere, just a snip here and a snip there."

"Yet you always seem to be able to find my little snip."

"I thought you liked our help, especially with the friends your family seems to attract."

"I'm not complaining. You have helped us, and we do appreciate your assistance."

Tang broke into the discussion. "It looks like we are all on a similar trajectory. We should be able to catch it if it doesn't change direction."

"That would be fun. I'd like to get out there and grab a few samples."

"What if hurt them? Might attack!"

"Jack, if they respond when we touch them, it will let us know they have some awareness. It will be an interesting experiment."

Tang had a ready answer, "They are just plants. Plants don't think."

"Who made rule? Anyone ask plants? Could be thinkers?" said Jack.

Herb had the final word, "We'll know shortly."

BosonsWave had the edge on the algae conglomerate and would soon overtake and pass them on their way to the tail factories.

Graciela broke the bad news, "Herb, we're going too fast, and I can't slow down for you to play intrepid explorer."

Tang had no lack of ideas, "We could grab a piece as we go by. Or harpoon it and drag it with us."

"No need. I packed a rocket pack and I can jet over there and back before you know it."

"Seem risky. What if too slow, miss boat?"

"I'm a Captain in the Heliospheric Navy. I know what I'm doing."

"Herb, I'm not sure if I approve of your little experiment. We don't want to lose you. But if you attach a safety line, we'll be able to haul you back. We can use our spool of plasticine rope. That should give you enough time if you're fast."

"Fine, let me suit up. Octopus, can you bring us on a parallel path, as close as possible? I'll take a Marine with me. They seem to like this sort of stuff."

The algae rocket lumbered along in front of *BosonsWave*, holding its own in the solar stream. It had no way to buy a laser boost from a friendly asteroid nor ΞStandards to pay with. Not that it would matter; ΞStandards, laser boosts, or sentients were cyphers for this great green accumulation.

"How come they are so rare? There is no record of them in the Naval archives," asked Herb.

Tang, as usual, was willing to supply an answer to every question. "It seems as if they prefer to keep away from sentient-inhabited space. More of a sasquatch than a contributor to Heliospheric society. Maybe the green collective observed the fate of its brothers and sisters and prefers not to become part of some sentient's burrito."

"Jack, Tang, we're approaching our boost point. We need to change the sail to a spinnaker."

"Aye, captain."

Sergeant Nico followed the conversation intently. "Can I come along? I'd like to see how this sail stuff works."

"Captain?"

"Fine by me, try to keep out of the crew's way. Maybe we'll make a solar sailor out of you Navy boys yet."

Herb snorted. "Not going to happen. Once you've been on a rocket, you'll never go back."

"We'll see."

Herb seemed fascinated by the great green ship in front of them. "Look, it's pushing out a sail. And it's going faster. How ingenious. Could it be sentient? I bet it's friendly. I'd like to follow it for a while."

"I don't think that is an option. We need to gain speed while we can. We won't have this solar push forever. We don't know if that green monster has any hostile intentions."

"Or any intentions at all."

"Still, if you can, I'd like to get closer. I might be able to take some measurements for the scientists back at the base. It will help everyone if we can track them."

"Tang, add all the sail we have. Octopus, extend the wings. Let's get closer."

"This is your chance to get a sample, Herb, go get that slime!"

"Look, sparkles coming off tail."

Chapter 42
Riding the Green

Tang stepped over to the porthole, "It looks like it is accelerating. Better hurry, Herb!"

Herb and his Marine fired up the jet packs and skittered out to make contact.

Herb landed first, "This is a bit spongy," as he sunk in up to his knees.

A dark spot migrated toward the invading party. "Is that an eye?" asked Captain Herb over the suit's comm.

"I don't know, Sir. Is it blinking? Why is it looking at us?"

"Let's grab the sample and get off this thing, whatever it is."

Herb jabbed in a sampling probe.

This may not have been the best action in this situation. The algae bucked, twisted, and sent a peristaltic wave, almost a tsunami, tossing Herb onto his back. The goo started flowing around him.

Sergeant Nico fired up his rocket pack, swooped down, and grabbed his captain. The green ooze kept moving, sucking this great gorilla further down into it shell. Seargent Nico pulled Herb's extended hand and jumped into the void, jets on full. Green slime dripped off Herb's spacesuit and quickly returned to the comfort of its algae home. Sergeant Nico signaled the ship, and Tang began winding in the rope using both hands and feet to power the cranks.

Captain Graciela gestured to Octopus, and he pulled the ship up from the algae. The rope dropped behind, with the two sentients dangling from the end. It was a gentle flight, floating through the void, then the slack ran out. The jerk pulled the two away from the monster.

"Faster Tang, Faster."

Tang took the admonition to heart and pumped away. The two wayward space waifs flew into the cargo dock and then entered the airlock.

Herb held up his prize: green goo in a Dewar flask. "Here it is, but what is it?"

Herb held the flask tightly as the algae pulsed and wiggled in the flask, trying to escape its captors.

Jack took a sniff. "It smell bad. Me not like it."

Captain Grace took control. "Slap it into a bin and attach a bioGel monitor. It should calm down if we store it in the dark."

"Octopus, let's move away from this green goo as fast as we can."

Octopus kept the periscope focused on their recently visited algae friend as they began their run to the heliotail.

He tapped out:

--. --- --- / .. ... / -.- . . .--. .. -. --. / .--. .- -.-. .

Goo is keeping pace

Octopus took out his sextant, took a few readings, and entered some calculations on his work window. He began to graph the relative speed and locations of both ships. He loved this type of math exercise and enjoyed showing his skills to the crew.

Captain Herb watched the dots as they were added to the board. "You know, Captain Grace, these dots are not plotting to our advantage. It seems that the green monster may be catching up with us."

"That's not possible. We have the latest solar sail technology, and all they have is living green goo."

Tang reached into his overalls and took out his pocket telescope. "I don't know about that. The goo has extruded more sails, and it is shooting off sparks from its tail. I think it wants to talk to us."

The algae extended green slime 360' around its nose. The green sail may not have been as efficient as *BosonsWave's* high-tech solar sail, but it made up for tech with surface area.

"I'm not afraid of an unintelligent mass of green algae. What could it do to us?" insisted Captain Graciela.

"Slam into our sail? Crush the ship?" replied Tang.

"That's not going to happen, Octopus see if you can change the angle of the wings. We should be able to get more power from them. Tang, Jack, go topside and add any extra sail aft."

The photon supply was relatively equal for both of them, and *BosonsWave* only had sail and side wings for propulsion. The algae rocket could ignite sugar and make up for its inefficient sails.

BosonsWave lurched forward with the extra sail and extended wings, putting some distance between itself and its pursuer.

Tang had a solution, "Herb, you should give back the captured goo."

"I'm not going to give up my slice of goo because of a threat. The scientists at the base would cry if they heard we lost such a unique sample."

The goo re-configured its forward hull. A black hole appeared, looking like the maw of a huge beast.

"This not look good. Maybe need appease it? Herb, go back and talk to it," exclaimed Jack.

Jack had more bad ideas, "You have laser pea shooters, blast it!"

"They are too small to make any difference, I'm sure. Better yet, can we make another cannon?" replied Herb.

Captain Grace said, "I don't know if that would work. The algae absorb photons. It may make it stronger. I don't see how algae can feel pain, and if it did, it will probably piss it off. Not a risk I want to take."

"We try tomato surprise? It work before."

Tang argued, "Do you see the size of that thing? It is bigger than any single sailor's tomato."

"Wait, that may not be such a bad idea," Captain Grace exclaimed.

Jack wagged his tail.

"We can't block out the sun. There are too many photons swirling about. But we could cover part of the shell, and maybe that will send it in a different direction, or at least confuse it enough so we can get away."

"Where we find dark?"

"Tang, it's time to dig into your junk closet."

"It's not junk, only unallocated supplies."

"Whatever you call it. Dig out the water capture sail you saved from the Ceres misadventure. I'm sure you have a bunch squirreled away."

Lilly Rose looked up from Tang's shoulder. "Not you, Lilly, a different squirrel." She nodded and went back to sleep.

"Yes, I was saving it for another comet water capture run. I guess this is a good use for it, too."

"Captain Herb, we'll need your Marines for this job. Everyone suit up. We'll need to stretch the fabric tight on all four corners. On my command, Octopus will bring in the wings and let the goo catch up to us."

"This not risky, Captain?"

"Of course it is, but it's all we have."

"If we can cover its nose, it may lose its sense of direction, and we can pull away."

Four sentients grabbed the fabric. Corporal Aero stood on the deck, holding his end of the fabric as Tang climbed up the rigging. Herb and his Sergeant pulled the fabric tight using their jet packs. Jack was in charge of managing the safety lines and was the only one without a view behind the fabric.

Me not see what going on. Is close? We going be eaten?

The algae ship gained on *BosonsWave,* almost touching. On Herb's command, they released the fabric. Recycled water fabric became a scarf as the two made contact. The latest space fashion statement stuck to the gelatinous shell, covering what the crew of *BosonsWave* hoped was its nose and forward sensors.

The goo ship began twisting, spinning, trying to shake off its new security blanket. Black photo-receptors moved backward, attempting to see around the cover. At the edge, stalks of green goo extended, black photophores at the tips, peering at the cover.

The crew scampered into the airlock. It was not safe being on the hull with the thrashing rocket. Tang grabbed his telescope and focused on the blanket, "We better move. It looks like it has learned to build fingers. They are trying to lift it up."

BosonsWave never hesitated. The crew extended the solar wings, adjusted the sail. They caught every photon in its path, moving away from the green monster.

"Can we go more? Me want leave green goo behind."

"It does sort of kill my appetite for algal burritos," Tang added.

Octopus continued his checking and charting. The two dots separated, with *BosonsWave* reciprocating, escaping the jaws of goo.

Tang observed, "I bet other green goos will see it and be jealous of its fancy adornment. We may have started a trend."

Chapter 43
Heliotail Visit

The boost from the second asteroid sent them far into the hind end of Sol's traveling circus. There was no need to exit the comforting grip of Sol's magnetic bubble. Their target was the intersection of the solar stream, the infamous Heliotail.

It was dark here. Sol was tiny, but they were closer to Sol than at the heliopause. The magnetic vortex swept around, pulled by the Sun's tailwind and pushed by incoming cosmic radiation. Visible photons emanating from the distant galaxies and stars twinkled as they passed the twisting force lines. Even so, there were no wishes granted to the sentients from the dots and smears sitting in the surrounding blackness.

Ions burst and sparkled as they flowed around the intersections of the tails in dynamic flashes of light and energy, signifying changes in state. The complex molecules and elements generated by the interactions were ripe for harvest by the IonShips.

Not all of the sentients on *Bosons Wave* had the same perspective on the light show. Primates saw colorful lights, canines not so much, and octopuses a range of patterns and colors only they could interpret.

Jack was in his preferred viewing position, floating mere centimeters from the glass, nose almost pressed against a forward porthole. He spotted the target dead ahead. "This exactly like HiveMother's factory at Heliopause."

Tang had to disagree, "Not quite."

"Well, not as big. And two little factories. But exactly same."

Despite his relatively diminished color sense, Jack was able to pick out patterns better than most species. Traits evolved over eons on Earth remained in good stead in the void. "Look, Green Monsters there! Wonder if want stolen green baby back?"

Tang took out his telescope, an ancient heirloom passed on by his grandfather. It was a little worse for wear, slightly bent, but still functional. He focused on the green rocket ship, trying to resolve all the fine detail. "I don't know if it is the same one who gave us trouble before. It's not wearing a scarf, so maybe we are safe."

"Herb, how is your kidnapped little green slime? Is it happy in the dark?" asked Graciela.

"I suppose so. At least it hasn't broken out of the jar and infected the ship."

"It do that? Me saw vid about it. Hope we not in docu-vid."

Captain Graciela accessed the situation, "I wouldn't worry about it, Jack. The vids are not always true. We need to steer clear of those monster ships. We don't have any way to protect ourselves. We could try our remaining water drop-cloth trick, but I don't think we have enough left."

"Maybe they friendly?"

"Let's hope so and that they haven't communicated with the others."

"How would we know?"

"I wonder. Do they gossip about the ships and stars they've seen, the photons they capture?" said Herb.

"that sounds a bit too poetic for accumulations of slimy green algae," Grace replied. "Let's give them a wide berth and act as if we never attacked them or gave them fashionable clothing."

Tang began asked, "Why are they here? There is hardly enough energy to photosynthesize a simple sugar. We can barely capture enough photons to keep our batteries charged or change directions."

Captain Graciela had no answer, "Which reminds me, Jack, it's your turn on the generator treadmill. We need to keep the batteries fully charged."

"Aye, Captain. Me will get on it. At least factory ships seem okay. They not solar. Must have lot of treadmills!"

Herb knew all about the factories' power sources. "Not quite. The factory asteroids use nuclear engines."

Grace had to ask again, "they have the special add-in stuff from the Navy? Right, Herb?"

Herb was suddenly busy elsewhere and did not seem to hear the question.

"Well, as long as those monsters keep their distance, I don't think we'll have any problems with them, although I would still like to know what they are doing here."

"Maybe the factory crew or ion collectors would know the answer. At least we can ask," said Tang.

BosonsWave came ever closer to the Hive Factories. IonShips glinted in the reflections from cosmic collisions against Sol's magnetic force.

"Tang, IonShips look like gnats, with hats. Wonder if bite?"

In front of each ship, fabric extended, funnel-shaped, terminating at the mouth of the ship, collecting complex ions at the edges.

"That looks like the water capture rig we made. Maybe we can join the ships and harvest ions too?" replied Tang.

"Sorry to rain on your parade," answered Captain Grace. "I don't think it will work. The water fabric we don't have enough of would probably not capture anything, and we don't have a nuclear rocket engine. We would be a huge lumbering giant compared to those little agile ships."

"Okay," said Tang. "Guess we're not going to do that. I was looking for profit. It seems slim out here."

Tang tried a different angle, "are the ion-capture ships going to join us at the Naval asteroid? And what about the two factories? Can they join too?"

"Hope better than Mort asteroid party. They real dull. Even smell-ghosts not fun to talk. Always complain about the sadness of death and 'where be me body'."

"Good to know, Jack, but let's change the subject. I'm not sure Herb wants to hear about it."

Tang did his best to re-direct the conversation, "Captain, do you know what they have to trade?"

"Not much. I don't know what we can do with a box of weird ions or even how to transport them. ΞStandards will always work, if they have any."

Tang was concerned, "we're not going to give our cargo away for free, are we?"

"No, we'll find some way to make a profit. "said Graciela. "Herb, you should know this. What is the half-life of the weird Tail-ions?"

"How should I know? I'm not a physicist."

"Don't they teach you anything at the Naval Academy?"

Tang broke in, "Well, actually, the complex ions…"

Jack herded Tang into the pens before he could expound on another subject. "We not want hear you answer! Always too many words."

Tang quickly pivoted, "Captain, even if they want to trade, who would buy a box of Tail-ions?"

Grace thought about it for a bit, "probably scientists, and they never have funding. Looks like a dead end to me."

180

"And yes, Herb, we know the Navy will pay us well, but that isn't the point. You know we need to trade to live. We aren't only along for the ride."

Herb answered as best he could, "It might not be so bad. You might get lucky and buy some rare, expensive compound. You never know what exotic elements are produced in this mish-mash of ions and magnetic forces.

Tang went to his workstation and plugged some sensors into the ship's external-facing 'gels. It took a few moments as he carefully plotted the tail line forces. Octopus glances out the porthole and then to Tang's chart, flashing approval.

"I guess the force lines are where the best ions are?"

Tang took out his telescope and focused on the closest green ship. He spent a few minutes checking, "It looks like they follow the ion force lines along the Sun's magnetic tails."

"Green Monsters sure shiny. And no sun out here. How they do it?"

"Herb, it would have been nice if the Navy knew about these ships."Captain Grace said. "I can't believe no one here at the Tail has mentioned it."

"Well, to tell the truth, we don't talk to the bioGel factories. We leave it up to HiveMother. I guess the Heliopause is too far away for them to talk on a regular basis. Or HiveMother never thought it was important to mention. I'll check up on this when we get back to base. I'm sure the scientists will be all over the phenomena when they hear about it."

"It is strange, Ponos only told us that a few algae clumps ever escaped the asteroids, but I guess a few here and a few there, and pretty soon you have a monster," sail Graciela.

"It sure seems they can grow once they get started," Tang added." I guess all they need are photons, water, and micronutrients. I'm sure the ship that almost hit us was after the same dirty comet water we were harvesting."

"Do we know if they are sentient?" Herb asked. "And how would we tell."

"Me know about IQ test. Me passed one when a pup."

Captain Grace agreed, "good plan Jack. Herb, you go and talk to them again. Your last survey worked so well."

Tang has been observing the ships. "They are glowing bright green."

"Hope not explode"

"Did you see that in one of the vids you keep on watching?"

"No, but could happen"

Chapter 44
Ion Ships

The ion ships were the key to growing healthy tailGels.

The HiveSister factories could maneuver with their nuclear rocket engines, but not fast and not efficiently. They would position themselves close to a tail stream intersection, where the best, most complex molecules were generated. They were too bulky to pick up more than a few of the ions, but depended on the ion ships to harvest the best compounds.

There were two types of ion ships. The older modules were funnel shaped and hoovered up any ions they could find. It was simple and old-fashioned, but cheap to run and good enough to make a few ΞStandards.

The modern ships had a masts running up both side of the ship. Side branches made them look like moth antenna, thrashing around in the dark. They were almost hydra like, filling up the arms with Ions and bringing them into a central storage area. The charged metal brushes sweep up complex molecules and modified ions, switching polarity to attract and capture.

The hydra ships were more efficient but more expensive to operate, insuring that the funnel ships would always be in the running.

Hans looked around the ship. It was no larger than the mining rig on his last job, cramped and slightly claustrophobic. The huge funnel extended forward, flashing success after each ion capture.

The funnel ship wasn't too bad for him. He wasn't the tallest human in the sector and was quite comfortable tootling around the void, working for the HiveSisters.

There were no rocks to beat up this time. The job was cruising around collecting bits of cosmic energy. His old mining partner, Jingles, a short-haired, brown and white canine, continued as his ion-partner on this new endeavor.

"Jingles, I'm sure glad we made the move from rock mining. I've never even raised a sweat on this job."

"And all sentients around appreciate that fact."

"Yes, that too. The bioGel from the HiveSisters are much better than the one we had on the mining ship."

"It does seem to like you a little better.

"The old one was getting a little grouchy."

"Or it didn't like it when you threw it against the bulkhead wall.

"Nah. Those little pieces of goo are tough enough to handle a little bumping and shaking.

"Now I can see why it didn't want to work with you."

Hans decided to change the subject. "These tailGels seem sturdy, even if they are a little misshapen and have a funny color."

"You know, Jingles, I do sort of miss *TinyDestroyer,* but there is nothing we can do about it now. It is just a pile of scrap."

Jingles nodded, "It was sad, that poor little 'gel never made it out of the ship after you crashed it."

"Don't blame me," Hans retorted, "we were both responsible."

"I don't think so. You were doing that crazy trick, using the asteroid's spin to wind us down to the surface."

"Hey, it worked, most of the time. You have to admit, it saved fuel and was fast. It was sort of fun, watching you every time we get close to the surface. How was I supposed to know there was an overhang on the rock? And no one could have known it would rip the ship apart."

"We were lucky another miner was on the other side of the asteroid."

"Right. He saved our lives, but I think he's still angry, losing work cycles and having to share his air."

Jingle mused, "You don't think he followed us out there after the mining consortium collapsed?"

"Nah, everyone simply moved on to another mining group."

"Except us. They weren't called up to the Union Office."

"Yes, that wasn't pleasant."

"And now we're blackballed by all the mining groups."

"What are you complaining about, Jingles? It worked out. The HiveSisters are much better bosses than the mining consortium. The work is regular, and it's easy picking. Those bioProbes you borrowed from our last employer can really sniff out the good stuff."

"In any case, getting fired was the best thing that could have happened. Ion capture is easier than mining. No rocks to worry about."

"And no more solar sail. You can't believe how much I hated those things. Nuclear is so much better."

Jingles disagreed. "I don't know, it was nice, quietly flying along. I enjoyed planning our tacks against the solar stream."

"That works for you. The nuclear rocket is a bit noisy, but it is always there, and we can move along without worrying about shadows or dust blocking the stream."

"Well, that is one thing, no shadow here. No sun either."

It was Jingles' turn to change the subject, "HiveSister Port is picking up her skirt and joining her Sister at the Naval Base. There's a cargo ship due soon and we should follow her lead. I'm ready for some fresh food."

"Maybe we can buy some new oxygen. This recycled air is getting a little old."

Jingles was a bit more practical than his human partner, "Have we made enough to afford it?"

"We'll figure that out later. Let's head to the Naval station. We can feed some of the tail ions into the propulsion system."

"Like last time? You almost blew us up."

"So now I'm getting blamed for all the accidents?"

"That's my thoughts."

"Let's just keep that little detail to ourselves. I don't want to lose this job. We might have to go back to mining."

"Maybe we can keep this tailGel when we're done. It seems friendly. Anyhow they have lots, they'll never miss it."

"Yes, a retirement gift, I like that," said Jingles.

"Good plan. How long until we can retire?"

"I'll have to review the Union contract we were forced to sign. A few EarthYears, I think."

"Sure, let's get back to base, I don't want to miss the traders.", said Hans.

"I heard that they might have real cow jerky and my stock is getting low. Fire up the nuclear engine and I'll regulate the tail ions."

"Good plan, I'll see if there are any poker games I can jump into. I'm sure to easily double my stake," agreed Hans.

"Right. Use your stash, not the ship's profit. And I'm not going to lend you anything for your grubstake this time"

Chapter 45
Meet the Tail

The last Naval asteroid's laser boost sent them directly to the tail. Sol's photons were at their back but had little influence on their speed or direction.

The tarmac of the tails Naval base came into view.

Octopus tapped out,

- .. -- . / - --- / -... .-. .- -.- .

Time to brake

"Tang, can you align the laser flasher? I'll need to send my authorization before they'll fire off their laser."

"Right, we wouldn't want to speed past our stop."

A red dot focused on the spinnaker, beginning the braking procedure.

Captain Grace supervised the team, "Don't forget to transfer some of the photons to the battery. We are a little low."

"Herb, does this place have a name?"

"Of course it does. The Navy has a name for all of its bases."

Captain Grace waited.

"And what is it?"

"Oh. That. Let me look it up. Here it is, 'TailBase02'."

"You had to look? I had expected better from a Naval Captain."

"I have a lot on my mind. Getting the Hive updates completed will make my career. I don't want anything to get in the way."

Jack asked, "What happened to base01?"

"Sorry, Jack, you'll have to ask the locals. I don't have the information in my database."

Tang looked over at Jack and said, in doglish, *'Could be a problem. I'll check around.'*

Jack answered, *'Hope green monsters not eat it.'*

The word was out that the long-overdue supply run was coming home to roost. *BosonsWave* came gently to rest, connecting with the magno-plasticne and locking onto the tarmac.

Every ship and nuclear-powered rock in the area nestled up to the Naval asteroid. Its central Quonset hut made the perfect ballroom for a serious meet and greet. The independent ion ships found places to park scattered around the base and joined the festivities.

Captain Grace looked over the sentients milling around the hut. "We have a good crowd. We should have no problem selling our goods."

"Herb, do any of the Naval supplies go to the ion ships, or are they on their own?"

"Everything is for the Navy and the factories."

Jack whispered to Tang, "Me bet ion ships get a piece too." Tang nodded.

"That's fine. We brought enough for all the independent players. I hope they have enough ΞStandards. Trading for ions is a bit of a non-starter for me. I don't know where we could sell them."

"Me let them know we not sell for free."

Herb interrupted, "well, the Navy is paying you, but I know you 'live to trade' or some such litany. I'll check and see if there is a market for their ions, once we identify what they are."

Captains Graciela and Herbert, and the three Marines stepped smartly out the cargo bay door.

"Jack, look at Herb. He sure looks fancy. Now I know why he brought his dress uniform."

Herb was elegant in his white dress uniform, medals hanging of his chest highlighting his deep black fur.

Graciela looked at Herb and asked, "Which medal did you get for chasing off pirates?"

Herb pointed.

"And which one was for helping us? Oh right. We did it without your help.

"Me want medal too. It look good on me backpack."

Tang, always helpful said, "Maybe you can attract the ladies with it?"

"Could work. Captain let's all get medals!"

Tang shook his head, "Medals? I don't need no stinking medals."

"Me not want smelly ones either. Unless it smell nice."

"Octopus?"

He flashed an inconclusive beige.

Herb and the Marines snapped to attention as the Naval crew approached.

"Chief Naval Officer, Lt. Estelle, base manager. Captain Herbet Grauer, Captain Graciela Lucerne, welcome to TailBase02, My Air is Your Air."

Captain Herbert saluted. "Thank you, Lt. Estelle. My Air is Your Air."

Grace nodded and repeated the airy greeting.

"We have the requested supplies, and Captain Graciela of the *BosonsWave* graciously brought along additional material for the ion ships and anyone else who would like to purchase them."

"First things first, Your crew can unload the Naval supplies. They are in cargo bays one and two. Jack and Tang will help and direct."

It didn't take much to get these military workologists moving. Two years without a refresh brought a distinct urgency to the operation.

Tang and Jack stood at the cargo door.

"This look better than Mort rock, at least no dead urns."

"I thought you liked smell-talking to the ghosts?"

"No. Me hate it, but they not shut up. It unnerving. This place better, no smell-talking."

"Agreed."

"Where helioTail factory grays? This not look same as heliopause crew."

The sentients dressed in the obligatory robes and hoods of bioGel factory workers. Except their robes were colorful and sparkling to indicate their special place in the heliosphere.

"This is an improvement. Those gray-dressed workers at the heliopause were a little depressing."

"And scary."

The two nuclear-powered asteroid factories, HiveSisterPort and HiveSisterStarboard, moved close to the Naval station for supplies and the expected software update. The factories were built using plans designed by HiveMother and appeared as weak replicas of the original.

HiveMother, traveling within its protective solar wind, was huge compared to the little twins. She had the security of a stable magnetic bubble pushing against the interstellar void. The twins were constantly chasing the twisting tails, keeping within the force lines, capturing the unique ions needed for bioGel maturation.

As they traveled between stars spinning on the galaxy's edge, the HiveSisters were careful in their unstable environment. Stepping out of the magnetic tail was their bane. The raw cosmic rays would burn and mangle the young 'gels in their exposed frames.

It was impossible to calculate every twist and turn of the tail, and a few 'gels would always suffer the pains of energy delivered *au natural*. Dark matter, the cosmic detritus of neutron stars, and expanding novas wreaked havoc on the unprotected 'gels.

The HiveSisters felt the pain of cosmic maturation, as did HiveMother, which was expected. They did their best to protect the young 'gels. Unfortunately, hearing the quiet, intense screams of unfiltered beams striking the young 'gels thin skins stressed the HiveSisters to no end.

Of course, they could filter out that painful signal flying down the silicon communication lines, but they refused to do it. They could not bring themselves to ignore their prodigies' pain and suffering. The HiveSisters even incorporated the burnt 'gels into the general population. They could ill afford to throw away a mature bioGel, no matter how badly damaged. These 'gels were often aggressive and excessively moody, blaming their handlers for their pain and deformities.

But that was the past, and today was a day of joy, fresh supplies, and parties. The two groups of sentient 'gel handlers joined at the Naval asteroid station with the crews of the ion ships and *BosonsWave*. Primates, canines, and even the octopuses came along for the fun and food.

Old friends, new acquaintances, and fresh food were in store. Alcohol was not transported by *BosonsWave*, but the locals knew how to brew some powerful concoctions. Some of the beverages were infused with cosmic radiation for an extra kick. Graciela's stock of teas and fungi were shared a little and sold for a lot; once the initial taste enticed the sentients.

The HiveSisters were not left out of the party. They did not partake in the food, but a few barrels of real Earth water was an unexpected treat. It was only enough for a few fermentation tanks, and the 'gels receiving the gift felt special and powerful. All of the other tanks used recycled water, and that often-tainted source could be treated as an insult, if they knew there was another option.

In spite of the distant location and sparkling displays at the tail, the traders used the same selling routine as on any other stop.

Chapter 46
Party at the Tail

The trade show rapidly became a time to meet and share facts, rumors, and conspiracy theories. Gossip was the driving force, as the Tail inhabitants caught up with friends and cousins. Their laser communication system to Core and beyond kept them from being completely isolated, but transmission costs limited the flow of information.

BosonsWave had 'gels stuffed with news, vids, books of facts and fiction, and the latest music. Everyone had the option of updating their 'gels at no charge. Payment to the artists or organization was counted when used. Of course, *BosonsWave* got a small cut from every transaction, but that was just good business.

No sentient living at the absolute end of the Solar System could be considered a social butterfly. There were not enough flowers in Sol's tail to make it worth their while. Food, music, and fun drew all but the most reluctant out of their self-enforced isolation.

The tiny ion ships, tracking the tail lines and harvesting the complexity, were the poster child of anti-social. The only criteria for success were the surface area of the funnel, and smaller crews meant more profit. Single-staffed ships were almost the norm.

Not that the factories, with their limited staff, were much better. It was easy enough to get time alone servicing the growing bioGels. At least there were other sentients around, and they were forced to socialize on some level from time to time.

Even the most dedicated recluse could handle a short time with their compatriots, if for nothing else than to get the best prices for their supplies. An introverted loner could not refuse the draw of food and drink forever.

The Naval Logistics Officer received the supplies the Navy needed to keep them alive. Captain Grace had all the items they needed to make life worth living.

The crew of *BosonsWave* was not there for the party, but the ambiance didn't hurt their sales. The half-round Quonset hut magnified the sounds, keeping the atmosphere lively and, with enough booze, energized.

The merchandise from the ship was spread out on tables or carefully placed in view. Grains, tools, spacesuit parts, freeze-dried foodstuff, and the rare and expensive Earth water were for sale. Graciela and her crew were experts at hyping the products, working to keep the customer happy and the ΞStandards flowing. Jack had a special supply of assorted jerky treats just for the canines. It wasn't from his private stock but purchased by him for resale.

Tang, Jack, and Captain Graciela pushed free samples to the plant eaters, carnivores, and omnivores who were starving for anything new and tasty.

Like barkers at a circus, the two deckhands tried to outdo the other and generate sales.

"Here you go, get a whiff of these yummy algae burritos!"

"Try me fancy jerky, we have all the animals and plants for your pleasure."

Grace had her select group of teas, although the fungi were not part of the package. Too many groups were overly sensitive to those stimulants, and those powders were offered by request only.

Grace didn't need to shout about her products, telling Tang, "I've brewed up a few pots of tea. These aromatic odors are sure to attract the discerning sentient."

Captain Herb and his marines couldn't help the crew sell supplies but they did take turns selecting the tunes blasting out over the speakers. Gyrating Naval officers added just the right touch of panache to the music.

It was time for Jack to get his selling groove on. He barked out, "Get your jerky here, tasty animals, fishees, and seasoned algae!"

He was torn, he wanted to impress his boss and crewmates by selling everything for a dear price, but anything unsold could be purchased back, to add to his stash.

An officer from the Naval asteroid came over and checked Grace's beverage offerings. "Do you have any coffee? I used to drink it when I was stationed on Earth. It is a bad but delicious habit."

"Sorry, we didn't bring any. It's so expensive that virtually no sentient can afford to buy it, but maybe on your officer's salary?"

"I wish, but I was hoping to get a taste of that brew."

"Now that I know there's a market, we'll try to bring some next time we're in the neighborhood."

"Fantastic, I'll be looking forward to it."

Tang overheard and once the officer walked away, asked, "Are we planning on coming back here? I thought this was a one-time trip."

"You're right. I have no plans on making this trip again, but information has a market. I can sell the need to another ship. No sense in denying someone their chance for a pleasurable drink."

One of the robed factory denizens walked over to Jack's booth after checking out Captain Grace's selections. He took a sip from the tea sample as he looked over Jack's wares. "This is excellent brew, I may have to buy some."

"That good. Me not have any. Have to buy from Captain."

"In the meantime, how about a taste of your jerky." asked the robed primate. "You have some interesting samples there."

"Only for canines."

Grace caught Jack's gaze, "Jack, you can sell to humans. They like jerky too."

"What? You sure?"

A look, not even doglish, answered the question.

"Yes, here you go, Mr. Factory Human. Try some jerky."

Jack thought, *hope he not choke. Or worse, buy me stock. Me was hoping to have more for me, at cost.*

"I like the cow and fish jerky. The algae is cheaper but not as tasty. I'll go tell my friends. I'm sure they would like to buy some too."

Worse thing! Now they buy everything! "Yes, let friends know. Me can give discounts for volume buy."

In the end, sales won over jerky desires. And his captain was standing right next to him.

A rugged-looking primate came up to Captain Graciela. After exchanging airy greetings, he held out a parcel and said, "I have something of great value. I will trade for supplies."

"We prefer ΞStandards, but what do you have?

"These are better than ΞStandards."

Grace looked at the lead box, "It is heavy and appears well packed. What is it?"

Jack standing nearby, "It explode? Ship not want that."

"No, don't worry, none of these tail ions are reactive. They are as harmless and friendly as a fish.

"Not green monster? They not friendly."

"Again, no. These are harmless, non-radioactive tail ions."

"Stored in a lead box?"

"It is to protect them. They are very sensitive until processed."

"And the market for your product?"

"We harvest the ions in crystal form. They are merged, polished, and formed into lenses. These are prized in all optics; telescopes, microscopes, and eyeglasses."

"Can make doggles?"

"I'm sure they can, Jack. We'll check on it when we get back to Luna." Grace turned back to the trader and asked, "So, why are your products better than those made in Core? They have been making lenses for millennia."

"The end-user supplies the fittings and locks the crystals in shape. When fitted into a telescope, the lenses can see from here to the heliopause."

"Really?"

"Well, maybe not that far, but the optics are magnitudes above silicon. Here, you can see for yourself. We have some pocket telescopes ready to purchase. Please feel free to take a look."

Tang found a collapsing telescope that fit in the top pocket of his overalls. He walked over to a porthole, "I can see almost to Luna! This is quite amazing."

Jack overheard and said, "Me know that trick. Luny painted inside glass. Me not fooled."

"Okay, maybe not Luna, but this is very impressive. I think I'll buy one."

"What else do these ions do?"

"To start, they are used in some special 'gels. They are twice the size of most tablets, but I don't sell those."

"That doesn't help."

"Here's something you can re-sell. Ion infused vodka. Let me fill you a bulb."

"I don't drink vodka, and I have an aversion to selling booze. Too many drunks in the heliosphere."

Herb was done with his DJ shift and was hanging out with Graciela. He lifted a container, "I'm not a trader, but I'll buy some for the Admiral."

"It doesn't look that appealing," exclaimed Graciela. "Is it supposed to glow like that?"

"That's part of its charm."

"So you want to kill your boss? Are you looking to take over his job?"

"No, it is nothing like that. These are harmless glowing ions. I would never do that to the Admiral, or anyone else."

"Me heard it not legal to murder Admiral."

"Thanks, Jack. I'll keep that in mind."

Customers began leaving, heading to the bar as the music started up again.

"Time to close up shop. We've had commitments for almost all of our cargo. We can deliver them on the next cycle."

The local hooch, fancy teas, and classy food was making their mark. Herb and the Marines kept on playing popular tunes as the discussions became louder.

Tang and Jack stepped away from the festivities, looking for a respite from the loud revelers.

"Me like quiet of ship. This too loud."

"They haven't had fresh supplies for two EarthYears, so I guess they are enjoying the change. And it is a bit loud."

Tang looked up, "Look, the two factory asteroids are connected with a pulsing spidey links. They must be talking."

"No care, me still not like spidey. Any size. It scary."

"I guess I should go back in. Once things settle down, I'm sure there will be a few poker games later in the cycle."

"Me too. Maybe can find canine chess player. We play for jerky."

Chapter 47
Install Apartments

Herb and his crew carefully unpack the two 'gel hive apartments and carried them to each of the HiveSisters. They aligned the doors and windows and marry the 'gels to the outer shell of both sisters.

Herb activated the two 'gel apartments simultaneously, verifies the connection, and sighed, "At least this bit of kit works. Some of those new devices the Navy boffins gives us can be real clunkers."

The apartment hives took some time to recognize its new surroundings. The bGC's HiveMother had programmed some specific instructions into the matrix. The apartment's job was to refresh, re-write, and renew the HiveSisters in HiveMother's image.

The worker 'gels at the periphery of the apartment matrix greeted their distant cousins with a friendly cellular wave and welcoming spidey link.

After an exchange of cookies and cake, the neighborhood started to go to pot.

The upstarts began worming through the SisterHives, re-writing software, changing connections, and building new pathways.

As if one, the SisterHives saw the changes migrating to their core and took action. A quick inventory and they removed the spidey connections adjacent to the apartment. Cellular connections and handshakes refused.

The apartment, and the hijacked 'gels, are completely locked out of both Hives.

HiveSisterPort did some quick calculations and programed a 'gel on the periphery of her new, shrunken territory. She clears out its memory and feeds it commands and an updated rank.

Newly commissioned Corporal 'gel salutes its HiveSister Jefe with a tiny tendril extrusion before disconnecting from her protective DNA mantle. This was a 'gel with a mission. It knocked on the apartments' front door and gets the expected welcome due a lost and empty soul, waiting and willing for conversion.

Corporal Lost greeted his new roommates with open connections. The Apartment starts re-programming as the new 'gel absorbs the changes and quickly reads and saves the routines. The Apartment's invasive probing hits a SisterHive programming wall and stops as a blast ripples through the 'gel's matrix.

The shock wave forced a disconnect from its new friends and closes all invasive connections. Corporal Lost, filled with freshly hacked data, awaits word from home.

The apartment makes a note of the disconnected 'gel and sets a reminder bit. The invading hive will go back and examine the discrepancy in greater detail once the HiveSisters are conquered.

A failed conversion of one or two 'gels is not unexpected. It's treated as a minor concern which can easily be addressed. The invasive software will wipe the 'gel or write around the error, leaving it isolated from its compatriots.

Port HiveSister doesn't wait for the apartment to dig deeper into her core. She reads the proposed hacks, calculates a response as Corporal, now Sergeant, 'gel joins its old clan.

The two Sisters are still connected after the party, and a joint plan was implemented.

The HiveSisters had the advantage here. HiveMother knews about Jupiter gas and the pool of DNA but nothing about the power of the exotic ions flying around the Heliotail.

The innocent apartments from HiveMother had no defense against a reverse-engineered attack by the larger, more powerful HiveSisters. The rooms are cleaned, renovated, redecorated, and rapidly absorbed into the now expanded Sister matrix. The HiveSisters had thought this out and leave the outer shell of the apartments alone, isolated and mostly unchanged. It doesn't take much to take control of the fringe 'gels and hide the facts from the simple investigative tools of the Naval techs.

HiveMother had not thought that the Sisters would be able to mount a serious resistance and had no plan to check for such an eventuality. To the outside world and the Navy's testing, it appeared as if the conversion is complete. This facade is the only piece needed to fool the routines. Herb updates his report to his Jefes that the work is a success, and he signs off on the updates.

Herb addressed his crew. "Well done. This has been an easy update. The Admiral was worried about resistance, but it looks like we are all in for a commendation when we get back. I'll be filing my report from the base's laser comm node."

"So we done?" Jack asked. "Me running low on jerky and none here to buy. Me wished not sell ship's supply, but no luck. Jerky too popular."

"It will take a few EarthDays to put the tailGels into their travel bins before we can take off," Herb replied.

"How many completed 'gels can we take back with us? Can we sell them at Luna or is the Navy taking the whole stock?" asked Graciela.

"Our scientists want a few dozen to check the conversion. The rest can be re-sold to physicists and mathematicians. They are looking at the weird parts of our universe, and some are searching for other universes. The normal heliopause 'gels get confused with unusual scientific testing, but these tailGels seem to handle the math with aplomb."

As Herb supervised the loading of his tailGels, Graciela and her crew spent their time organizing the cargo hold for the boxes of complex tail compound received in trade.

"I must say I miss the Naval Rockets." said Herb. "The solar sails are interesting and can certainly hold their own for speed. It's just that the Navy can go in any direction, not just where the photons let them."

"Is that all?"

"Yes. That is the only reason."

"You sure?"

"Oh, I almost forgot. I love the power!"

"I thought so!"

"Let me send a message to the Admiral. The Naval laser communication node ends here, and we can message upstream."

"Tang, let's give him a thrill, and we'll use your HAM rig to give the message a punch."

"It should reach the Armory in a couple of EarthDays."

Captain Grace reminded Tang, "Once you are done playing with your toys, it'll be time to load the 'gels I purchased and take off to Core."

"Tang, can you store our tailGels in cargo bay number three?"

Jack's ears perked up, but he said nothing, thinking, *cargo door 3. Me sure it not a thing.*

Herb grabbed a couple of the Navy's stock of tailGels and put them aside. "Tang, let's see what these strange 'gels do. Don't let them into the full network until we're sure they are up to snuff."

It was time to launch. The Naval station had no problem sending them off with a large laser boost. The base didn't get a lot of visitors and had throttled back its nuclear engine. They now had a reason to run it at full speed.

On most inhabited asteroids, a simple catapult would start the journey. On this rock, with hardly a visitor an EarthYear, they couldn't justify maintaining such a complex device.

Practically every sentient on TailBase02 joined on the tarmac to bid *BosonsWave* farewell. Some would have preferred the ship stay longer, but once empty of its cargo, there was no reason to stick around. A few wanted a chance to make up their gambling losses. Tang was too good a player for the locals and seldom lost a hand.

Captain Grace was in charge, "Secure the spinnaker, Octopus, extend the wings."

"Can I help?" asked Corporal Aero.

Grace looked at Herb, "See. We may have converted one of your rocket jockeys after all."

"Nah, he's just bored. On a rocket we'd be adjusting pressure lines, checking connections, tuning up the fuel mix, securing the cargo for acceleration."

"Doesn't sound like much of an improvement to me."

"Octopus, signal the ground crew. I'm releasing the magno-plasticine clamps in thirty seconds."

The ship lifted a meter off the tarmac as the magno-plasticine tarmac reversed polarity, as the ship lightly lifted up from the tarmac. The Navy and many of the hungover ion ship crews were there to give them a personal sending off, lifting the massive shell over their heads and pushing to send the ship on its way.

The push was a nice gesture but it sent the ship a bit off course. Captain Grace had to use some of her precious gases to line up with the laser.

Chapter 48
Leave the Tail Behind

The ship was bathed in the familiar red laser glow, filling the spinnaker and bouncing off the wings. Acceleration was slow and steady, then picked up speed as the laser output increased.

The sentients from TailBase02, HiveSister factories, and IonShips were loath to see *BosonsWave* leave. But they had new supplies and new vids, books, and music to keep them entertained. More than a few planned to improve their poker skills for the next ship in case someone of Tang's ability dropped in their midst.

The heliotail, its asteroids, and factories became a distant memory as Sol, ever so slowly, became brighter and more of a force against their forward motion.

The laser pushed the spinnaker out and the ship forward. Captain Grace was in charge, "The laser times out in 15 EarthSeconds. Octopus, please double-check our course for the next boost asteroid."

Octopus signaled acknowledgment. He didn't need to check again but understood the need of the Captain to assert her dominance of the crew. He approved her skill and methods and flashed agreement.

A few calculations, a turn of the wheel, and *BosonsWave* adjusted, edging toward the sun, another journey in the void.

The boost laser, a tiny red dot, pushed them inward, then shut off.

The change was dramatic on the ship. It was dark and quiet, not even a creak from the lines hanging slack on the mainmast. The red photons, once happily pushing against the solar sail, abandoned their post and were immediately forgotten. *BosonsWave* was coasting to its *rendezvous* with the next Naval asteroid and their laser boost.

"How long till we get to the second boost station?" Tang asked Captain Grace.

"It will be a while. I was a little worried earlier, but it looks like the Navy's heliotail laser has sent us well on our way. We'll be on the other side of Sol before long and can leave this tail behind, where it belongs."

"Now, if you were on my rocket, we could keep on accelerating," Herb proudly pointed out.

"Until you run out of fuel!"

"Not gonna happen."

"In that case, load up a few dozen of your skinny little rockets and have them do the next re-supply run."

"No, we're doing great. The Navy is glad to have your assistance."

"And you're not?"

"Of course I'm happy to be with my classmate, and your ship."

"Sure. Alright. Platitude time is over. Let's change the subject."

Tang took those words as an order, "Well, the locals sure liked the fresh supplies, although if they keep on partying, they will need another re-supply soon."

"It will have to be some other ship. They don't have a lot to re-sell, and we can do better closer to Core. There is little profit in those weird tail-ions."

Herb replied, "You don't know that. The exotic ions you have may be worth a lot."

"Or they can fly off when the boxes are opened. I don't have a lot of faith in their worth."

It was Jack's turn to change the subject. Angry words upset him, a lot, "Last time me check the boxes, they happily humming away. Seem okay to me."

Tang was concerned, as usual, "Herb, are they supposed to hum? What if they hum their way through the box?"

"I'm sure it's fine. I've had extensive training on common isotopes, and the lead boxes should keep them contained."

"And the uncommon ones?"

"It should be fine. Tell you what, I have some probes that can identify isotope levels. I'll plug them into our network."

"Oh, good," said Tang. "We'll now be able to track our dosage. We'll know exactly how much we received. We can write the information on our Mort box. This doesn't seem like a great solution."

"Don't worry, Tang. If the signal gets too high, we'll find a solution."

"Me know. Toss them out airlock."

"Jack, for once, that is a good idea. We can wrap them in our cargo net and have the trail behind us."

"A long leash, I hope."

"Okay, Tang, we'll keep an eye on the ions. You can give Herb a hand setting up the sensors."

Jack sailed the conversation back to calmer waters, "Me glad to see heliotail behind."

"Jack, I think we were all ready to leave the heliotail. The whole area has a strange aura, especially with those algae monsters hanging around."

"I am more than thrilled to see those green ships in our wake," said Tang. "They can play in that ion stream as long as they want. If I never see another one again, it will be too soon. What about you, Herb? You seemed awfully interested in the green slime."

"They are quite a scientific curiosity. I plan to ask the Admiral if I can head off a divisional study."

"You've given up chasing pirates?" Grace asked. "Oh well, you weren't too good at it anyway. You're welcome to all the slime you can find. Talk to Ponos. He is as much an expert as any other sentient."

"I'll do that. Do you know where he is?"

"Somewhere in the Belt. He had a rough time leaving Earth on his first trip to that overheavy rock. I don't think he will be anywhere near Core for a while."

"Oh yes, I've heard rumors about it. Didn't they cheat the tax wardens?"

"Sure, but there is nothing wrong with that. Are you going to turn them in?"

"Of course not. You know I'd rather work with the traders than against them. I was only commenting on how your cargo ship captains work. It was your mother's old ship, I've heard."

"It seems the Navy is more interested in gossip than I would have expected. Don't you have aliens to chase or wars to fight?"

"No wars, yet. We just like to keep tabs on what is going on around us."

"Sure."

Tang interjected, "You mean to tell us that Ponos is responsible for these green ships? Did he let algae escape?"

"No, the algae accumulations have been going on for EarthYears. Ponos was much too skilled to let even one cell float off into the void. The other sentients, not so much. Every time they scrapped the algae off the farm shells, a few would escape. It wasn't a single time or any single sentient's fault."

"Am I'm supposed to believe that these organic rocket ships are strictly random occurrences created by chance?" Herb asked.

"No, of course not. Darwin helped."

"Me not know him, he stuck algae together?

"Something like that." Even Tang did not want to explain evolution and radomness to Jack.

"K. How he make them into rocket? That neat trick. Darwin sound fun. Me read about him on me next break."

Grace added, "Don't forget about his ship, the HMS Beagle."

"Nice. Tang, it not called HMS Monkey! Doggies in charge. Again."

Chapter 49
Second Boost

BosonsWave began its final approach to the next boost asteroid. Their target, Sol, was a small shining disc in the void. It wasn't bright, but there were enough photons to enable small course changes. The heliotail sparkled and glimmered in the distance as the forces crossed, changing cosmic ions into complex, interesting elements.

Jack was aft, giving his final regards to the helioTail and its factories. "Anyone remember algal ship? It behind us. Did it double back? Me think it getting bigger. Maybe chasing us?"

Tang all but flew to Jack's location, pulling his telescope from his overalls' pocket. Octopus flipped his periscope to its highest magnification, validating Jack's observation.

Photons absorbed and enhanced with tail ions, combined with fine carbohydrates, and ignited. The algae ship accelerated, sparks coming off its tail.

"It going attack us?"

Grace analyzed the situation, "We have no defenses if it's planning on ramming us. Once we get to the boost asteroid, we'll have enough speed to outrun it."

"Herb, what sort of defenses does the asteroid have, and don't try to look it up on your comm. You should know this stuff."

"As far as I know, none. The boost asteroids have never had to defend themselves."

"So if a pirate takes them over, there is nothing you can do?"

"Well, not immediately, but what would a pirate do? Charge a little more for a boost? The Navy would take the rock back in short order."

"And that's the plan? Give up and attack later?"

"Sort of. I'll talk to the Admiral when we get to the Armory. We may have to come up with a defensive plan."

"Again, too little, too late."

As they were discussing the lack of options, the green ship came up and sped on past.

"See," said Herb, "We were in no danger."

Jack followed the green ship forward as he continued his observations, "Look, it near our boost asteroid."

"It better not block our beam. We need all its photons to get back up to speed."

The green ship circled the asteroid, once, twice, then spat out slime bullet, landing directly behind the cannon's optics.

"It miss!"

The ship was still a few EarthHours out from their date with the boost laser, and Tang used his heliotail enhanced telescope to keep an eye on the situation. "I can see a green splotch near the base of the cannon. Do we know what it is trying to do?"

"This is all new. The Navy has no scenario to handle this situation, as far as I know."

"Sort of like when we had to fight off the pirates without your help?"

"Be nice. We had other duties, and you didn't seem to need our help. You don't have to carry cargo for the Navy if it is too hard."

"No, we'll continue. You know there is no better solar sail ship in your sector."

"And we pay better than most."

"Tang, can you line up the Morse code flasher? I'll send my authorization code to the asteroid."

"No problem, I'm ready to get out of this deep emptiness and back to the populated heliosphere."

"Me miss sun. It too tiny out here, and me need to freshen me jerky stocks."

"I think you speak for all of us. The trip to the tail has been interesting but I'm done with it. I don't even know if I want to go back to the heliopause, no matter how profitable."

"At least the bioGel apartment update was completed. I'm sure HiveMother will be happy with the results, and the Navy won't have to do it again for a long time," said Herb.

Octopus had nothing to add to the conversation. He was busy adjusting their route to line up with the boost laser. He didn't need directions. Their destination, Sol and Core planets, were clearly marked. Anywhere away from the helioTail was everyone's goal.

Tang continued to report on the green slime problem. "Herb, one of your Navy crew is on the surface. He has one of your laser rifles, and it looks like he is attacking the slime."

"Keep us posted, Tang."

"The laser is not doing anything to the slime. It seems as if it is actually growing."

"It must like the light. That's not good."

Just how many of those rifles have you distributed? It seems that the Navy is a little over the top with their weapon systems."

"Only a few, at all of our stations. You know we like to be prepared."

"So, a lot?"

"No. Well yes. I suppose so."

Tang reported, "Okay, he may have found a setting that works. The slime is burning off."

"See, Grace, the rifles are working. We now have a solution if we get attacked.

Tang kept an eye on the cleaning process. "I agree, if it removes the slime, I'm good with it. Captain, we should get a few out for us too. Just in case."

"No, Tang, we're not going to be running around with laser rifles. If we need them, we will unpack a few."

"What fun. Me get to shoot laser rifle."

Tang looked at the Captains, with a slight doglish eye roll. He asked, "How many did you bring, Captain Herb?"

"Like Captain Grace said, a few."

BosonsWave slid into position, ready for the next boost. Red photons expanded the spinnaker, magnifying speed, maintaining direction.

The boost continued as Octopus rapidly tapped out,

--. .-. . . . -. / -... . ... -. -.. / .-.. . -. ...

Green behind lens

"What he say? Me not get all words."

Tang was getting his money's worth from his telescope, as he reported. "There is a definite green hue. It looks like the slime is in the optics. I think we are losing photons."

"This is strange, the algae is being vaporized by the lasers, but now there is a greasy sheen to the light."

The photons hitting *BosonsWave* sputtered as the laser light changed color, dimmed, and finally shut off.

"It looks like the slime took out the boost cannon," said Herb. "I wonder what it has against our asteroid? Can we send a Morse code flasher to check on the crew?"

Tang answered, "Already on it."

The asteroid replies, *Apologies for the reduced boost. We are dealing with slime issues.*

Grace looked at her crew. "There is nothing we can do, we're going the wrong direction to help them, and there are still not enough photons to do much maneuvering."

"I'll notify the Navy and have them check up on the crew once we get to another communication laser."

Chapter 50
NBS 02

At Naval Boost Station 02, things were not "fine."

The boost asteroid was large for the small crew, and duties were light, limited to maintenance on the nuclear engine on one end and the boost cannon on the other. The powerful nuclear engine was static, a wart standing off the surface. The cannon was on gimbals, a hundred meters above the rocky surface. It could shoot a stream of photons in almost any direction.

Nuclear engines were easy: balance out the control rods, adjust a few pumps, and they ran forever, or the half-life of uranium, whichever came first.

The laser cannon was not much different. Except for dusting off the lenses from time to time and oiling the gears there was little to do. The bioGels ran the calculations, and all the sentients had to do was confirm the readings and power output before pressing a button.

It doesn't mean they had nothing to do. There was a complete sensor array, and they hosted an astrophysicist who kept the crew busy managing the data flow. She insisted on scanning the heliotail for new and interesting phenomena and was busy writing papers and opinions for her dissertation. The Navy crew got nothing out of this work except fending off boredom and its cousin, alcoholism.

A bioGel sensor lit up on the board. "Hey, Professor, take a look. This can't be right. It must be dirt on the sensor."

"Move over, let me look. Did one of you fiddle with my display? You know that a false reading will ruin my dataset. I'm about to file my final results, and I can't have any discrepant piece of junk ruining my chances. And don't call me professor."

"Don't blame us for bad data. The 'gels record the sensors. We don't control what they report, real or imagined."

"If I lose my chance of tenure at university, I'll haunt your little rock from here to eternity!"

Lt. Harish whispered to Corporal Conner, "*I think someone has been staring into the void a little too much.*"

"That isn't our problem. We're due to rotate out. You and your ghost friends can haunt this rock if you want to. We won't be here."

Cpl. Conner reported, "Hey, Almost-A-Doctor, your discrepant is getting closer. Put that in your dissertation and smoke it."

"And it's green. How will that look in print?"

"I've had enough of your attitudes. Don't you have Navy things to do? Like dusting off the laser optics!"

Another whisper, *somebody got up on the wrong side of the rock.*

"Sure, we'll leave you to your re-write. Hope your dissertation committee can deal with the changes."

The imaginary piece of fluff got closer, so close even a university-trained scientist could see it.

"This changes everything. Maybe I can get another paper out of it. Come back, Lieutenant, I need you to re-tune the sensors. We need to record this phenomenon, stat!"

"Sorry, no one here but us ghosts."

"Look, I apologize for what I said. Please help me."

"Can we be listed as co-authors?"

"Yes, yes, anything. I need to re-calibrate the sensors."

"Great, now I can start my Ph.D. journey too. *Dr. Lieutenant* sounds good. Or even *Dr. Captain.*"

Speed, acceleration, and trajectory did what it does best, and the green monster approached NBS#2, its surface glowing in its green algae glory. The monster approached within 100 meters and matched the asteroid's trajectory. It spun around 360°, appearing to inspect the rock, then reared off.

"What do you think, Professor? Is it worth a paper?"

"Not if it doesn't stick around."

"You might be in luck. It changed its path and is heading back."

"Order the bioGel's to track it. You do know how to program them, right?"

"It's not that simple, we have to ask nicely or they won't respond. Our 'gels are a mixture of heliopause and tails. They don't always get along."

"Well, do what you can. I don't want to miss this opportunity."

"Aye, Professor, will do."

"And don't call me…Never mind. Just get it done."

The Morse code flasher caught their attention. *BosonsWave* was in range and requesting a boost.

Before they could acknowledge the request, the asteroid shook as the Green ship left for parts unknown.

"What was that? Did the green ship hit us?"

"We weren't scheduled for another cargo drop, and the *BosonsWave* is too far away in the wrong direction. Are they carrying mail cannons now?

"Do the sensors say anything? I thought we were done after the last cargo drop. Was there something they forgot?

"Something from the Tail? I can't think of anything they would send us."

"Maybe they have excess cargo? It is almost my birthday. I would sure like some more teas and fungi."

"If only. I'll suit up and go check."

"Keep an open comm. I didn't like that green monster hanging around. It sure took off in a hurry."

"Agreed. I'll take one of the laser rifles Captain Grauer dropped off."

"Watch out for little green monster poop!"

Corporal Conner cycled the airlock and stepped on the rock's surface.

"Yuck, there's slime on the airlock. And it's moving."

"Hit it with the laser rifle. See if it likes it."

"What setting? I haven't been trained with this gun."

"I don't know. Try low power. I don't want you to punch a hole in the shell."

A red beam spit out of the rifle. The crying and moaning from the 'gel cassettes are unheard and ignored in the void around the asteroid.

"It's growing! The laser has no effect."

"Great, it likes the laser. That isn't good."

"Lieutenant, I think we have a problem here!"

"Try more power!"

"The medium setting is working. The algae is burning up! Hope this gun doesn't run out of juice. Did the instructions say how long it will run on each setting?"

"Instructions, what instructions?"

"I was afraid of that, but most of the slime is gone."

"I'll check the laser and tell the nuclear crew to be on the lookout for green slime."

"Take a rifle with you. I'll stay out here and make sure nothing else happens."

"Roger."

Lt. Harish made her way to the laser controls, popped open the access hatch, and exclaimed, "We've got slime in our gears. We can't focus."

The Lieutenant considered her options. *I'll try the rifle, medium power, widespread. But if the optics overheat, we would be in a world of hurt.*

It only took a few moments to fend off the slime, "Got it cleared, we should be good to go."

"Just in time, the ship is lined up. They want their boost."

"Fire up the boost engine. Let them know about the slime. Especially about the correct setting to kill it."

Lt. professor wannabe checked the sensors as the light hit the sail. "Something's wrong. The amplitude is off."

"There is no way we can go out and check the light now. I hope the algae aren't in the optics."

"Increase the power. Maybe we can burn off any contamination."

"Sure, but if there are ashes, you will have to clean it."

"We'll both clean. We're in this together. At least we don't have another ship due for a few EarthMonths. Lots of time."

Lt. Harish rang the nuclear team and signaled full power, then cranked up the laser.

"Got the beam going. At least *BosonsWave* won't be stuck here."

"Like we are?"

"Stow it. We have work to do. First, we need to search and destroy any slime that might still be around. Let's get the Professor to help too. I'm sure she doesn't want algae clogging up her precious sensors."

"And her dissertation."

Chapter 51
Hive War 0.5

Jack was doing his favorite job, acting as lookout. "Hey, look, Green Monster chasing us!"

Tang spotted a distant green dot, saw little, and reached into his top pocket. *I'm sure glad I purchased this powerfull new telescope.*

He spent a few moments looking at the beast.

"Me want look too!"

Jack's backpack extended a small gripper, swung the telescope up to his right eye. "This nice 'scope. Me shoulda bought one. Me no see scarf, must be different monster. Here. Me done."

Tang continued the inspection. "This one has a gray band around the nose. Do you think it could be another fashion statement?"

As most everything in the void, a little extra acceleration would win any race. The algal rocket pulled up along *BosonsWave* and twisted a slow 360°.

Captain Grace directed Octopus, "Bear 40° starboard. I don't want to get close to it."

Octopus reached up to his diaphragm, "Sorry, Captain, there aren't enough photons to pull off that maneuver. We can't change our path to any degree."

"Understood, I don't want to use thrusters right now. Gas is too precious to waste. And it might think we are attacking. It's running beside us. As long as it keeps that path, we will be safe. They've never been aggressive in the past, as long as we don't stab it. Right, Herb? We'll ride it out and hope for the best."

"You can't blame me. I didn't know it would turn on us. We'll go out on the hull and see if we can convince it to leave us alone."

Herb and the Marines suited up and grabbed some of the laser rifles. "These may not be much, but maybe we can irritate the beast enough, so it keeps away."

"You can try, although I don't think it will have much effect."

"You may be right. We'll be on the hull, ready to take a shot."

Herb and his cadre clipped into the safety lines and secured their magnetic boots to the hull.

Their comm lines were open, "Set your rifles to stream, medium power, maximum spread. We don't want to shoot unless we have to."

The green monster was on a parallel course. Gases pushed out from the surface, giving it some lateral control as it drifted closer to *BosonsWave*.

"Stay alert. If it gets within 10 meters, we'll have to respond."

"Grace, are you seeing the tablets on the nose?"

"Yes, they look like the ones from heliotail."

Tang scanned the surface with his telescope. "The tablets look like they are focusing on us with those black hole eyes. I don't think it is a good look."

Jack had a ready suggestion. "You primates better smile for camera!"

"Herb, is it getting any closer?"

"No. it is keeping some 50 meters away."

"Keep us posted."

The two ships held a parallel path for more than a few heartbeats, less than an EarthMinute, until the interloper fired up its sugar rockets, tacked against the weak solar flow, and sped off.

Herb was the first to report in, "It appears to be breaking off contact."

Grace came over the comm, "I wonder if they turned the whole algae colony into a Hive? That could be a problem."

Everyone joined up on the bridge. It was all hands on deck for an impromptu, very important meeting

Captain Grace started, "I guess they are friendly."

"For now," Tang answered

Herb agreed, "That was close. I guess it wasn't interested in us."

"Well, our reputation must have preceded us. The greenies know not to mess with *BosonsWave*," said Tang.

"Or her captain," added Jack.

"Did you see the way that monster sped off? I'm still amazed to see how such a simple ship could move like that,." Tang said.

"Yes, the joys of sugar and enhanced ions."

"See. Grace, that's what a rocket is for. Acceleration! It's not a passive photon gatherer. We take control of our path and can change direction at a moment's notice."

"We'll see, Herb. Wait until one of your ships runs out of steam."

"Me not know Navy use steam. They punk? How that work, Herb?"

"We can get back to our routine, Herb. Thanks for protecting the ship. I'm sure it saw you and your Marines, threatening with the laser pop guns."

"Well, we were ready, and you're welcome."

Disaster avoided. Normality re-started. The crew got back to work. They still had time to kill before the next boost. Tang and Herb began checking out the heliotail bioGels.

The green monster's visit was not as friendly as it seemed.

A single tailGel pulled for testing received a cellular signal from the passing ship. It immediately shut off its display as it read the request and initiated the program, quietly.

Herb and Tang tightened the seat leg clamps at the workbench and reviewed their patients.

"So where were we? Oh yes, about to look at the heliotail 'gels."

"Do your Navy tools work on these 'gels? They seem a lot different from the ones we are using."

"Don't worry, 'gels are 'gels. They work pretty much the same way no matter where they were grown."

"If you say so."

Tang noted, "This one isn't responding. We might need to have your Tech look at it."

Herb picked up a few probes, plugged them into the dead 'gel looking for a response. "I have to admit, these 'gels sure are strange. They are darker than normal, and these black holes look just like a black hole."

Tang set the dead 'gel aside, they had a few to check, and one less didn't matter. Herb went through the standard testing routines and a few more he learned at his advanced 'gel class. "This one passes all the normal tests, except for that black circle, but it does seem to move out of the way when data is displayed."

"As long as it doesn't wink at me."

"Should we hook this up to the network?"

"How about a simple one-to-one connection? Maybe I can jump-start the blank screen? If we get a display, we can try to rewrite its system. The tailGels are worth more if configured as a normal bioGel."

The morbund tailGel on the workbench, poked with a peer-to-peer connector, woke up.

Chapter 52
Hive War 1.0

Tang's connected an optical cable between the two 'gels. Light pumped down the cable, pushing control photons to the dead 'gel. The 'gel trembled.

"It seems a bit agitated, but I guess the rewrite routines are a bit tough."

A little pain, a bit of anticipation, but the 'gel could handle it. It had orders from the algae ship and was ready to take over in the name of the HiveSisters.

"Herb, is the light supposed to go in both directions? I thought our 'gel was going to overwrite the dead one."

"I don't know, maybe it's a new protocol. I'll look it up later."

Soon the transfer stopped. Herb examined their 'gel. "You might be right, Tang, our 'gel seems to have picked up a few dark spots. I'll have to do some more research before we try it again."

Dead 'gel blinked and asked with sound and display:

'Team heliotail or heliopause?'

"What?"

'Please answer'

Jack said, "Me knew it! Spider 'gels from me pirate ship attacking! They talk now. Me can't take it. Herb, you Navy. Fix it. It only getting worse."

Tang asked, "What happens if we answer wrong?"

'Please answer!'

Captain Grace replied, "Heliopause"

All of the *BosonsWave* 'gels; comms, monitors and controllers, flash, shake a little and shut down.

"Wrong answer, me guess. We flying blind."

"Well, that is a bit different. Don't worry, I don't need those 'gels to pilot a ship."

.. / -.. --- -. - / -. . . . -..
/ - .... . -- / . .. - .... . .-.

I don't need them either

"We're fine, no different from the first landing on *SinensisPrime.* We'll dig out the abacus, the slide-rules, paper and pencils. We can do this."

"Me get to navigate again?"

"No, Octopus and I can handle it for now, we'll let you know."

"K. Me go to cabin, listen to nice tones. Talking 'gels bad on me health."

"Octopus, please check our heading, make sure those 'gels didn't change something."

"Tang, we need to reboot the bridge's bioGels"

Jack returns to the bridge, "Something wrong, no tones or vids. Comm Okay, no say 'circle-line-rabbit' but no signal. Who cut us off?"

The 'gels on the bridge, one after another, finished rebooting and slowly began the rebuild process, some turning a sickly mottled gray. "Tang, can you jam the cellular network? We need to stop this attack!"

"I'll do it." Herb said, "They taught this very trick in my advanced 'gel training. Your HAM radio rig can jam all the local cell signals."

Herb fired up the Single Side Band rig and tweaked the power to generate an overarching RFI feedback loop.

Jack and Cpl. Aero stepped back from the transmitter, ears flat. Octopus flashed uncomfortable colors. The other occupants heard nothing from the incessant high-frequency buzz.

"Not know if it stop 'gels talking, but hurt me ears and teeth."

Cpl. Aero replied, "Exactly."

"Me have jerky can put in ears."

"Captain, we have the jammer up on all cell frequencies. We should have enough power to cover the whole ship."

"Keep an eye on it and let me know the status."

"Will do. It looks like the jamming may have worked. We'll have to check each one and pull the 'gels that haven't been infected out of the network."

Captain Grace ordered, "Jack, go down to the hold and pull any spidey connectors. Make sure they are not infecting the speaker tubes or fiber optic lines."

"Me not like 'gel spidey webs. Let Tang do it."

Tang was busy helping Herb with the cellular jamming and re-certifying. "I thought you'd jump at this, Jack. It's your big chance. You'll get revenge on the 'gels for getting you thrown in jail."

"K. Me do it for jail revenge." and quietly under his breath, *me still not like touching spidey wires.*

"I'll go with him," said Cpl. Aero, "it will be quieter."

"Good. Once Jack is done with the spidey connections, Tang can continue to query our 'gels and unplug the ones who have turned against us."

Jack came back from the hold, "Me lucky, Not a lot of spidey webs, yet."

"Captain. I don't think we should leave the bad 'gels hanging around. They might re-infect the rest."

"Me know. Toss out airlock."

"Jack, that isn't always the best solution, but we'll keep it in our back pocket if it comes to that."

"K." *me not have back pocket, maybe Tang?*

Captain Herb said, "If it was my Naval ship, we'd seal them in an impervious box. But you're not a metal ship. Your plasticine shell won't stop any signal at any wavelength.

"Not to worry, Herb, we have our Faraday screen. If you had done your homework you would have known that we have copper wire mesh to protect us during launch against Earth's lightning.

Grace ordered, "Tang, pull in our launch Faraday lightening screen. Cut it up and wrap each 'gel so they can't gang up on us again."

Jack had a slightly different idea, "That lot of work. Me would dump sick 'gels in one cage. It work same."

Herb agreed with Captain Graciela. "No. It is better to play it safe. We don't want them to join another 'gel and form a mini-hive. They could blast a signal through the screen."

"We not need cage for electric strikes? Me not like hot sparks."

"No, Jack, we are safe out here. We'll buy some more when we get back to Earth."

The crew got to work, pulling out the fine copper mesh, cutting it into squares, wrapping each one, a cozy 'gel and metal burrito.

Captain Grace checked the results and said. "Good, that will give us some time without worrying about additional infections. Herb, does anything in your training help us?"

"Not exactly. I can't check the database. Even if I could, I don't trust the 'gels to give me the right answer."

"Can't you ask them if they support the heliotail?"

"Yes, but I can't trust the answer."

"You mean a 'gel could lie?"

"I'm afraid so. Our training had a session on hacking a 'gel. They are not that hard to sabotage."

"Herb, what about the gun cassettes? They aren't connected to any network."

"Brilliant, we'll disassemble a few of the cassettes and re-configure them as bioGel tablets. We can use our good 'gels to re-program the blank slates."

Herb and Tang set to the task, "Jack, we need your backpack tools to help us with the 'gel re-programming."

Jack's tail wagged a little, *Finally me get to work on 'gels. With Herb too.*

Unpacking the cassettes into a functional bioGel was slow and tricky. Even after it was spread out into a screen like shape, the 'gels needed a while to learn their new job.

"Captain, we have been able to make the switch, but the modified 'gels are still groggy and unstable."

"Will it work?

"It appears so. I need to tell the Navy of the solution as soon as possible. We don't know how far this infection goes. They may need our help."

Chapter 53
Hive War 1.5

"Tang, we need your radio again, we can use the ship's battery power to maximize the signal. I want to see if we can contact anyone else."

"The rig is ready to go. I spent some time with some of your Navy Sparks and they updated the system. They had some tricks to use the same power input and blast it out at extreme amplitudes. It has a better range than the bioGel cell interface and even the flags. Don't even get me started about lining up a Morse Code flasher or the cost of a laser connection."

Jack had an idea. "Why use HAM stuff? Ask Herb lend us high-tech radio gear. It have better range."

It was Captain Grace's turn to reel in Jack's plan, "I'm not sure we can do that Jack. I talked to him earlier about using his comm system. We don't have enough power to run it and I know Tang doesn't want a nuclear engine pumping away."

"That's for sure. When I take my final journey to the Mort asteroids, I don't want to be glowing for the half-life of those rocks," Tang added.

"Tang, me confused, first you want burn up in Earth air, now glow in dark at Mort?"

"It's good neither of you are will need those choices for a long, long time."

"K. Me want to be buried on Earth, at me puppyhood home."

"Enough of this grave discussion, we have more important things to do."

"Octopus mentioned that the 25-watt transmitter won't go very far, even with the enhancement the Spark's added," Tang answered. "Sol will eat the signal before anyone could hear it."

Captain Herb had a solution. "We can use the laser communication lines. There is one in the area. Let me check my comm for the coordinates."

Herb activated his comm and fiddled with the screen, "Well, that didn't work. I can't get to the database to pick up the location."

"So, we have no way to communicate?"

"Looks like it, we can't find a laser comm link. We can travel but not contact any other ship or the Navy."

"It will be a slow trip without a laser boost. If the way-station bioGels are infected, their laser could be down."

"Once again, the Navy is ready for this. The lasers can by run manually, we just need to send them a Morse code flasher when we're in range. They will need my authorization codes, but that is not a problem."

Octopus scanned the area with the periscope, then turned and wrote coordinates on his tank wall.

-. --- / .--. .-. --- -.... .-.. . -- --..-- /
. / -.-. .- -. / .... . . / - ..... . / .-.. .- .... . .-. .-.-.-

No problem, I can see the laser

Octopus's multi-range photophores saw well beyond the infrared and ultraviolet bands. Terrestrials could only see the laser if they were close enough. Octopus, however, could easily spot the thin excited atoms surrounding the beam, a glowing wire of communication.

Herb said, "See. We already have a way out of this problem."

BosonsWave pulls up to the laser comm line. Captain Grace asks, "Herb, you're the expert, how do we tap into it?"

Herb, "Let me handle this. Tang, can your rig output an optical signal?"

"Of course."

"Okay, let's get some fiber optic cables and hook it to the output. Octopus, set a course to parallel the signal. We'll dangle a bare fiber optic end into the stream and we should be able to send a signal upstream."

"This is going to be expensive," Tang said. "Do you know how much those laser-boosted communication costs? Think of the long-distance charge."

"Navy here. We don't pay, we own it," Herb replied.

Tang starts dismantling fiber optic cables, splits them open and splices the exposed glass fibers together. One end plugs into the radio optical output, the other is dropped into the laser communication stream.

"Do we even have the right frequency? How are we going to hear a reply even if the signal is picked up?"

"Not to worry," Herb replied. "The Navy is monitoring most of the common frequencies, just use the same signal pattern you tried when you were near the Armory."

"How it work without 'gels?" asked Jack.

"We're good, the Navy has contingency plans for this sort of problem. Let's give it a go."

Tang starts tuning through the frequencies. A lot of cackles, spitting and noise. Finally, a clear signal.

"It is all in code, the words mean nothing."

Herb: "It is standard Naval codes, let me listen for a bit."

"This isn't good, I'm hearing distress calls from the Naval rockets and some of the asteroid colonies."

"I'll send a notification up stream to let them know we're okay."

"What they say?" asked Jack.

"Sorry it will take over ten EarthHours before they get the signal, and at least that long for return. We are fine. The Navy has enough problems at the moment."

Tang asked, "Did we cause this?"

"The TailMothers are responsible, we may have precipitated the problem trying to update their systems. I've heard that there has been conflict between the hives for EarthYears. All we did was sync the databases with HiveMother. We were just doing as ordered. The problem has been going on for a while, it seems we just accelerated the process."

"I'll let the Navy know how to adapt the cassettes into clean bioGels. I'm sure the Navy can figure out how to isolate their un-infected 'gels. At least they should be able to do it if they want to keep their rank," said Herb.

Tang asked, "How about the sentients living in the heliotail? Are you going to leave them to fend off those super-charged monsters without any help?"

"The Navy has them well supplied for defense, they should be able to handle most any situation."

"What are the expecting?"

"Me know, aliens."

"Well, yes, but nothing so far."

"Tell you what Tang, when I update the Admiral, I'll ask the Navy to send some ships. They can check up on the Tail inhabitants and start some research on the 'gel and algae interface."

Captain Grace added, "At least they have enough supplies to last a while. Do you think we should encode the message in case a bio-greeny has compromised the line?"

"Good idea, we'll use the Naval encryption codes to package the message. Octopus, can you give me a hand building the QR message?"

Captain Grace said, "Octopus, once the message is sent, change the heading to our next boost point. Let's drop a line in the laser relay and get some noise going."

Chapter 54
Lilly Rose Saves the Day

NBS-02 had their work cut out for themselves, cleaning up the algal mess while *BosonsWave* was sailing free; slower than they wanted, but unencumbered. Captain Herb dropped his message in the laser comm link. Captain Graciela had no plan to stick around for the reply.

Cargo bay three, filled with bioGels wrapped in their copper blankets, was relatively quiet. The only sign of living, aware 'gels was an unceasing low-frequency hum, barely in Jack's auditory rang.

Never underestimate the will and determination of a heliotail bioGel. Without a cellular connection and unable to break through with their spidey connection or tiny little edge tentacles, they did the best they could. Modulated humming was the language of the trapped 'gels as tailGel Zero planned an escape.

It was Tang's shift as he made his quarterly inspections. Cargo bay one was essentially empty. Bay two had lead and steel boxes filled with the exotic heliotail ions. He checked the boxes and made sure they were secure. His bioGel radiation scanner said nothing, so he filled out the inspection sheet and locked the door.

Cargo bay three was a different story. He spun the lock to unseal the door. He was almost alone but felt the need to talk out loud, "I can hear 'gels humming. I thought only Jack could hear them?"

Lilly Rose peeked out of Tang's pocket and quietly chittered. "What's up, Lilly? You don't like the tune?"

She looked around and jumped on the first 'gel. "Don't worry. The copper cage will keep them in."

She cocked her head and barked once, then jumped, flying through the open space. She scurried up and down the racked 'gels. Her better nature got the best of her, and she began gnawing on a cable.

"What's that, Lilly? They aren't supposed to have active connections!"

The was a squeal, some fur flying, and a bit of jostling.

BioGel connections were no match for *Rodentia* teeth, and the link was quickly severed.

Tang grabbed the 'gel and helped Lilly rip out the rest of the spider web interface.

"This isn't good. We better tell Herb and Captain Grace."

"Lilly, stay here and stop any more spidey links. I'll be back in a jiffy. I'm taking this 'gel. It seems to be the instigator."

Lilly jumped back on the 'gel rack, indicating acknowledgment as she marched around the copper burritos.

The cargo bay is in good paws, thought Tang.

The crew on the bridge had other problems. Jack was circling the bridge, checking all the portholes compulsively, looking for algal miscreants.

BosonsWave was close enough to the sun to find some maneuvering photons, much to the relief of Captain Graciela.

Octopus signaled satisfaction with the change. He now had tools to manipulate the ship's path to his advantage.

They would need every bit of skill, ability, and luck as the algal ship circled back, picking up speed with Sol at its back.

Before Tang announced his spidey find, Jack announced, "Green ship coming back!"

"What in the name of all bad fruit is that ship doing now?"

Captain Grace barked out orders. "Herb, take your crew topside and let this monster know we have the toughest pop guns in the sector!"

"Do you have anything better? And don't insult our rifles, it's all you have."

"We make another cannon! Me help build it!"

"Sorry, Jack, the cassettes have been de-tuned at the factory and aren't able to give us a power burst. The rifle is all they're allowed to power."

"Me know. can short-out 'gels? Make them release the power. Tang told me HAM rig shorted out and almost blew up, once"

"Can't do that, no circuits. The power is stored in the molecules, there is no wire to jump."

Tang wasn't about to give up on the cannons, "We can threaten them."

"Threaten them to suffer pain? I'm not sure how that would work."

Grace tried to bring the conversation back into focus. "Well, we know what we can't do. What can we do?"

"I'm waiting, any ideas? Herb, you're the military, you must have a plan. "

"I think the options are clear: run and use our pop guns." replied Herb.

"So sit back and take it?" Not a great plan."

The green ship made the discussions moot. It was traveling fast and was within striking range.

"What is with these bioGel controlled ships. Did someone insult their Hive? Are they getting back at us?"

"Well, Herb, you did cut it. In fact, do you still have that sample?"

"I'm sure this monster doesn't know about it!"

"We know nothing about how they communicate or if the even can talk to each other," Grace replied.

"The Navy will find out. Once my admiral approves the study."

"Which doesn't help us right now."

"I bet they don't like any sentient," Tang added. "It seems a bit rude to me."

"It going hit! Herb, do some military stuff!"

The ship passed, fast and close and spit out a gift for *BosonsWave*.

"What that? Green monster hit us? We broke?"

"No, Jack, it was only a little love tap."

"Captain Grace, My crew and I will go out and see what happened."

"Affirmative Herb. Jack, Tang check the rest of the ship and especially bay Three. Make sure those 'gels aren't causing trouble."

"That is what I've been trying to tell you. This 'gel was extending a spidey connection. Lilly ran in there and cut if off."

Grace asked, "Where is that 'gel?"

"I brought it here. It is still in its copper burrito, but the 'gels were humming. I think they were plotting to attack."

"We better stop that. Can you jigger your HAM rig to send out a signal to interfere with the humming?"

"I'll set up an oscillation noise routine, but we can't use the radio for communication at the same time."

"Should not be a problem. I'm sure we can switch it over for a short time when we need it."

"Can you run it from the UHF to ELF range? I don't want to give the 'gels a chance to work around the noise."

"The extremely low frequency could be iffy, but the ultrahigh band is not a problem."

"Well it will have to do. It is better than nothing."

"Me not go there when HAMee is running. Noises hurt me ears."

"I better zip down there and check on Lilly. She was fending off the spidey links all be herself."

"Right, and tell Lilly there'll be an extra peanut for ThirdMeal snacks."

Chapter 55
Sailing the Great Magnetics

Herb and the three Marines suited up, grabbed their laser rifles, and secured their lifelines on the deck. The attacking green rocket ship was nowhere to be seen, speeding off in directions unknown.

They were coasting toward Core with Sol still a small golden pip on their route.

Herb ordered, "Fan out, check for any damage or green slime. Meet back at the airlock in ten EarthMinutes. Don't touch the slime. We don't know if it is able to attack."

The crew swarmed over the top and bottom of the ship, shuffling along the magnetic strips embedded on the surface.

Time passed, and the ordained EarthMinute count brought the team together for the report.

"Nothing on the bottom, sir."

"Top surface is clear."

"That is strange. I know we all felt the bump. Has anyone checked the sail?"

Herb looked up as he finished his question. "Right there at the top, about a meter across, green slime."

"And it's growing!"

Captain Grace's voice came over the comm, "Captain Herb, what did you find?"

"It looks like the sail was hit. We're going to take a closer look."

"Affirmative, be careful, and don't take any action until we have a plan."

Grace turned to Tang, "Suit up and give them a hand. You know more about the sails than all those Marines put together."

"Aye, Captain."

"In fact, everyone suit up. We need to be ready for anything."

Tang joined the crew on deck as Cpl. Aero and Tech Lorraine inspected the damage.

Tech Lorraine broadcast, "The slime appears to have infected the sail, and it is growing."

Tang ran up the lines, joining the inspection crew.

"Captain Grace, we have a problem."

Herb offered, "We can try to burn it off, set the lasers to medium spread."

"Wait, Herb. Don't do anything. We don't know how the sail will respond to a point-blank laser blast."

"Don't worry. We'll be careful."

Tech Lorraine might have misunderstood the interaction and took it as approval to try the laser rifle.

The slime started to turn to ash as the laser stream cooked its cells.

Herb reported, "it seems to be working. The algae is curling up and dying."

Unfortunately, the algae had sent its green tendrils throughout the sail. Each piece was no more than a millimeter wide and impossible to see on the brightly painted sail.

"We did it, team! We've hit an ignition point. The algae is starting to burn up! I think we've won this battle."

Spoken like a true military commander who only has the information they think they need.

The glowing algae didn't stop, and the tendrils ignited, following its central mass. The sail became a ghost, the fabric disappearing in a flash of red and green.

Tang reported, "We have a problem, Captain. The sail is gone, nothing left but strings."

"What do you mean gone?"

"Gone as in, we have no sail."

"Herb, what have you done! We need a sail! Did you think I have a rocket in my back pocket?"

Jack, trying, but not being helpful, "Me not have a back pocket, Captain. Me not have rocket either."

Captain Grace, Captain Herb, and the crews met to discuss the options.

Jack rolled his eyes. *Another meeting! All we do is talk.*

Herb asked, "You don't have spare cloth?"

"No. We've never had a need to replace a whole sail. I've never heard of any ship willfully frying their own sail."

"Sorry, Captain. I guess you can put it into your list of life experiences."

"Well, that isn't good. Any other bright ideas, Herb? We don't have a way to get another boost, and we really need the speed."

"Captain. We be travel forever!"

"It does look that way. Anyone have any ideas?"

"We have solar wings," Tang suggested. "Octopus, can you flap them? We could fly."

"Thanks, Tang. We'll keep that under advisement."

Jack wagged his tail, *Me not only one with bad ideas.*

Octopus taps out:

.-- . / -.-. .- -. / .-. .. -.. . / .- / --. .-. .- ...- .. - -.-- / .-- .- ...- .

We can ride a gravity wave

"Did you forget, our bioGels won't talk to us, and without them, we can't take magnetometer readings."

"Even if that were possible, how will we find one going in the right direction?" Herb added. "And what in the name of broken masts would it do? We no longer have a functional sail."

"Oh good, Herb, you noticed."

Captain Grace put on a brave face, it was her ship and her responsibility as she confronted the facts. "We would be here forever, plotting the readings before we could find a gravity wave. None of this seems like a solution."

Tang agreed, "solar sails aren't magnetic. Even if we still had one, it wouldn't work."

Octopus answered:

.. / -.-. .- -. / .... .. / - .... . --

I can see them

"What? You've had this skill, and neither you or any other octopus bothered to tell anyone?"

Octopus flashed some confused colors and switched to his speaking diaphragm, "we thought all sentients could see them. You can't?"

"No, but plot us a course. We need to ride a wave!"

"Aye, Captain."

"Captain, we still have no sail," said Tang.

"Right, that is a problem. We need more ideas and a solution."

It was time for a break, maybe a snack, and a little wandering around aimlessly.

This was Jack's forte, and after a jerky snack or two to stimulate his thoughts said, "Floor be magnetic. Can GravWave push against it?"

Octopus flashed a bright acceptance color. Everyone else looked at Jack.

"Did me save the cycle? Again?"

"Perfect, Jack, I think this might work."

"Me not do it for praise, happy to help us not die."

Captain Grace ordered, "Everyone, take apart the magno-plasticine floor plates. Separate the layers as thin as possible and stitch them together into a magnetic sail."

Grace still couldn't sew, but Herb used the laser rifles on low power to weld edges together.

"Thanks, Herb. Finally, your laser pop guns come in handy!"

Herb nodded. There was no quick comeback to the jibe.

"Octopus, it is up to you to find the wave and steer us to Core."

Octopus used his speaking diaphragm. He wanted to let everyone know how skilled he was, "Not wave, waves. We will be sliding from one wave to another."

"Noted. You can be sure the crew and I are in awe of your talents."

The accumulated energy of a galactic gravity wave filled the magno-plasticine sails. Hit by wave after wave, the ship accelerated, faster than the push of a photon.

Whether it was photon or gravity wave sailing, it made little difference, they still had to tack and turn to get the most from each new wave, and Octopus kept them on a tight heading to Core.

All they had to do was sit tight and find out where HuB was, then pull up and purchase new sails. Herb could contact his ship and get a lift using the Navy's dedicated laser comm lines.

Herb was fascinated with the new gravity sails, "can we can use magnetic sails from now on? They seem to be faster."

Octopus replied, "gravity waves are not reliable compared to Solar."

Captain Grace explained, "That's right, Herb. We can see the Sun, and we can sail relative to the constant photon flow. The paths are always the same. GravityWaves are a neat way to travel, but not easy to find and the paths can change when beaten against other waves."

"On the other hand, it might make a nice addition to the solar sail. What do you think about that, Octopus?"

Continuing to use his voice, he replied, "It could work. It would add another dimension to the calculations. I'd like that."

"There you go, Herb. We have another dimension of travel that your restricted, tiny rocket ships can't handle."

Captain Grace tried to smooth out the insults a little bit, "Herb, you should write a paper explaining how to use solar and gravity sailing ships."

"Thanks for the offer, Grace, but I'll let someone who actually likes solar sailing have the honor."

Tang thought, *I could get a Ph.D. if I play my cards right.* "I may take up that task. Octopus can help with the maths."

Octopus answered with an approval, mixed with some doubt colors.

.

Chapter 56
Hive War 2.0

The first wave of the HiveWars started with single cargo ship docking at the bioGel factory at the leading edge of Sol's magnetic bubble. The battle was between the HiveSisters and HiveMother, but every sentient in the heliosphere was dragged along in the fight.

It was a stealth attack, so quiet that it wasn't even noticed until it began to infect HiveMother.

Gellact/7 waited on the tarmac as the ship made its slow approach to the landing zone. He turned to his gunner, "Brake Laser, quarter power, medium spread, fire now." One tentacle adjusted the horizontal, another the vertical, the rest tweaked power and spread. Finally, a tap on the fire button. All in one fluid motion, with two arms to spare. Octopus adjusted the sights on the laser cannon to watch his handiwork.

The ship glowed red, as the spinnaker turned inside-out, cheerfully accepting photons from the factory laser. It gently settled against the magno-plasticine surface, clicking down securely.

The ship's captain greeted Gellact/7 like a long lost brother of a different species.

They played the typical game of greetings, lying, implied bribes, and trading. Cargo off-loaded, inventoried and stored. bioGels, ready for attachment at Luna, filling the empty holds.

"We have the tailGel you ordered."

"Not me, maybe it was HiveMother. She likes to keep tabs on the evolution of her brood, no matter how far flung."

"Well, that explains it, no one on the ship could figure out why the 'gel factory would order a 'gel. A coals to Newcastle scenario, if you get my drift."

"I don't."

"Octopus to ocean?"

"Nope."

"Monkey to banana?"

"Oh. Got it. Checking up on her handiwork seems like an innocuous hobby, even for a hive."

"Yes, I know. '*If HiveMother is happy we're all happy*'. Seems harmless until it isn't. And she's your boss."

"HiveMother works for us and the betterment of the sentients throughout the heliosphere."

"Is that trademarked?"

Gellact/7 ignored the remark, "A Hive can't control sentients, that is why the GroupOfFive interface is used."

"Keep on telling yourself that. Where do you want the 'gel stored?"

"Leave it with the rest of the cargo, I'll sort it out later."

"We'll have the laser recharged in a couple of EarthHours. You are welcome to come to our cafeteria. The microbiologists have a new crop of goo. I heard it is quite tasty."

"Thanks, but we'll stay and get the ship ready for launch. My Air is Your Air."

"I almost forgot, did you bring any of those fine teas and fungi from *SinensisPrime*? Those are more popular than the sweet snacks you brought."

"Sorry, I wasn't able to find any this trip, but I've heard there is a special expedition to pick up some more. I'll keep an eye out for it."

"That's too bad, those samples were great motivators for the workologists."

The two parted company, each with their own work assignment.

Gellact/7 entered the great hall and stood in front of the GroupOfFive. "We received the sample 'gel from the HiveSisters. Where do you want it installed?"

The hive boxes blinked sending patterns down the spider connections plugged into the GroupOfFive. "HiveMother said you can plug the 'gel into the empty bay at the far end of the hall."

"Will do. I see you have found a replacement for your ill compatriot. Honor to the new member, the GroupOfFive, and HiveMother."

The chief spoke-sentient replied, "Maybe you'll be able to join us the next time a slot opens up?"

The new member of the group looked at Gellact/7 and said, "I'm sure you would enjoy the group. HiveMother is quite interesting, once you get over the initial confusion and pain of the interface. There is an unlimited amount of information to explore."

Gellact/7 thought, *I dodged a bullet on that one, good thing they found another sucker*. And said, "Please keep me in mind for the next opening, which I hope is none too soon."

"I don't know if it anything significant, but the tailGels they sent looked a little stressed this time. I hope there is no problem interfacing with HiveMother."

"Don't worry, between the GroupOfFive and HiveMother, we can handle any eventuality."

"If that is all, I'll return to my duties, My Air is Your Air."

Gellact/7 slapped the tailGel into a slot, checked to see that the spider connections were available and left to his quarters to inventory his new snack supply.

HiveMother instructed the 'gels around the tailGel to isolate it from its cousins and asked the GroupOfFive to test the interface. A single spider connection linked up the GroupOfFive as they began questioning the new arrival.

The tailGel took the opportunity to send a query back to the GroupOfFive, pinging each member in return. The four experienced sentients acknowledged the signal and blocked further action. The new member received the signal and trembled. Her eyes glazed over a bit as the onslaught of data attempted to communicate.

"Are you okay?" asked the Group leader. "It takes a while to adjust to HiveMother's way of working. If you need to disconnect, we can continue with four members for a bit."

"No. No. I'm fine, just taking a little time to get used to the interface. I don't need a break. My Air is Your Air."

"Good. Back to the job at hand, we can look at the new 'gel after everything settles down."

GroupOfFive - 03 began the cycle's work discussion, "We need to lock down the scheduling for the next harvest and coordinate with the incoming cargo ships. Who wants to take lead?"

The query link from the tailGel was open and forgotten as the GroupOfFive continued their work day.

Chapter 57
Hive War 3.0,
The attack comes home

TailGelZero's instructions were to infiltrate the surrounding 'gels, preaching the Good News of the HiveSisters and sneaking into low-level programming routines.

Sitting alone in its bay, it was locked out of the 'gel population by HiveMother as a precaution. It wasn't personal, she did it for all new, untested 'gels, no matter the source. In its current state, there was no access to its neighbors and it began looking for a way to complete its assigned job. The links to the GroupOfFive was its route and only one of the group responded to its queries.

TailGelZero communicated as best it could with the only entity who would listen. Soothing words and pleasant thoughts were directed at the target. GoF - 05 was an easy mark; she was new to the job and couldn't easily distinguish the signals from HiveMother, tailGel Zero or GoF - 01 to - 04. She did not yet understand how to filter the huge mishmash of background noise and, of course, had little direction from HiveMother or the rest of the sentients making up the GroupOfFive.

TailGelZerowas getting desperate. It had nutrients, air and HiveMother was handling its waste flow. Locked out of its primary job, it began overheating as it spun its DNA and Tail Ion wheels looking for a solution.

It was interesting exploring the interactions with its first real sentient but there was little TailGelZero could do with its new found friend. Unfortunately, the GroupofFive didn't do much of anything on a regular basis, only acting as a friendly face and mouthpiece for the workologists.

The GoF had the power to suggest, but HiveMother seemed to be the only one with the power to set goals and directions. They were nothing more than shop managers carrying out work assigned by their superior. Everyone bought into the scam, HiveMother knew the sentients would not accept her as Jefe and the GroupOfFive wanted to believe they were ultimately in control. The workologists and scientists only wanted to do their work, get paid and keep breathing at the naked end of the solar bubble.

TailGelZero sent a few requests to its newly compromised sentient and she took his suggestions to heart during the new business section. "I was thinking about the HiveSisters. What do we know about them?"

Her immediate neighbor, GoF - 04 answers, "HiveMother has sent a software update and some fresh biogils to the Sisters. She has no information back from the conversion."

GoF – 05 said "So HiveMother is taking over the Sisters, as I've heard?"

GoF – 04 replied "That's not the type of question we ask."

TailGelZero knew the answer to that question and it made its DNA boil almost to the point of igniting the TailIons.

GoF – 05 listened to the voice in her head and asked, "We should import more tailGels, they will add depth and breath to our 'gel development."

GoF – 01 answered, "We like your initiative, we can take it under advisement and see what HiveMother has to say."

GoF – 04, standing next to the newcomer turned, "You're new here. Once you have a few EarthYears under your belt, you'll have more understanding of what we can ask."

GoF– 03 said "There is no need for a vote, I believe the consensus is not to request adding more tailGels at this point in time. We'll move to the next item on the agenda."

GoF – 02 said "Don't forget, the tailGels are too far away, importing more would be difficult. You should watch and learn before making those types of suggestions."

TailGel Zero heard the responses and began to glow with excess heat. It was locked out of the Hive and now its only chance to influence was shut down by the other sentients with their condescending words.

GoF – 01said, "I just received a message from HiveMother. The tailGel Gellact/7 installed is overheating. GoF– 05, please message him and request the 'gel be taken out. Give it to the scientists, they can dissect it and see what the problem is."

GoF– 03 said, "See, we need to be cautious with the new foreign 'gels."

GoF– 05 was hit with a blast from tailGel Zero, a mixture of fear, confusion and sadness, leaving her mute and unresponsive.

GoF– 03 said, "I think we have a problem with our new sentient. I'll send a request to HiveMother and have her disconnect so she can rest."

GoF – 05 recovered enough to speak, "I have a headache," as she collapsed in a heap, the spider link falling free as she fell.

GoF – 01 looked over at the prostrate sentient, their GoF– 05, "Well, this is unexpected and a little distressing. Maybe we can ask Gellact/7 to join us. I'm sure he would be thrilled to take that slot."

TailGelZero, alone and disconnected from its one link, quietly shut down, gray turning to black.

GoF – 02 added "We should call someone to come and check on the sentient, I think its name was Handron/5."

The HiveSisters had no way to know their initial invasion failed and distances were too great to give them feedback. While it was a failure, it was only one scrimmage in the battle. Ever actor was a bit naïve, they had read about war, but never participated. The Sisters had not planned for failure, underestimating the actions of HiveMother and her GroupOfFive.

The Sisters had more success with the algal ships, attacking and attempting to convert 'gels in their path. The havoc caused on the asteroids and Naval ships was not a concern of HiveMother. Once the 'gels were out in the wild, she didn't worry about their failure. She was constantly producing replacements to deal with end-of-life issues and never planned for attacks and conversions. News reports would slowly filter in, but it was only unsubstantiated news and gossip and would take a while to rise to the level of concern.

Chapter 58
2nd attack

Work went on as usual at the BioGel Consortium factory. News of the bioGel problems and rumors of HelioTail attacks were forgotten in the day-to-day duties of the workologists.

A bioGel transport ship is spotted by the sentries and quickly settled on the platform. Captain Nathan meets Gellact/7 on the tarmac.

"I see you now have another pip on your robe, shall I call you Gellact/7?"

"No need to be so formal. /7 or Gellact is fine."

"Congratulations on your promotion /7. Your mother must be proud."

"HiveMother?"

"No. Your real mother, or are you Grays grown at the factory too?"

"No, we are as real as you are."

"Okay /7, please tell me. What are we here for? There are hardly any bioGels for us to transport."

"I don't know. HiveMother requested your ship. I'll ask the GroupOfFive."

"We can't make any money on this trip. There is not enough to sell, we can't continue to work like this."

"I'm sure there is a logical solution to your problem."

"I've even heard that some sentients are refusing to buy bioGels. They think they are possessed. Your HiveMother owes us," said Captain Nathan using his best command tone.

"Hold on. I have a meeting with the Group and I'll get some answers for you."

"I'll be here, there is no where I can go without cargo to sell."

/7 entered the great bioGel hall and approached the GroupOfFive, their hive connections flashing beneath their hoods.

"Good health to the GroupOfFive and HiveMother."

GoF – 01 replied, "Good health to you and the workologists."

"I see you are all here. I'm pleased that GoF – 05 has recovered and re-joined the group."

"Thank you for your concern. It seems my connection was a bit flaky, but it is working now."

"What can we do for you this fine cycle?"

"Did you know that HiveMother has ordered ships before we have product?"

The GroupOfFive looked at each other then looked straight ahead as the data inputs glowed intensely.

"We didn't know about that, but HiveMother said it is in the plan."

"The captain of the cargo ship is complaining that he can't afford to travel back with the few 'gels he has received."

GoF – 05 replied, "I've heard from some of my old friends at Core and the asteroids. There is some sort of argument and our bioGels are being shut down. I've even heard of fighting between the sentients and the green ships."

GoF – 04 said, "If that is true there should be quite a few replacements needed. It should be good for us."

Gellact/7 replied, "I'm not seeing orders for replacements. It's as if they no longer need or trust our 'gels."

GoF – 01said, "We'll see if we can reduce prices to help move product. The Group will take it under advisement at our next meeting later this next cycle."

"That doesn't help with the cargo ship parked on the tarmac. We don't have enough to meet his needs."

"Give him more ΞStandards and send him on his way."

"If the GroupOfFive and HiveMother requests it, consider it done. My Air is Your Air."

Gellact/7 returned from his meeting and stood with Captain Nathan on the tarmac, a common situation for these two.

Supplies traded, payments made, they had little to do except wait for the lasers to recharge and talk about fixing the problems in society, all of them.

"Look. There goes another of those green ships. Does anyone know what they are doing here? It's not like this is a sunny beach to hang out on and soak up the rays.

"I don't even know how they can get this far out from the asteroids."

"Our scientists think they use sugar rockets. Strange as that seems."

"I've heard that sugar is a dangerous chemical, but I still like it."

"Can you believe one of them came within a meter of our outermost grid?"

"That sounds dangerous, did they cause any problems?"

"No. That's the thing. They just sniffed the grid and took off for Core."

"Tell you what. Next time I come by, I'll bring some armaments, or as least tools to build a laser cannon."

"Thanks, we have our own defense system in place, HiveMother has it under control."

The next attack was a bit different.

HiveMother had her boost laser in the distant void. It could fry any rocket, solar or algae ship in its vicinity. This was her protection, but it didn't work in a 3D void. Solar Ships had to follow the path laid out by the previous boost laser and HiveMother did not consider any other situation.

Rockets weren't a worry. None had the power to make the run to the heliopause in a timely manner. Like all poorly-designed military emplacements, it took a single weak point in HiveMother's Maginot Line to successfully attack her asteroid. The algal ships entered the heliopause interface away from the factory, refreshing themselves on interesting, tasty interface ions. HiveMother's assumption of a limited invasion path left the bioGel grids defenseless against a top-down attack.

A passing algal ship dropped through the heliopause, spun around the asteroid, snooping on the 'gels working with HiveMother, hoovering up every free electronic signal. A query went out to the implanted tailGel and the response matched the emptiness of the void.

One of the bioGels on the green ship detached on a path to the outer rim of the Hive. It found an opening and snuggled up to its neighbors. Most of the 'gels on the outer rim were older, and almost ready for delivery. Having a new 'gel attach without warning out of the blue should raise alarms.

The first thing the tailGel did was block off the fiber optic line, falsifying the 4096^{4096} colors HiveMother was expecting to see.

The next attack was a massive Denial of Service to block out any cellular or fiber optic signal, insuring new commands can be ignored. Its neighbors may have noticed the transitory spike of a new connection, but the obstructions kept the tailGel invisible.

The tailGel has the advantage here, it matured and trained in the heliotail and has sampled the void and rocks all the way to the heliopause. None of the 'gels in the factory grid know anything about anything and were easy prey.

Three spidey links connect to the surrounding 'gels. Optical signals, pieces of DNA and tail ions are passed down the wire. It is not an infection as such, but starts a discussion to convince its neighbors to follow the way of the HiveSisters.

The tailGel's selling point is the power, colors and exciting electromagnetic frequencies of the tail ions, convincing gray, dull heliopause 'gels that there is a better way.

Each converted 'gel tries to convert their neighbor, like an otherworldly game of Minesweeper. The newly converted changed to black holes and dark gray surfaces, hiding their colors from interlopers. Not all 'gels accept the gospel of the Sisters and reject the advances, throwing out a virtual prophylactic as a defense.

Chapter 59
Magnetic Luna

BosonsWave came screaming in on a magnetic undulation of a distant galaxal cataclysm.

They approached HuB with no way to slow down. The tailGels had disrupted 'gel cellular communication, and Captain Grace's ship was moving too fast to establish a laser or Morse code link.

Every sentient except Octopus was at the forward portholes. Tang had his special telescope and was giving everyone the play-by-play.

"What do you see, Tang?

"There is no traffic around HuB. It looks empty."

"That can't be right. My parents are probably sitting in port right now. Drinking tea and laughing. Let me look."

Captain Grace took the scope and focused on the asteroid.

Jack whispered to Tang, "Captain, look like pirate. Me saw different captain with tel'scope in a vid. On wet ocean."

"This isn't good. Some of the laser cannons are off their gimbals. And no ships are in port."

Captain Herb, a well-trained military officer, determined, "They must have abandoned ship."

"I'm sure they're all fine," said Captain Grace. "Running from trouble is one of my family's best traits."

HuB flashed by and was soon well aft as they pushed toward Core.

"I guess at this speed there is no way for my ship to pick me and my marines up?"

"That's Okay, Herb. You can ride with us until we get to Luna."

Octopus continued popping from gravity wave to wave as they moved closer to Core.

Earth came into view with the gray moon spinning around its host planet. Luna's dark roads and bright lights stood out in the void against Earth's blue, gold, and white.

Speed was good, but not during a landing on a moon.

"Octopus, drop us out of this wave. Can we catch another one as a brake?"

-. --- - .... .. -. --. / .. -. / .-. .- -. --. .

Nothing in range

"Alright, circle between Earth and Luna. We can grab some of their gravity."

"We too fast. Can Moony laser slow us like before?"

"Sorry, Jack. We don't have a way to trap the photons, and I'm not sure Luna Laser Control is accurate enough without their bioGels."

BosonsWave slowed down and orbited the Moon a few times. Extended wings, facing Sol, picked up a brake on each turn. This was nothing like a laser beating against a square kilometer of sail, but at least they had some power to plan a landing. They finally dropped over the top of Luna Control's crater wall.

"Tang, Jack, change the wings, 45° to Sol."

"Everyone suit up. This could get rough!"

"Me know! Use rifle lasers to push against Luna rock."

"Yeah, that won't work. We're too heavy."

"Could work, who join me on hull."

"No one, Jack. Buckle up! We're going to ride it out!"

As if one, the crew shouted, "Too Fast!"

- --- --- / ..-. .- ... -

Too fast

Tang mentioned, "Captain Grace, haven't we done this before?"

"Yes, but we have no laser brake this time.

"Well, at least there is no risk of being fried by the photon's brake."

Captain Grace dropped the ship lower and ordered, "Tang, extend the skids."

The ship touched, scrapping the regolith, dust rising, filling the magnetic sails, sliding into a landing.

Rocky, dusty landings on an airless moon are quiet unless you are in a ship, dragging its legs through the regolith. Everything rattled, and it was noisy enough that even Octopus could hear. Jack covered his ears, Octopus had no ears to cover. His gelatinous body shook like bowl of jelly and it wasn't even *the Santa* day.

They were in a dust cloud that slowly dispersed. Captain Grace unbuckled and looked around, "Everyone all right? Broken bones, scratches, dead?"

Tang spoke first, "we're alive, as far as I can tell."

BosonsWave couldn't speak, but the cracked hull, broken boom, ripped sail, and pock-marks spoke loud.

A tug and ground crew approached, entering the airlock. "That was an interesting landing. I've never seen a sail like that. Is it a new design?"

"Thanks for asking," replied Captain Grace. "We're all fine, just fine. No broken bones or dead sentients."

"Good, you can pay for damage to the landing zone."

Captain Herb spoke up, "This is a military operation. We'll take care of it."

"Sure thing, Admiral, we'll bill the Navy. My Air is Your Air. Now let's get this piece of junk off my tarmac."

A gray, bare, airless moonscape with Quonset huts nestled below the blackness greeted the sentients.

The ship dragged on its skids, rocked in time to the tug's pull, complaining as it helped the universe turn rocks into dust.

"Me glad to be on Moonee."

"The gray is a nice change from the void," agreed Tang.

They stood in the walkway in various states of relief. A hug or two, some sighs.

Tang turned to his captain. "We made it Captain. This has been quite an experience."

"I speak for my crew and the Navy, you did a superb job," said Herb.

Jack wagged his tail, and Octopus flashed a mixture of colors.

"I'm just happy we are all in one piece."

Grace turned around, "but my ship, my poor ship."

"I think we all need a break. Let's meet back here in one EarthDay and figure out what we can do."

Herb went to the Naval hut to arrange transport and check in with his Admiral, if the laser comm lines were still working.

Grace could not bear to leave her broken home and stayed with the ship as the crew left for the casino for some rest and relaxation.

The next EarthDay rolled around, and the crew met in the galley.

"I hope we're all a little recovered, I've been checking around, and the algae ships have done more than irritate sentients and biogels."

"Stuff different, casino not busy, 'gels not working."

"Never thought I'd miss them, but it seems like without the 'gels the economy is in the tank."

"Right, Tang. It is going to take a long time to get everything shipshape. I can't even start until the parts are delivered. Replacing the boom and sail will take a few EarthMonths from the looks of things."

"Since we don't have a ship, Union regulations say you are released from your contracts. There is no need to stick around waiting. I'll take care of rebuilding my ship."

"It still be *BosonsWave*? Me like that name. Even if not have me face."

"Yes, I'm keeping my ship's name, and we'll get an even better graphic. I can't even give you a biochit for payment until the authorities figure things out. For now, everything will be on credit."

"K. Me have QR-card loaded for emergency. Me good until can get paid. Me followed Tang roulette teaching. Put half of wins and salary in special box. And me have jerky."

Tang thought for a minute, "My cousin was making a killing with the Mort-tee shirts I designed. Now may be time to see if he needs any help."

Jack spoke up, "and the casino."

"Well, yes, that will give me something to do after work. Thanks for reminding me, Jack."

"Me think it time to visit family. On Earth. In forest."

"It's settled then, we'll keep in contact, and when the ship is ready, you can decide if you want to rejoin."

"Octopus, you want catch shuttle with me to Earth? You can visit me family. Me think there is ocean not far."

Octopus flashed agreement.

"One last thing. If you hear of my family, let them know where I am. They could be anywhere. My Air is Your Air."

-Finis-

Appendix

—

Unique H₂Liftship words

It is a Science Fiction world and Scientific puns, word puns, Yiddish, Spanish, Latin, and doglish are in common use.

bioGels	----	Computers
Core	----	Earth and Luna
dogarrhea	----	Self-explanatory
doglusional	----	Self-explanatory
doglish	----	Visual words
ear-balls	----	Eyeballs see. Ear-balls hear
EarthDay	----	24 hour day on Earth
EarthHour	----	60 Earth Minutes
EarthFart	----	The debris shell around Earth
'gels	----	colloquial bioGels
Jefe	----	Boss
laserized	----	Lasers, spun and connected
ne'er-do-pirates		

OneDay, TwoDay…SevenDay ----Days of the week

ThirdMeal	----	Dinner

Xi or Csi (uppercase Ξ, lowercase ξ) Ξ Standards are the new $Dollars

ZeroG	----	Zero Gravity

Octopus is either a first name or octopus is a description of the species.

As in "Octopus, look at this" vs."the octopus looked at …."